# NEVER SAY GOODBYE

Claire Lorrimer

This first world edition published in Great Britain 2000 by
SEVERN HOUSE PUBLISHERS LTD of
9–15 High Street, Sutton, Surrey SM1 1DF.
This first world edition published in the U.S.A. 2000 by
SEVERN HOUSE PUBLISHERS INC of
595 Madison Avenue, New York, N.Y. 10022.

British Library Cataloguing in Publication Data

Lorrimer,   Claire,   1921-
    Never say goodbye
    1.Love stories
    I. Title
    823.9'14 [F]

    ISBN 0-7278-5535-2

All situations in this publication are fictitious and
any resemblance to living persons is purely coincidental.

Typeset by Palimpsest Book Production Ltd.
Polmont, Stirlingshire, Scotland.
Printed and bound in Great Britain by
MPG Books Ltd, Bodmin, Cornwall.

# 1954

# One

The girl sat on the huge concrete block that marked the furthermost point of the Mole. Around her on three sides the brilliant transparency of the blue Mediterranean swirled and gurgled gently in and out of the rocks. A light breeze ruffled the chestnut curls that surrounded a thin *gamine* face. She might have been seventeen or twenty-seven; in the olive-green swim-suit she had the appearance of a schoolgirl and yet the eyes that stared out across the water were not the eyes of a young girl . . . there was too much unhappiness in their depth, too much introspection.

The hazel eyes looked for a moment at a tiny sailing boat that was tacking slowly towards her . . . or rather towards the little harbour that the Mole afforded. It seemed to be moving very slowly and she guessed that if the breeze lessened at all, the occupants would find themselves becalmed. But her thoughts were not really on the boat . . . they were on herself.

She had been in Benghazi for two months now. It seemed much longer since she had left England behind and flown out to Libya with her sister Kathie and the children. At the time, she had felt a lifting of her spirits, an expectancy, a hope for the future that in this moment of self-analysis appeared rather stupid.

You're a fool, Scilla! she told herself with feeling. You have always been a fool!

Kathie, had she heard that unspoken thought, would have chided her with her usual common sense and honesty. Scilla could imagine Kathie's warm reproachful voice saying:

"That's absurd, Scilla. You've far more intelligence than I have, and anyway, you're only a kid . . . a baby. You can't expect to go through life without making some mistakes."

But she wasn't a baby now, Scilla told herself bitterly. She was nearly twenty-seven and old enough to be able to decide what she wished to make of her life. At seventeen she had decided and made the mistake that only later had she realised was so drastic and so irredeemable.

'I won't think about the past! I've come out here to a new life! I'm going to enjoy myself . . . be happy!' she thought with a fierceness of purpose that to Kathie, who knew her so well, would have betrayed the fear and doubt with which she was viewing the prospect.

The girl watched the boat drawing closer and could see now the two men who were sailing her . . . tall, bronzed by the May sun and looking from a distance a little like Greek gods silhouetted against the amazing blue of the sky.

Her attention waned again and she thought of Bill . . . dark, sunburned as the two yachtsmen, undoubtedly handsome and already in love with her; Bill, who was taking her tonight to the Officers' Club for dinner and, because it was Saturday night, afterwards to dance. She knew she would flirt a little with him and enjoy herself . . . enjoy the flattery of his affection for her; knew that Kathie and her nice brother-in-law Pete would be looking on pleased and happy with her enjoyment which really they had planned for her. Perhaps that was one of the reasons why she could not really take Bill very seriously. He was so obviously the perfect 'tonic' that Kathie thought she needed. She could recall her elder sister's words when it had first been suggested that Scilla accompany her to Benghazi.

"It would be so wonderful for me, Scilla. You could give me a hand with the children and we'd be company for one another. Besides, you know you're fed up with that silly modelling job of yours and you're thin as a rake. Mother was only saying the other day that you ought to take a long holiday somewhere in the sun. Do come, Scilla. It will be a new life. We'll find some

2

handsome young army officers to amuse you and you're almost sure to have a good time. Pete says the unmarried chaps will be crying out for girls to 'date'. It isn't as if you have anything to keep you in England."

True, there wasn't any*one*.

"There's my job!" she had argued feebly.

Kathie just grinned. Both knew that Scilla had taken up modelling only because she was bored doing nothing. The allowances given to them by their wealthy car-manufacturing father were more than adequate for all their demands. In fact, they were more than most people nowadays had to live on.

Kathie, good-natured, easy-going, placid and pliable, took what her father offered her with gratitude and an easy acceptance. Scilla, highly-strung, emotional, sensitive, could not. Perhaps it was because of the interference that her parents had permitted themselves in the past. That interference might have been warranted when she was only seventeen. But as she had grown up, she had realised how wrongly they had judged her . . . and for her; and her independence of thought and deed had become an obsession. For that reason she had got herself a job and refused to draw the allowance her father still paid with obstinate regularity into her untouched bank account.

Kathie knew this and, guessing Scilla's reluctance to go with her to Libya to be based partly on the fact that she would be forced to accept financial help once more from their parents, she quickly suggested that Scilla would, in fact, be doing her a good turn if she could see her way to being employed by her as nanny or governess to her nephew and niece.

"I'd have a hard job to find someone suitable at a moment's notice and it would be a risk taking out some strange girl. If she wasn't satisfactory I'd have to pay her fare back home. Besides, Pete and I are none too keen on the idea of a stranger living in with us and we'll have to have someone. Now Pete is a full colonel we'll have to do some entertaining and be out a bit. Do come, Scilla darling!"

Because of this, because she was deeply devoted to Kathie

and because she had nothing at all to keep her in England, Scilla had come. Anything would be better than staying in London, brooding over the ghastly mess she had made of her life . . . regretting the decision of nine years ago . . .

So long ago, yet it did not seem that long since the war had ended; since the day Dallas had sailed home to Australia in the giant troopship that unknown to him she had watched leave port, taking her heart with it. Dallas . . . Dallas . . . She still loved him!

Her thin hands clenched together round the bare, brown knees. Her eyes blinked with tears that were out of place in this calm, lazy May afternoon with the sea sparkling brilliantly and far behind her at the Sailing Club the excited happy shouting of the kids playing and splashing about in the paddling pool.

She brushed them away rapidly before they could fall, a little incredulous that she could still weep for a love lost so long ago. Dallas had never written . . . never tried to see her again. She would not even have known he was leaving England for his native Australia if a fellow officer in his squadron had not written a friendly word of farewell mentioning that he and Dallas would be leaving on the *Windrush* and thanking her for the hospitality she and her family had shown them both in the past.

"If he'd really loved me, he would not have given in so easily," she told herself for the hundredth, or was it thousandth, time. "Such a very very little persuasion would have been necessary to bring me to my senses. I was so young, Dallas . . . and you were the first man I had ever loved. How was I to know it would last for always? How was I to know that it was love and not infatuation as Mother and Dad said? How was I to know that I wouldn't forget . . . couldn't forget when they promised me I would? If you'd really loved me, you'd have known deep down inside you that I could not ever change."

Yet she had doubted herself . . . and because of that she could not blame him for her own weakness. She could only despair that with his seven years' superiority he had not stood firmer for them both instead of accepting, as he had done, her parents' wishes.

With a little sigh of resignation, she looked out to sea again and saw the sailing boat almost opposite her as it changed course and swung in towards the Club. She recognised one of the men but the second, acting crew, had his back to her and she did not see who it was. The wind had freshened a little and she felt it against her body, still wet from her swim, and shivered. Then she stood up and started to clamber back along to the Mole to the changing rooms. Soon it would be tea-time and she must get back to the flat and help Kathie with the children.

She had just completed her brief dressing and pushed her slim arms into a white cardigan when she heard the men's voices outside the door of the changing room. For a moment her heart stopped and then it began to beat at double its pace. It could not be . . . and yet the accent was unmistakable.

"I'm going crazy!" she told herself as she sought for and feverishly lit a cigarette. Benghazi was not the kind of place where she might meet an Australian grazier! But nor was it the place where one heard an Australian accent. There were many strange tongues in this tiny country, English, Scots, Greek, Italian, French, German, American . . . but not Australian.

Reassured that she had made a mistake, she pushed open the changing-room door and entering the Mess walked almost directly into a table at which the two men she had seen in the sailing boat were being served tea. One of them was Dallas.

The blood rushed to her cheeks, then receded quickly leaving her deathly pale. Robert Hendry, the young Federal Government lawyer, stood up to greet her and she could not walk by. Then his companion looked up and after a moment's intake of breath, said:

"Great heavens, Scilla . . . *you!*"

"You two know each other? Sit down and have a cupper with us, Scilla. We've just been out for a sail . . . bit slow . . . no wind . . ."

"I was on the end of the Mole . . . I saw you!"

Somehow the words had come out and made sense. Somehow she was sitting down at the table, Mohammed bringing the tea Robert Hendry had called for. Her eyes, however, would not be controlled so easily and were still fastened unbelievingly on Dallas. He, too, was staring at her, his eyes fathomless, unreadable.

Perhaps sensing that all was not quite straightforward, Robert said to break the silence:

"Queer world! Always running into people I know out here. Ran into a chap the other day who I'd known years ago in training camp. Couldn't remember his name or where I'd seen him but he recognised me, too. We thrashed it out and found it was twelve years ago we shared the same Nissen hut for a fortnight!"

"It must be all of nine years since I last saw Scilla!"

The Australian leaned back with easy grace in the basket chair. Everything about him was easy but assured and somehow graceful. No longer the boy Scilla remembered but a man of thirty-three, he seemed to her to have grown even taller than the six foot she recalled. His face had lost its smoothness and was deeply lined round his eyes, but they had not changed. They were startlingly grey eyes which could be translucent and gentle like calm water, or hard and unreadable and a little frightening.

*"If that's the way you want it, Scilla, then there's nothing more for me to say except goodbye!"* Words she had forgotten came crowding back into her mind, confusing her.

"You've . . . changed!" she said at last, breathlessly.

*"Anno Domini!"* he replied with an easy laugh. "We all get older, I guess!"

"Except Scilla! She looks like a school kid!" Robert Hendry said admiringly.

"I expect I've changed, too!" Scilla said with difficulty. "I was seventeen when I last saw Dallas!"

"Well, I expect you two have a lot to mull over," Robert said tactfully. "I must be pushing off anyway."

6

"I'll have to go, too!" Dallas said, standing up abruptly. "No doubt we shall run into each other again, Scilla. You must tell me sometime how you manage to be in this tiny corner of the world. Thanks for the ride, Bob. So long, you two!"

White as death beneath her sun-tan, Scilla watched him disappear through the gate out of sight.

"What's eaten him!" Robert said with a look of surprise. "I call that pretty abrupt!"

Scilla bit her lip.

"I'm no doubt responsible. As a matter of fact . . . it's rather hard to explain, Robert . . . we were engaged to be married once. We broke it off . . . that is, I broke it off." Her voice trailed away.

The young lawyer whistled softly.

"Now I begin to understand. I don't imagine that fellow much enjoyed being jilted. Never knew such a proud man in all my life. Funny you hadn't run into him before now, Scilla. He's been down here at the Club several times . . . must have just missed each other, I suppose. Matter of fact, he's going great guns at the moment with our glamour-girl, Nancy. You know the one I mean?"

Scilla shook her head, her heart like a ton weight in her throat choking her.

"The dark woman with the Jane Russell figure . . . or perhaps that's a bit catty . . . she really is a stunner. I just don't happen to care for the type myself, but I can see what Dallas sees in her. In any case, she's one of the few eligible girls around here . . . except your sweet self!"

"I know who you mean!" Scilla said suddenly. "She is stunning. But I thought she was Mrs Harold!"

"Was, but not is. There was a divorce in England about six months ago. The husband went to Egypt and she stayed on here . . . has a good job with the Embassy. Frankly, I think Dallas was the main reason she has stayed on here. Benghazi isn't really her cup of tea . . . not sophisticated enough if you

7

ask me. Still, it must have its compensations, viz Dallas, or she wouldn't be here."

"What . . . what is he doing here?"

"Don't you know? But of course not. He's over with the F.A.O. . . . Food and Agricultural Organization. Now much as I love you, my sweet, I must depart homewards. My better half will be wondering what I'm doing. Incidentally, when are you coming round to see us again?"

"Soon!" Scilla promised, for she liked Robert and was even more friendly with his young attractive wife, Isobel. "I'll come with you!" she added as Robert stood up. "I promised Kathie to see to the children's tea and it's nearly five now."

They parted at the road running north around the harbour, Scilla crossing over the piece of waste land that fronted the large block of flats which, for the time being, constituted home. She ran up the stairs, opened the front door swiftly and, as quietly as she could and without Kathie or the children hearing her, slipped into her bedroom, closing the door behind her.

She stood with her back to it, her hands pressed against her cheeks, her eyes wide and with an expression of acute pain. It was as if half her mind was unable to credit the happenings of the last hour . . . that Dallas, *Dallas*, should be here in Benghazi was an event momentous enough in itself. That she should have seen him, sat with him, heard his voice . . . not the voice she remembered, saying, '*Darling, I love you so much . . . marry me, please marry me!*' but a cool, unhurried, hard voice saying, '*Good heavens, Scilla, you!*' as if she were the last person he wanted to meet again.

Of course, it's probably true! she told herself with sudden understanding. She couldn't have expected him to stay in love with her for the nine absurdly long years they had been apart. And yet because *she* had never really stopped loving *him*, she had hoped for at least some sign of pleasure in seeing her again.

The girl moved across to her bed and sat down as if she were suddenly too weary to support her own slight weight. She had lived so long in her dreams of the past . . . dreams of the days when she and Dallas had first met and fallen so deeply in love, that even now she found it hard to believe that this was now, the present, that she could see and talk to Dallas again . . . not the romantic young airman, which was her memory of him, but Dallas, a man of thirty-three, different and yet somehow unmistakably the same man she had once loved as a young man.

The door opened suddenly and Kathie came in. Seeing Scilla on the bed, she gave a little start of surprise and her round, rather plump face crinkled in perplexity.

"Darling, I thought you were out swimming! Whatever are you doing here? I came to see if Dina's dressing-gown had got into your cupboard. Scilla, is anything wrong?"

The whiteness of her young sister's face and the tense attitude of her body had given Kathie cause for anxiety as well as surprise.

"I've just seen Dallas!" Scilla said flatly.

"You've just . . . what did you say, Scilla? Are you mad? It can't have been . . . not Dallas . . ." Her voice trailed away as she saw the brief shake of Scilla's bronze curls.

Kathie Henshaw drew in her breath and walked slowly across the tiled floor to the window, where she stared out across the harbour. This, if it were really fact, was a dreadful mishap, to put it mildly. None knew better than she, who had always had Scilla's confidence, what this must mean to her sister . . . moreover what fresh unhappiness might be lying in wait for her. Surely . . . surely it could not be true! Dallas Poulten had gone back to Australia after the war to work on his father's sheep farm. What could he possibly be doing here in Benghazi? It was incredible.

Her mind shot back to the past . . . to the last time she had set eyes on the young Australian pilot . . . how many years ago now? Nine? Ten? She had been the unfortunate one who had had to deliver Scilla's last unhappy letter to Dallas. She knew every word of it and could remember it now as clearly as she could remember the lost, angry bitter look on the young man's face.

> *Darling Dallas,*
>
> *I believe Mummy and Daddy are right about us . . . we ought not to rush into marriage. I do love you . . . I shall always love you but can't you wait a few years . . . until I am nineteen at least? I think Mummy and Daddy will eventually give their consent if only you could wait. I don't doubt my love for you and I don't really doubt yours for me but if we do truly both care, then two years' wait is not so terrible. But we've talked this over so many times, haven't we? You, I know, feel that I would marry you and come to Australia with you when you go if I loved you as much as I believe I do. I truly think that my love would weather a separation of two years and I should have thought that if you loved me as much as you say, then you would rather wait than lose me. If you change your mind, Dallas, before you go home, then I shall be the happiest girl in the world. If not, then it is goodbye. I do love you, so very much, but I can't marry you yet.*
>
> 

*Ever your own,*<br>
*Scilla.*

And the few weeks that remained before Dallas was to return to Australia were a nightmare Kathie would never forget; Scilla, desperate, hugging the telephone, watching every post; her mother and father reiterating for the thousandth time, 'If that's the way he is, you're well rid of him . . . he doesn't love you enough to wait . . . he's not our kind . . . you know in your own heart, Scilla, that any reasonable man would wait . . . he's just a rough, uncouth Australian from the backs or whatever you call them . . .'

If only her parents, well-intentioned no doubt, could have refrained from making those remarks and left Scilla alone. They had both seemed utterly unaware of the dreadful torment their words caused their daughter. Slowly but surely as the weeks went by, Scilla's spirits drooped as hope waned. At one time, she might have sunk her pride and written again to Dallas, perhaps phoned him. But her mother's warnings made an issue of his silence which gradually influenced her young daughter to the extent of believing at least part of what she said so many times: *'If he loves you, he'll wait . . . he'll get in touch with you. If not, you're better rid of him.'* So it developed into that single issue . . . if Dallas really loved her, he would not let her go so easily.

Then the letter came from Dallas' close friend saying they were sailing next day. It was the end. Privately, Kathie had felt relieved that at least the waiting was over for her pathetically distressed young sister. She had hoped, as her mother and father did, that it would be a case of 'out of sight, out of mind'. And, indeed, for a little while it did seem as if Scilla had picked up her spirits and belief in the future. She no longer mooned round the house with tear-swollen eyes . . . no longer went off for long walks on her own, coming back late to meals and leaving her food untouched. Instead, she began to talk, a little feverishly, but at least to talk to members of her family, and then announced that she wished to take a course of modelling which her parents eagerly agreed to her doing, knowing nothing of the reason.

It was six months later when Scilla was running round London, drinking a little too much, staying out a little too late, with young men who were not exactly the companions that Kathie or her parents would have chosen for her, that Kathie began to see beneath the surface of this new Scilla. The girls now shared a small flat in town, necessary because of Scilla's classes and permitted since Kathie had agreed to live in town, too. One night, when Kathie had waited up until the early hours for Scilla and reprimanded her when she came in for her behaviour, Scilla had turned on her with a savage speech that had left poor Kathie floundering, dismayed and at last desperately sorry for her sister.

"Did I ask you to wait up for me, Kathie? You're not responsible for what I do . . . no one is. I'm my own master now. I've had quite enough interference from my family. Between you, you've ruined my life. If you don't like the results of your meddling, then that's your look-out. I'm going to get a job as soon as I can. Then I shall be self-supporting. I shan't touch a penny of Father's money . . . not ever . . . never again. He can control my life until I'm twenty-one, but only on the bigger issues. I intend to be independent of all Dad's money from now on. If it wasn't for him . . ." her voice began to rise dangerously, ". . . I'd be married to Dallas now . . . in Australia with him. I hate you . . . all of you . . . hate you . . ."

In the ensuing bout of weeping that bordered on a nervous breakdown, Kathie tried to reason with her sister. But deep in her heart she was no longer so sure that her parents had done the right thing. When Scilla had first met young Dallas Poulten and taken him home to meet her parents, her mother had been charmed by him. He was a tall, handsome enough young man with broad shoulders but an otherwise slim, graceful figure. His face was sun-tanned and the brilliant grey eyes that crinkled so frequently into a boyish grin were very attractive. His near-Cockney sounding drawl was a little off-putting at first but one had grown used to it and he had been a regular visitor to the large country house near his station in Lincolnshire. When it became apparent to the family that Dallas and Scilla were falling in love . . . or rather were already head-over-heels in love, Scilla's parents began to make discreet enquiries about him. It was not, Kathie thought, that they were really snobs . . . not that they counted wealth, which they themselves had, as being all important; but, not unnaturally, they had hoped for a 'good marriage' for herself and Scilla, by which they meant that they wanted for them at least the same standard of living to which the girls had been accustomed. They were sensible enough to realise that their income was well above average and that the war, while impoverishing many, had increased their own assets enormously; that it would be near impossible to find any eligible young men who could, on return to civvy life, match their income. But there were, nevertheless, quite a large number of young men left whose families had money and a distinct social position that placed them on an equal or better footing than they had themselves. Dallas, as a son-in-law, did not fit into this pattern of their hopes and so he was unwelcome and distressing to them.

Dallas, it seemed, had very little of what *they* believed necessary to make Scilla happy. His father, it transpired, was a not-too-well-off sheep grazier. There would be years of hard work and roughing, as Dallas put it, before he could offer Scilla very much. If his father did well, then naturally he, the son, would prosper too, and they had great hopes for the future. It was only natural to expect that the inflated price of wool would continue for quite a time after the war, if not rocket higher in a free market. Yes, Dallas Poulten was full of hopes, but he had nothing very much to offer at present except himself, Scilla's father pointed out bluntly.

There was no arguing that Dallas was a very personable and attractive young man. He had charm, lots of it, and he seemed genuinely devoted to Scilla. He had been to a good school . . . although none of them recognised its name as they would have recognised any of the English boys' public schools. Dallas would have gone on to university if he had not disappointed his father, who had high hopes for his academic future, by running away to join the R.A.A.F. Since then, he had served in the ranks until he qualified as a pilot and, miraculously enough, survived the war and risen to the rank of Squadron Leader.

Socially he was a little difficult to place. His manners were impeccable but he lacked the polish of the young men they had been used to having around the house. Scilla, of course, at seventeen had had no real friendships before. She had been friendly with many young boys from the neighbouring large houses when they were home from school or university, or on leave. But Dallas was the first young man who could be termed a suitor. The others had been Kathie's friends, older since she herself was Scilla's senior by seven years. Compared with them, Dallas was at times a little gauche, a little aggressive, self-assertive, perhaps. It might only have been his extreme youth and his inexperience by virtue of the war of smart dinner-table conversation and manners that made him seem a trifle uncouth. But Scilla's parents, first and foremost loath to consider letting her go to the other end of the world, unwilling to accept what they believed to be second-best for her, and lastly doubting her own knowledge of herself, arrived at the conclusion that Dallas Poulten was unsuitable as a husband for their daughter.

They had been too sensible to let Scilla see immediately that they disapproved of him as a possible husband. They had hoped, up until the day Dallas proposed and Scilla accepted him, that she might tire of him and find someone else. When it came to the point where Scilla, radiant, and Dallas, anxious, asked her father's permission to marry, they were taken off guard by the speed at which the affair had run its course.

Even then, they kept their heads. Quietly, their father told Dallas that he considered Scilla a good deal too young and inexperienced to know her own mind . . . that he would prefer them to wait . . . not even to announce an engagement as yet. Their mother, talking to a starry-eyed Scilla, sought to discount Dallas in various subtle ways. Was Scilla sure this was not just a flash-in-the-pan? It was well known that these young dare-devil pilots did not take life very seriously. Did Scilla realise how different life on an Australian sheep farm would be from the world she had been used to? Did she realise that her family and those who loved her would be twelve thousand miles away if anything went wrong? Was she, Scilla, equipped to be a domestic drudge to a young farmer? She couldn't cook, sew, had never had to keep house, to chop wood, draw well water. She might even have to have babies year after year without even a doctor to attend the births.

Scilla, worried, went straight to Dallas and asked him outright what conditions would be like in Australia. She knew she was not trained to be a farmer's wife and it had never occurred to her to look at a future with Dallas in such a realistic light. But Dallas had reassured her with laughter and also an oddly hard look in his grey eyes. She would have a nice house, one or two servants, a horse to ride, modern sanitation and reasonable comforts. She could have her babies . . . or none if she preferred, in a good hospital with the best medical attention.

"We don't live like the Aborigines, you know," he said at last in a tone of voice that caused Scilla to look at him in dismay.

"Darling, don't be hurt. I just wanted to know what life would be like. Mother thought . . ."

"Yes, I guessed it was your mother. She doesn't think I'm good enough for you. Well, that's okay by me . . . I'll push . . ."

"Dallas!"

With his arms around her, everything had seemed right again and even if she had known she would have to draw well water and chop wood, since it would be for him, she would gladly have done it.

But slowly, her mother's carefully chosen words, her far more insidious attack on Dallas himself, began to make Scilla afraid. How could Scilla be sure Dallas really loved her? She had his word for it but she was not experienced herself to know. Did anyone ever know?

Again and again, Scilla had gone to Kathie for advice. Might Dallas just be infatuated with her? Would he have still wanted to marry her if the war had been prolonged and he had not at the psychological moment of boredom suddenly met her? It was true that flying was virtually ended . . . that the excitement of missions was over and that Dallas, grounded now, was bored to tears with hanging about in England and mad keen to get home. It was true that he himself had said meeting her had made a world become dull and stale, radiant again. Was she just an antidote to boredom, a replacement for the heady excitement of flying? Did he only want to marry her because to go home without a girl would make it seem to his friends and relations there as if he hadn't been able to get one? Or because so many of his friends in the squadron had suddenly married the girlfriends they had never dared marry before in case their wives were widowed in the next week? War marriages were not a good thing . . . post-war marriages could be dangerous, too.

Kathie had felt unable to cope with these late-night dissertations from Scilla. All she could say was: "If you really love him and he loves you, then why not marry him? I wouldn't let Mother and Father stop me if I really wanted to marry a man."

"But you're over twenty-one, Kathie."

"You could marry him the day before he leaves for Australia. Mother and Father wouldn't chase you all the way out there."

For a time, Scilla lived on just that plan. Dallas made the necessary arrangements. Then a week before this secret wedding, Scilla lost her nerve. As if they guessed intuitively their daughter's thoughts, both parents redoubled their efforts to dissuade Scilla from marrying a man she knew so little about.

"After all, Scilla, if he really loves you, he'll be willing to wait a couple of years. Your father said if you hadn't changed your mind after just one year, he would reconsider the matter. That's not unreasonable, darling. You're very young . . . seventeen is young, you must admit, to decide on the whole future of your life. Surely to wait a year is the most sensible thing. You can write to each other . . . Daddy and I aren't against Dallas and you being in love. It's just that we don't want you to rush into marriage and regret it later. If he loves you, he'll understand and appreciate our sentiments . . . and what I truly believe to be your own."

"In a way, I agree with Mummy," Scilla said that night to Kathie. "I love Dallas . . . desperately. I know I'll never love anyone else. But I've only known him three months. I wish . . . oh, I do wish he wasn't going back to Australia . . . that we could have had a long engagement and then been married quietly and beautifully here . . . from my home. I hate the thought of a secret registry office wedding. Kathie, suppose he doesn't love me enough to wait?"

"Then you're better rid of him!" Kathie said with her usual common-sense outlook. "I think you'd be wise to wait and be sure."

"Dallas, I want to wait . . . I'd be happier to wait!" she had told him the next night, his arm tightly around her as they stood in the mild June darkness at the top of Cop Hill behind her home. It was a beautiful night, yet with those words she shattered the beauty of the evening for them both. Dallas suddenly withdrew his arm and said bitterly:

"So they've won; I guessed they might. They've talked you out of it!"

"Darling, don't . . . don't say that. It isn't true. Mummy and Daddy know nothing of our plan to get married. Mummy has nothing against *you*, Dallas . . . only against our marrying hurriedly."

"To your people, I'm an uncouth, rough, tough sheep farmer who isn't good enough or wealthy enough for their daughter. That's the truth, Scilla. I've always hated snobs!"

"Dallas! You can withdraw that remark. You know it isn't true!"

"Look, Scilla, I'm not prepared to argue the point. In any case it's wrong to set a girl against her folks. Besides, it isn't the point. The point is whether or not you love me and want to marry me. Do you?"

"Dallas, you know I do."

"Then does anything else matter? You'll marry me next week and come to Australia as my wife?"

"I'd rather wait . . . just a year, Dallas. We can write . . .

17

every day. I'll write every day, I promise. Maybe six months will be enough."

"Enough for what?"

"Why, to be sure that we're not making a mistake . . . rushing things."

"Then you do doubt your love for me?"

"No, I don't. But perhaps I doubt your love for me, Dallas. If you really love me, you won't mind waiting."

"I wonder whom you are quoting now . . . Mother or Father? No, I'm sorry, but I'm not leaving England without you . . . or at least, if I do, then it's all finished . . . for always. I know you're young . . . but if one is truly in love, then deep in your heart you know it. If you love me, you'll come with me. If you don't love me enough . . . or don't trust my love for you, then six months of writing letters, or a year or two years, won't alter that. I'm taking you home now. Let me know what you decide. It's got to be one way or the other, Scilla."

Then, after many bitter tears, Scilla had written the letter and it had been Kathie who had had to keep their assignation and deliver it. Scilla refused to meet Dallas again. Kathie would never forget the look in Dallas Poulten's eyes . . . first unbelieving . . . then desperate and then, lastly, they had turned to that steely grey which had really frightened her.

"Okay! So that's the way it is. I suppose I've known all along that this was what would happen. Well, tell those parents of yours that I'd have made a damn sight better husband for Scilla than any of their namby-pamby young men from Eton and Harrow. Tell them they needn't worry that they'll see me back. This is the way Scilla wants it and this is the way it is."

"Shall I give Scilla any message, Dallas?" Kathie had been afraid and sorry and not unaware of the bitter blow to his pride.

"You can tell her goodbye and good luck . . . and that I shan't be writing!"

So it was all over. Kathie hoped it was for the best. She

hoped that in a few months . . . a year, Scilla would meet someone else and she would cease to mourn Dallas. Certainly her young sister did not lack friends. She was out every night, dancing, drinking, and Kathie sometimes wondered what else transpired, although she need not have done so.

A year after she, herself, had married Pete (fortunately an ex-Scots Guards officer now demobilised and trying out his hand on the Stock Exchange, backed by his wealthy father, and therefore considered a good 'catch' for Kathie), Scilla had announced her intention to marry a young barrister. It was clear to Kathie that Scilla was not the least in love with him and she was desperately concerned for her sister. The engagement was finally broken off by mutual consent and Scilla's confidences were limited to a brief:

"I just couldn't go through with it, Kathie. I want to forget him, so let's not talk about it."

After this episode, she had quietened down a little and given up the late nights and champagne. It was almost, Kathie confided anxiously to her husband, as if Scilla had resigned herself to becoming an old maid . . . and yet she was only twenty! A year later, when Kathie's first baby, young Paul, was born, Scilla became the perfect aunt and admitted openly to Kathie that the greatest pleasure in her life were the days she spent at their house playing with young Paul.

"It isn't natural!" Kathie bemoaned. "I wish she could fall in love again. She still hankers after that Australian."

"Did he never write?" Pete asked, for he had heard the story of his wife's young sister soon after their wedding.

"No! I didn't think he would. He was proud, and looking back, I suppose rather young and very hurt. Can't you find someone nice for her, Pete?"

But there had been no one nice enough . . . or at least whom Scilla was prepared to take seriously enough. Then three months ago, Pete, who had rejoined the army, having found he had no taste for civilian life after the war years, announced that he was posted to Benghazi.

"Wherever is that, darling?" Kathie said.

"In Libya. I'm told the climate is fine for kids and I'm rather looking forward to it. Sailing, shooting, hunting . . . and of course it's on the Mediterranean coast so there will be all the swimming you could want."

"I don't like to leave Scilla! She'll miss the children so much!" Kathie remarked at last, her only objection to the posting.

"Then bring her along!" Pete said good-naturedly.

So the idea had been conceived and born and now here, in this out-of-the-way spot, Scilla had had to run into Dallas Poulten again.

"Are you sure, Scilla? *Sure?*" she repeated, and wondered if she dared to ask if Dallas was married and, if not, what this meant to her sister after all these years.

"Sure! Quite sure!" Scilla said, and burst into tears.

# Two

Kathie watched her young sister covertly across the dinner-table. No mark of the tears she had shed showed through the careful make-up and there was no questioning the fact that Scilla looked most attractive. The small, pointed, rather elfin face was alive with vivacity and the sparkle suited her even more than her usual lost, dreamy expression.

Kathie, who knew Scilla well, and knew to her own concern the events of the day, feared that Scilla's radiance was of a very brittle variety; that it was a defence against her inner fear and tension and desperate unhappiness. She had confessed to Kathie that she still loved Dallas Poulten . . . that she had never forgotten or ceased to love him. But it had been quite clear to her in the brief meeting that he had not the least interest in her . . . far less affection for her, and Robert Hendry had told her flatly that Dallas was in love with Nancy Harold . . . that rather flamboyant woman whom everyone knew and talked about because she *was* flamboyant and completely unconcerned what anyone said or thought about her. Her divorce had been a somewhat unsavoury affair, gossip about which had reached Kathie's husband, Pete, and been duly related to Kathie when she had asked him about the beautiful Junoesque woman whom she had seen several times at the Sailing Club and at dances.

Really, Kathie could not find it in her heart to blame Dallas who, after all, must be in his middle thirties. It was surprising enough that such an attractive man was still single. It certainly did not surprise her to know that he had long since fallen out of love with Scilla. She wondered just exactly what he had felt, meeting her again so unexpectedly.

Bill and Scilla were dancing now. Bill was one of those

21

rather nondescript but charming young Englishmen whom everyone liked instinctively. One simply could not help liking him. Five foot ten in height, a neither long nor short, narrow nor broad face, one would not notice him in a crowd. But once one had spoken to him and come to know him a little, his obvious simplicity and charm and inherent niceness singled him out from his companions. Kathie had hoped that maybe Scilla would be attracted to him for there was little doubt that Bill would make the perfect husband . . . kind, considerate, attentive, amusing, and although only a captain he had a steady career ahead of him in the army. Scilla had liked him and Bill had certainly fallen with a bang for Scilla. The stage seemed perfectly set when Dallas Poulten turned up. Kathie felt rather bitterly that Fate played very unkind tricks on people's lives.

Watching Scilla and Bill dancing, Kathie noticed that Scilla was smiling rather brilliantly and unnaturally into Bill's adoring face. Had she not known Scilla's inner sentiments she would have turned to Pete and said: 'I really think Scilla is a little in love with our nice Bill!' As it was, she sent up a private prayer that the nice Bill would not have to suffer the consequences of Scilla on the rebound, if it could be called that!

Bill, when he rejoined the table, was on top of his form. He cracked jokes and teased Scilla gently and with obvious tenderness. They were completing their meal when he suddenly lifted a hand and waved to someone coming in the door.

"Hi, Dallas . . . come and have a drink with us. Are you alone?"

Scilla's face turned chalk white and then pink, then white again as the Australian threaded his way through the other tables.

"I'm waiting for Nancy . . . the girl's always late! 'Evening, Scilla . . . say, you're Kathie, of course! Hullo to you!"

"This is my husband, Peter Henshaw! Dallas Poulten!"

Dallas shook Peter's hand and then sat down opposite Scilla and turned to Bill.

"Don't want to barge in on your party, Bill. We'll find a table for ourselves when Nancy turns up."

"If you'd rather be *tête-à-tête* . . ." Bill began teasing and Dallas said quickly:

"If you put it like that, fellow, we'll join you."

No, no, no Scilla cried silently. Please go away, Dallas, leave me alone. I can't sit here all evening watching you and Nancy Harold . . . I can't . . .

"Care to dance, Scilla?"

She had forgotten the flat 'a' of his accent, making him sound for a moment American or Scots. She stood up with every outward appearance of calm and moved through the tables on to the small square dance floor. The dark-skinned Sudanese waiters passed by her with laden trays of food and drink. As Dallas' arm went round her, she heard him saying:

"You've lost weight, I think, Scilla. I suppose it was puppy fat that wore off . . . not that you were ever fat. Your face is thinner . . . I think it suits you!"

She did not reply, not daring to trust her voice. She had been surprised that Dallas had asked her to dance after his rather curt behaviour this afternoon. Then she understood because he said:

"Remember this tune? 'Cuddle up a Little Closer, Hold Me Tight!' They're so out of date here it's probably the latest thing! I don't think I've heard it since those war years. Remember?"

Yes, yes, yes! Scilla's heart throbbed with the memory. Dallas could not have recalled exactly that they had been dancing to this tune when he had proposed to her . . . 'Marry me, darling, please marry me!' His present tone of voice was far too casual . . . too untouched by nostalgia or longing. Desperately she tried to control the beat of her heart and to concentrate on the dancing rather than on the burning touch of his arm around her waist, his hand holding hers.

"I hear you are in the F.A.O. out here," she at last managed to force the words through her lips.

"Uh-huh! It's a far cry from Australia but I'm enjoying the experience."

"How did the farming go?"

He gave a short . . . was it a hard? . . . laugh!

"Fine and dandy. As I'd anticipated, wool rocketed and Dad and I made our fortune. We could sell up and retire now if we wanted to, but Dad loves the work for its own sake, and I'd be bored to death doing nothing. That's one of the reasons I took this job . . . for a change."

"When do you go home to Australia?"

"Not for some months. You know, you haven't told me what *you* are doing out here. I see you aren't married!"

"No!" It was almost a whisper and she repeated the word louder. "No! I came out with Kathie and her husband as nanny to her children."

"As nanny? Surely she could afford to hire someone for that menial task?"

She was stung by the sarcasm of his voice as much as by the implications behind his remark. Swiftly she retorted:

"But of course! However, I rather enjoy the 'menial task' and Kathie was good enough to bring me along. Shall we go back to the table?"

He gave her a long look from those unfathomable grey eyes and then, with a slight shrug of his shoulders, led her back to the table. Scilla sat down, trembling with anger, and had only just managed to control herself a little when Nancy Harold arrived. She made what might have been a film star's entrance. Every head in the room turned to watch the woman in the brilliant amethyst-coloured, low-cut evening dress as she stood in the doorway, searching unhurriedly among the diners for Dallas. He stood up immediately and went forward without self-consciousness to greet her and lead her back to the table. For a second, Scilla felt rather than thought what a perfect complement these two made of one another; Dallas, tall, rugged, handsome, the woman nearly as tall, full-busted but beautifully proportioned, a dark Juno to his fair, somewhat Grecian, Apollo.

Any girl must feel colourless and insignificant beside such a woman and Scilla was no exception. She became conscious of her own slightness, her rather childishly slim arms and small hands . . . of the unfeminine style of her boyishly cut curls. She believed she looked as unsophisticated as a schoolgirl.

Nancy Harold was certainly beautiful in her way. She consciously or unconsciously exuded sex-appeal and she was without any trace of timidity. It was as if she were fully aware of her own powers and completely in command of herself and any situation which might arise. Some men might find her, oddly enough, too masculine. Bill was one of them. He preferred a little less certainty and loudness in a woman even while he admitted Nancy's attraction. Partly because of this, partly because of her reputation, he would have refused any invitations that were forthcoming from her! Personally, he told himself, he infinitely preferred the dainty and not so obvious femininity of Scilla with her big, rather sad eyes and that large appealing childish mouth that was a trifle too big in so small a face for real beauty.

Introductions were being made and fresh drinks ordered. Then Dallas got up to dance with Nancy. Bill took Scilla on to the floor and Kathie and Pete, feeling a little middle-aged since they preferred to sit and give their digestions a chance after their large meal, watched the two couples.

"I'm worried, Pete!" Kathie told her tall, thin, distinctly 'army-looking' husband. "How's this going to end? I don't like that woman . . . and I'm equally sure that Dallas does!"

"I don't know very much about your Australian," Pete said calmly enough, "but if he marries Nancy Harold, I think he'll regret it. Still, that's his affair. In any case, I daresay Scilla is well rid of the fellow!"

"Don't say that!" Kathie cried sharply, then softened to put her hand on Pete's. "The whole family said it . . . not once but a dozen times. We all persuaded Scilla into thinking the same thing. But it isn't necessarily true and I think between us and that ghastly phrase, we've ruined her life."

"She'll get over it!" Pete said, and regretted his words on the next instant seeing his wife's expression. "No, I suppose not. If she hasn't forgotten the fellow in nine years, I suppose it went pretty deep after all."

Bill came back to the table with Scilla. The sparkle had left her face and she looked tired and strained. Kathie ordered coffee but Scilla left hers untouched. She was carefully not watching the other two dancers. At last, they came back and then Dallas departed for a few moments to speak to a fellow Australian who had just come in from the bar.

Nancy Harold said:

"Heavens, it's warm in here! Why don't they start the fans! You gave up soon, Miss Eldridge?"

Scilla murmured something about it being too hot for her.

"Queer how you and Dallas should run into one another here of all places," the older woman went on in her rather over-loud voice. "Dallas was telling me you'd known each other years ago when he was in England in the R.A.A.F. Were you a W.A.A.F.?"

The tone was faintly derisive. Scilla said sharply:

"No, I was too young. I was seventeen the week the war ended. Dallas was stationed quite near our home and was a frequent guest at our house."

So Dallas had not told her that he had once asked Scilla to marry him!

"A babe in arms!" Nancy Harold said with a brittle smile. "Sweet seventeen . . . and never been kissed! Oh, to be young again!"

"It had its compensations!" Scilla said quietly. The older woman gave her a quick glance and then laughed.

"I imagine it did with the war on and all those dashing young airmen in and out of the house. Oh, well, *tempus fugit* and here we all are. Don't you just love this place, Mrs Henshaw?" She turned her attention to Kathie, but Scilla still felt the words were for her. "I find it so amusing here. Dallas has promised to take me to Cyrene one weekend soon. I've been there before, of course, and it really is the most romantic place you can imagine, with all those incredible old ruins. I suppose you haven't been there yet?"

"No! We had planned to make a trip there on Pete's next leave!" Kathie replied smoothly. "I'm told the best time to go is in July or August when it's so hot here. Then the change of air and altitude would do the children good."

"Of course, I'd forgotten you were child-bound!" Somehow the remark contrived to give the impression that she felt sorry for Kathie in her domestic rut and that she, herself, was free to appreciate the romance of Cyrene unencumbered.

"You haven't danced with me, Bill darling!" she went on. "And you are such a good dancer. Are you afraid Dallas will object to one little dance? I can assure you he's sufficiently civilised not to make a scene about it even if he does."

Bill was on his feet, grinning, but neither Kathie nor Scilla, nor even the unimaginative Pete, had failed to digest the implications this time . . . that Nancy considered herself Dallas' girl and that she, at least, believed Dallas to be her man.

"A type I don't like!" Kathie said shortly.

"She's probably all right!" Scilla said faintly. "I think she's most attractive . . . or at least I can see that she must attract the opposite sex!"

"Excluding me!" Pete said firmly. "Not my type. I may be old-fashioned but I prefer my domestic rut and Kathie!"

The dance was a short one for Dallas had returned to the table and Nancy Harold was not leaving him alone for long. Bill asked Scilla to dance again and she took the opportunity to tell him that she was feeling rather hot and tired and would like to leave fairly early if he had no objection.

"It's only nine-thirty, Scilla!" he said in a disappointed tone. "I can't take you home yet. What about a ride in the car to cool off? You've never been in the car with me for a run. Don't you trust me?"

"You know I do, Bill!" Scilla raised a brief smile. "All right,

I'll come for a drive. I'm not really tired . . . I just don't want to stay in this hot, stuffy atmosphere."

Bill looked happy. At Scilla's request, they waited till ten o'clock and then made their excuses to the rest of the company.

"Scilla's rather tired so I'm taking her home!" Bill said to Kathie. Scilla's eyes were on her hands, clasped round the tiny evening bag she was holding, and she did not see Nancy Harold's smile, nor the sharp look that Dallas gave her. For a brief instant, their eyes met as she said goodnight, but his were again veiled and rather hard and Scilla quickly dropped her gaze and with a brief nod to Kathie, left the room.

Bill seemed content enough to drive for a few kilometres in silence. Without really registering the impressions, her eyes had taken in the lovely curve of the harbour, softened and lit by a brilliant moon. Then they were driving along the road to Benina.

"We could stop at the airport and get a cup of coffee!" Bill suggested, and Scilla agreed. By day, the scenery was not much to be admired, flat and rocky and with little vegetation. But by moonlight, it had a certain charm and the cool breeze of the evening blowing against her face was welcome and somehow comforting. The land looked desolate, but so was Scilla's heart and she could therefore feel an affinity for it tonight which she had not felt on her arrival here.

Within twenty minutes, the lights of the aerodrome became apparent, but a little to Scilla's consternation Bill drew up on the side of the road and stopped the car.

"You don't mind?" he said, turning to face her as he adjusted the brake.

She shook her head nervously.

"You know, I was fearfully bucked when you said you'd come for a drive. I'd begun to feel I wasn't making any headway with you at all, Scilla. Do you . . . like me . . . a little?"

"Oh, Bill, of course I like you. Very much. I'm sorry if I've behaved rather casually. The truth of the matter is, I . . . I don't want anything serious to happen and I was afraid . . ."

". . . that I was getting too fond of you?" Bill finished for her. "I'll admit it, Scilla. It isn't just that there aren't many girls out here and you're one of the few unmarried and very attractive ones available for bachelors like myself. I don't want you to think that. I am serious . . . much more so than I've ever been in my life before. I just don't seem able to get you off my mind. Scilla, is it silly of me to be talking like this? Have I frightened you? I know we haven't known each other long, but I wanted to tell you how I felt."

Scilla bit her lip. She didn't want to hurt Bill and yet what she had vaguely thought might be happening had apparently done so and it was too late to side-step the issue now. The least she could do was to be honest with him.

"I'm sorry, Bill. I do like you . . . better than anyone I've met for years. But I'm not in love with you, if that's what you want to know. I . . . I'm just not capable of loving anyone. I'm terribly sorry."

The man's pleasant, usually cheerful face, creased into a little frown of perplexity.

"That's no shock to me, Scilla . . . that you don't love me. I guessed as much . . . but I don't altogether understand you when you say you aren't capable of loving anyone. What did you mean? Is there some other chap?"

"There was . . . once . . . a long time ago . . . in the war. I don't seem to be the kind of girl to whom love happens twice."

"He died, then?"

"In a way . . . yes! It's all long ago . . . I wanted to forget it . . . oh, Bill, I want so much to forget it and be able to fall in love again!"

The appeal of her voice and the pain behind her words touched him as no coquetry could have done. With instinctive understanding, he took her in his arms firmly and yet gently and covered her lips with kisses.

For a brief while, Scilla responded. All her emotions had been aroused by this strange meeting with the man who had for so long haunted her dreams. She was desperately lonely, desperately afraid of the unhappiness that seemed to cling to her, and here was comfort, love, a simple passion that brought an instant of forgetfulness.

But only for an instant. When she realised that her eyes were closed the better to imagine that they were Dallas' and not Bill's arms around her, she broke away from him in a moment of self-loathing.

"I'm sorry!" she whispered. "That wasn't fair!"

A little perplexed, Bill drew out his cigarette-case and offered it to Scilla. He could not fully understand her. He had been willing to accept the fact that she was not in love with him . . . he'd known it in any case and had been content to let their relationship develop slowly. The fact that she wasn't even able to give him some hope for the future had been a disappointment. Yet when he had held her in his arms, he had felt her immediate and surprisingly passionate response to his love-making and for a moment hope had dawned again. Now here she was apologising! Strange, lovable, enigmatic little Scilla.

"Bill, you'd better take me home now. I ought not to have come for this drive. I . . . it wasn't fair!"

"All is fair in love and war!" Bill said the only thing that seemed appropriate, and then, as he spoke, some inkling of understanding reached him. "I can fight a ghost from the past just as easily as a solid man in the present. In fact, I think I'd prefer the ghost!" he said with a return of his cheerful smile. "Don't you worry about what's fair to me, Scilla. I know how you feel . . . at least, you've told me honestly what I'm up against. I'm not taking that for final. You'll go on seeing me, won't you . . . letting me take you out? Maybe I can lay your ghost in time!"

"I wish you could!" Scilla all but breathed the words. "I want so much to be free. Bill, don't count on anything. I honestly believe that love is over and done with for me. I suppose I could have married before now . . . if I'd wanted a marriage without love. I hoped once that just being very good friends with a man, liking him, respecting him, might be enough. But in my heart I knew it wouldn't have worked out for either of us. Love must be mutual if it's to last a lifetime."

"Yet you . . . well, let's not go back to the past. It's the present that concerns me," Bill said sensibly. "I've been warned, Scilla, so if I still choose to take the chance of getting hurt, that's my affair, isn't it? In any case, I'm too deep in now to avoid getting hurt if you finally throw me over. So let me have my chance, Scilla darling. Give me a chance to win your love. Will you?"

For a long moment she did not reply. What reply could she give him? Deep down inside her, she knew that her love for Dallas burned as brightly, as tormentingly as ever it had. In fact, the sureness of womanhood and of her knowledge of the world and other men, had only served to increase her understanding of the love she had once had and received from the Australian boy. She could see now that at seventeen, inexperienced, she had taken a lot for granted . . . and thrown everything away in one act of stupidness. Must she go on regretting it all her life? Could she not by sheer will-power forget the past and learn to love a man like Bill? Perhaps her inability to forget Dallas had been because she had never really wanted to forget him; because in the recesses of her heart and mind, she had thought that somewhere in the world his love for her existed, too; that they might meet again to mend the broken threads of their romance. Now she knew differently. Dallas had long ago ceased to love her . . . moreover he was in love with someone else . . . might soon marry Nancy Harold. With that thread of hope, that dream shattered, could she not herself shatter the rest of her dreams, and find a new happiness with Bill?

"All right!" she whispered. "All right!"

He bent to kiss her again but this time it was without passion

. . . or rather with a well-concealed passion of longing for her. It was a kiss of tenderness and it drew him far closer to her than any other kiss would have done at that moment. Then he restarted the engine and holding her hand tightly in one of his own, guided the car with the other at a slow companionable pace back along the road to Benghazi.

# Three

They were spending Sunday afternoon picnicking at Gun Cove, a small beach southwards from the harbour along the coast where there were fewer people than at the Sailing Club. Kathie's two children, four-year-old Geraldine or Dina as she was more often called, and six-year-old Paul, were splashing about in the water; the grown-ups were lying in bathing costumes soaking up the sunshine which still, as yet, seemed a daily miracle to them. To be able to count on fine weather next day when you went to sleep at night, was still an enjoyment that all three of them commented on with the frequency of all new arrivals from England.

Kathie had a fairer skin than Scilla and tended to burn rather than to brown. But Scilla was already golden from head to toe and her coppery-coloured hair was bleaching rapidly fairer as the days went by. She was very quiet . . . had been withdrawn and remote for the week since their Saturday night dance at the Officers' Club. If Scilla had seen Dallas since that night, she had not mentioned the fact to her sister, and Kathie rather doubted that she had. Scilla had obviously been avoiding any possible contact with the Australian and had had only two nights out . . . to a cinema with Bill, and to a private dinner party with Kathie and Pete where they had known there was only a young army officer and their host and hostess to be present.

Kathie wondered how long Scilla could go on avoiding Dallas in a place as small and restricted as Benghazi. Apart from the cinema, there were only the various sporting clubs – the Sailing Club, Saddle Club, Tennis and Golf Clubs, where one might go during the day and to the Officers' or the Barbary

Club at night. Even at private parties one was always running
into people one had been talking to during the day and sooner
or later Scilla would meet Dallas again.

Kathie was not wrong in supposing that Scilla had been
trying to avoid him. She had done some serious thinking since
their depressing last meeting and had resolved that she would
somehow or other will herself to stop thinking about him . . .
to stop caring. She wanted desperately to be able to fall in love
with Bill . . . dear, nice, comfortable Bill; to marry him and
have two lovely kids like Dina and Paul. But she had found
that it was one thing to avoid Dallas, but quite another to avoid
thinking about him, about the past, about Nancy Harold, about
her own betraying nerves when she caught sight of some man
from a distance who might be Dallas but was not. She longed
with all her heart to see him again, and yet her common sense
told her that such an occasion would bring her nothing but a
deepening of her misery and unhappiness. There had been no
spark of affection in Dallas' eyes, no sign that he felt anything
but the most casual interest in her. There was not even that
slight sentiment he might have felt for an old flame. Instead he
had been all but openly rude to her and she felt that whatever
love he had once had for her had long ago changed to active
dislike. Surely, she told herself for the hundredth time, her
pride would forbid her continuing to love such a man. And
yet pride had no control over her emotions . . . those betraying
nerves that trembled when he touched her . . . that heart racing
at the sight of his rugged, sunburnt, attractive face.

"Scilla!" Kathie's voice, low and urgent. Scilla looked up
from her reverie. "Isn't that Dallas Poulten and Nancy Harold
coming towards us?"

At least her warning helped Scilla to gather complete control
of herself by the time they came sliding down the sand bank
and stopped to speak to them.

"Been in yet?" Dallas was asking with a cheerful nod at all
of them. "Looks beautiful, eh, Nancy?"

Watching the older woman, Scilla thought she could detect

a flash of irritation in her expression. The thought crossed her mind that no doubt Nancy had been hoping for a *tête-à-tête* with Dallas and was annoyed that he had made a point of running into people he knew. Was it possible that Nancy was afraid of her, Scilla? Afraid of the past association with the man she undoubtedly hoped to marry? For a moment, Scilla felt a primitive elation at the prospect, but then almost immediately rejected it. Dallas must surely have given an adequate explanation of their love affair and had no doubt been able to say with sufficient truth and conviction that as far as he was concerned, it had ended many years ago.

Meanwhile, Dallas had sat down beside Kathie. The children, who had run up to see who was joining the party, were introducing themselves. Paul, although the elder, was the shyer of the two and was sitting with his damp little body pressed closely against Scilla's as he nervously admitted to being six, to have started at the Army school, to be able to swim a little bit! Then Dallas was on his feet again stripping off his shirt and shorts and shoes and was encouraging Nancy to join him in a swim.

Nancy quickly followed and Scilla, seeing her clad only in a clinging white swimsuit, knew a second of admiration for the magnificent figure she portrayed. Large though she might be, she was beautifully proportioned and her legs were sufficiently long and tapering to carry her height and stature. Standing beside Dallas, bronzed and Greeklike with his broad shoulders and narrow hips, they were without doubt a perfect pair. Nancy shook her black mane of hair away from her face and smiled up at the man beside her.

"Race you down, darling!"

"You coming, too, Scilla?"

Had it not been for the 'darling', flung so carelessly and possessively, Scilla might have refused, but she felt stung by the sheer pain of jealousy and knew if she remained lying there in the warm sand, she would bury her head in her arms and weep. So with a forced gaiety and a nervous speed, she jumped up and ran ahead of them into the waves that were washing the white sands. For a moment the coldness of the water took her breath away, but she dived forwards and a minute later felt real pleasure as she struck out strongly away from the beach. Behind her, she could hear voices . . . Nancy's . . . saying, "Heavens, Dallas, it's too cold for me!" Then Dallas' impatiently, "Come on, it's lovely." A few moments later, he was swimming beside her.

"You're a strong swimmer for your size, Scilla!" he shouted to her as she swam steadily forwards. "This is something we never did together in the old days!"

Scilla put her face down into the water, partly to aid her stroke, partly to hide the expression she feared might be on her face. When she lifted it, Dallas was on his back, floating, and with an entirely boyish grin was kicking water at her. Her heart raced and in a second the years had dropped away and she felt seventeen again. This smiling, teasing Dallas was the boy she remembered, the boy she had loved, and with all her old impulsiveness she threw away her careful control and turning rapidly on to her back, splashed water back at him. Then she felt his hand on her head and knew he was ducking her. She drew in her breath as she went under, a smile on her lips. But unmeaningly he kept her there a moment too long and when she came up to the surface again, she was choking for air and coughing up mouthfuls of sea-water at the same time. Panic seized her as she floundered in the water and then Dallas was beside her, holding her beneath the armpits, saying:

"My God, Scilla, I'm sorry! I never meant to keep you under for more than a second. Put your weight on me. I'll support you till you get your breath back. Heavens, I'm sorry, kid!"

His voice, his words, particularly the last one which she remembered so well, swept away her panic and she relaxed on her back, her head well supported by Dallas' firm hands. She could breathe freely now and said:

"I'm all right, Dallas. I can swim back now!"

But he made her float for a few minutes longer until he was

quite satisfied that she had recovered. During those moments Scilla lay with her eyes open upon the expanse of brilliant sky and sparkling water. She could not see the shore and she had a sudden dreamlike impression that she might be millions of miles away from it . . . out in a vast expanse of blue. Perhaps this calmness, this quiet, the soft lapping of the water against her face, was the reason that some people who wished to end their lives just swam out, onward and onward into the blue, knowing the same perfect feeling of peace.

I wouldn't mind, she thought. Not with Dallas beside me.

"Scilla!"

Something in the tone of his voice as he spoke her name, started her heart racing again. She struggled free of his hands and turning over, faced him.

"Scilla . . . I . . . I can't say how sorry I am . . . you might have drowned . . . it was a rotten trick to play. I'm terribly sorry!"

"I know you didn't mean it!" The words dropped from her lips, now suddenly cold and stiff. She had expected him to say something else . . . something different. She was not quite sure what she had expected might follow that soft, gentle 'Scilla' . . . but it was not the awkward apology. Mortified and with beaten pride, she began to swim slowly and steadily back to the shore. She could hear Dallas splashing a few yards behind her and knew that he was slowing his pace to hers.

So he should be solicitous, after nearly drowning me! she thought viciously.

As the water became warmer nearing the sand, she felt a deathly coldness and lethargy in her limbs. She must have been swimming longer than she expected . . . or else the moment of fright had tired her. She had to make a real effort to gain the last few yards to the sand. As she tried to make footfall on the rocks, she stumbled and then she felt Dallas' arms go round her and as easily as if she had been Dina, she was picked up and carried back to the others.

"I nearly drowned her!" Dallas was saying to an anxious

Kathie. "Darned stupid of me . . . better get some warm clothes on . . . shock . . ."

With an effort, Scilla denied that she was feeling ill . . . said she was just cold and would lie in the sun for a moment. But Kathie would have none of it. Shoving Dallas back down to the water's edge, she insisted that Scilla get out of her wet swimsuit and poured out a cup of tea from the thermos.

In her cotton frock and cardigan and with the tea inside her, Scilla felt better and only then realised just how ill she had felt for a few moments. But her spirits were low. Then Nancy Harold said in her odd, superior tone of voice:

"I think you were rather stupid, Miss Eldridge, to swim out so far. It's one thing to risk your own life but invariably you endanger other people's if you get into difficulties!"

Scilla felt a hot flame of antagonism fire her to retort:

"You need have no concern for Dallas, Mrs Harold; he holds most of the swimming trophies that were available in England in war-time. Perhaps you did not know he was an exceptionally strong and capable swimmer?"

There was undoubtedly open enmity between the two now. Kathie understood it and wondered what it might lead to. Secretly she sympathised with her sister. There was something in the possessive way in which Nancy flouted Dallas in their faces that was objectionable, even to Kathie who had no interest in the man. She wondered how Dallas liked it . . . presumably he did or he would not be so friendly with the woman. She could have wept for Scilla. In a contest between the two, Scilla would not stand a chance. Nancy had all the advantages of years, experience and a carelessness for her own reputation that must leave nothing barred. Maybe this would be her undoing, but Kathie doubted it. What man could be immune to this woman's attractions . . . her colour, her glamour? One had to admit it . . . she was beautiful and ruthless. Unless Dallas' experience matched hers, he would be unlikely to see beneath the façade she chose to present to him, and he would be caught in the trap. Maybe he wanted to be caught.

Maybe this was the type of woman he cared for. Scilla's youth and innocence might no longer appeal to him as it once had done. And Scilla would not fight . . . she had too much pride; whatever sharp reply she might be stung to in a verbal duel with her rival, she would never show Dallas that she cared. Of that Kathie was happily convinced.

The men had returned now and they settled down to the picnic tea. Conversation was general and on a fairly simple level since the two children were in the midst of it, but once Nancy Harold filled a gap in the conversation by saying:

"Where's your charming young man today, Miss Eldridge? We're all so fond of Bill and it's quite touching how much he adores you. Oh, you mustn't deny it . . . I daresay I know Bill a good deal better than you and you can take it from me, he's your complete slave. Can we expect a real romance? It would liven up life in Benghazi enormously to have a wedding!"

Conscious of Dallas' sharp look in her direction, Scilla was momentarily tongue-tied. Then she said quietly:

"Bill and I have only known each other three months. I'm afraid you are jumping to conclusions, Mrs Harold."

"Have *you* any babies?"

This innocent remark from the four-year-old Dina made everyone but Nancy Harold laugh.

"What made you think I might have!"

"Well, Mrs-es do have babies!" Dina said seriously. "A Daddy, who's a Mister, marries a Mummy who is a Mrs and then they have babies. I'm going to have twenty when I'm married!"

"I'm going to have thirty!" said Paul, not to be outdone.

"That's enough, children. Run off and have a play and you can swim later when the tea has gone down!" Kathie interrupted. When they were out of earshot, she apologised.

"They're both at an age to have started asking awkward questions. Very embarrassing when they make their findings public."

"I suppose I'm rather old-fashioned, but I must admit I

believe in the Victorian edict . . . kids should be seen and not heard!" Nancy said casually. "I don't mean yours, of course, Mrs Henshaw . . . they're charming! . . . But some of the children at the Sailing Club . . . oh, well, I suppose I don't really like kids much."

"Don't you?" asked Dallas. "I think they're fun. I'm a great believer in large families!"

Talk your way out of that! Kathie thought viciously.

"One's own, yes!" Nancy said smoothly. "I'd love a large family of my own, of course. But then one can bring them up as one wishes, whereas with other people's you have to take them as they are."

"I think children are fine . . . all of them!" Scilla joined the conversation. "If they are objectionable, then it's invariably the parents' fault."

"Modern psychology? It's gone too far in that direction. A good slap never did any child any harm!"

"I agree with that!" Pete Henshaw broke in. "We often give Paul a sharp smack when he needs it. But it's not always easy being a parent!"

"Well, I wouldn't know . . . I suppose that lies in the future," Nancy said, looking across at Dallas. But he was idly drawing pictures in the sand and appearing not to be much interested in the conversation. They let it drop and presently Dallas jumped up and called to the children to come and play ball. Pete went to join them and the three women sat alone, watching the children and the men.

Does Dallas love her? Does he? Scilla was asking herself. How can he? Can't he see she is as hard as nails, selfish, greedy? She'll take everything and give you nothing. Oh, Dallas . . .

She lay back in the sand, closing her eyes against the glare. She could hear his voice now, sometimes his laughter, mixing with the children's.

If they were ours . . . ! she thought. If I had not been such a fool, we might be married and living here and Paul and Dina ours. I threw it away . . . threw my happiness away. Now he'll marry *her* . . .

She felt a soft thud beside her and opening her eyes saw the big red ball at the edge of her skirt. A moment later, Paul fell in a heap on top of it, scattering sand over her, then Dallas was there, sprawled out beside her, laughing.

She caught her underlip and tried to sit up but a second later Dina was bowling into her like a small warm puppy and in spite of herself and the tension of the afternoon, she found herself laughing, too. But the smile left her face again as she found herself looking into Dallas' grey eyes.

"Feeling better?" he was saying quietly. "I really am sorry, Scilla."

"I'm quite all right!" she told him, and unable to bear his proximity and the intimacy of those few words, jumped to her feet and chased Paul up the sand bank. She felt a little mad . . . dangerously mad with exhilaration and despair and a teeming confusion of emotions all out of proportion to their cause. For half an hour she behaved like a child, running, laughing, teasing the children, splashing them with water while they paddled about on the edge, then chasing them again while they dried off before going home.

But when the afternoon was over and they were driving back in the car, following behind the grey Chevrolet that Dallas was driving with Nancy beside him, her spirits drooped again and she knew that she could easily give way to tears and weep and weep.

I'm over-tired! she consoled herself. But she knew in her heart that it was depression and not fatigue that sapped away the energy and *joie de vivre* of an hour ago. I'll have an early night . . . go to bed soon after the children. I'll feel better tomorrow!

It was barely seven o'clock when, stepping out of her bath, she was called to the phone by Kathie.

"Dallas!" Kathie said shortly. "Do you want to speak?"

Half her mind said 'no', but all her heart said 'yes',

and so she went to the phone, wrapped around in a big bath towel.

"Scilla? It's Dallas! I want first of all to apologise again for this afternoon."

"That's both forgiven and forgotten!" Scilla said with an ease she was far from feeling. She waited for him to continue.

"Then you're feeling okay?"

"Yes, thank you! I've just had a very hot bath and I'm feeling fine."

"Well enough to come dancing tonight?"

She was taken off guard. It had never for an instant occurred to her that Dallas might be inviting her out. She was speechless and before she could find words, Dallas said:

"Do come, Scilla. If you'd let me give you a good dinner . . . or rather as good a dinner as the Club can provide! . . . I'll feel I have atoned a little."

"There's really nothing to 'atone' for!" Scilla said more sharply. "As a matter of fact, I meant to have an early night!"

"Don't back out of it, Scilla. I've cut a cocktail party and a dinner party tonight just so's I could have a few hours' chin-wag with you. Do come along!"

Her hesitation was only brief for hope had been reborn. If Dallas had really cut two parties . . . then perhaps . . .

"All right!" she said. "What time?"

"Eight-thirty? I'll pick you up a little before then. Okay?"

She put down the receiver and fairly danced along the tiled passage to the children's bedroom. Her face was glowing and her eyes alight.

"Kathie, I'm going dancing . . . with Dallas . . . tonight!"

Kathie gave her young sister a sharp look . . . first of surprise, then of concern. If Scilla could glow like that at the mere thought of an evening out with Dallas, there was small hope for Bill. Moreover, Scilla might be most dreadfully hurt again. She had guessed immediately from Scilla's face as much as from her joyous words, that it was to be just the two of them . . . that Scilla was hoping now what she had not believed possible when she re-met Dallas a week ago . . . that he might still care . . . or learn to care again. But suppose he did not . . . was in fact in love with that Harold woman! Poor Scilla!

"Don't expect . . . too much!" she said. "I hope you have a wonderful time, darling!"

"No, I won't!" Scilla said, suddenly sobered. Then her face glowed again. "All the same, Kathie, an evening dancing with Dallas can't be anything else but heaven. Even if it's only this one evening, at least I shall have had that."

The somewhat reckless words gave Kathie fresh cause for worry. Something of it showed in her plump, kindly face, for Scilla laughed a little bitterly and said:

"Don't worry, Kathie, he'll never know what it means to me, unless *he* wants it to mean something!"

Her demeanour of calm disinterest lasted until the moment the door-bell rang. The moment Pete answered it and she could hear her brother-in-law offering Dallas a drink before they left, she was in a desperate flurry of nerves. None of it showed on her face when the two men came into the room but her hands trembled a little when Dallas said:

"You look charming, Scilla!"

She knew she looked her best. The dress she had chosen was her favourite and undoubtedly the most chic and the most sophisticated she possessed. She had not worn it since she had been in Benghazi, feeling that perhaps the rather limited furnishings of the Officers' Club hardly warranted such extravagance. But tonight she was dressed not for the room but for her escort and as Kathie had openly told her . . . she looked her prettiest. The dress was pure white stiffened organza, showing off the lovely golden colour of her skin. Black lace flowers were appliquéd over it and the skirt billowed out from the tight neat folds of the bodice and waist. To cover her bare shoulders, she had a black lace stole. In her ears and round her neck were tiny jet flowers. She wore no other jewellery.

The drink Pete gave her provided her with a return of assurance; calm. As she followed Dallas down the stairs to his car, she was pleased that her hands were quite still.

When she slipped into the seat beside him, Dallas said:

"You know, I'd forgotten how small you were, Scilla."

She could not help wondering if the comparison were with Nancy Harold. For once she was glad she *was* small; that her bones were fine and delicate.

"It was good of you to come," Dallas went on talking in his slow drawl. "I'd thought maybe you wouldn't be feeling up to it, or that you already had a date with Bill."

"He's Duty Officer!" Scilla said simply. She left the implication that were Bill not otherwise engaged she might have been going out with him, although in fact she would not have done so; she would have pleaded tiredness and gone to bed.

"Nancy seems to think that chap is pretty serious about you."

It was almost a question. Scilla countered it carefully by saying:

"Does she?"

"Yes! As a matter of fact I was rather surprised to find you weren't already married. I can't believe you lacked proposals."

She countered that by saying cleverly:

"Thank you for the compliment, Dallas."

He seemed a little put out by her unwillingness to discuss her private life with him. In the ensuing silence, Scilla said:

"Where is Nancy tonight?"

A moment later she wished she had not asked, for Dallas replied:

"Her boss was giving a dinner party and she had to go, poor dear . . . be pretty dull from what I hear . . ."

So he had not cut a date with Nancy to take her out. He had merely cut a dull evening elsewhere. Her spirits drooped.

Ten minutes later they were in the bar of the Club, drinking Pimms. Scilla began to feel a little light-headed and the fact that Dallas was staring at her rather markedly, made her even more so. She suggested they eat and they went through to the dining-room and ordered dinner from the Sudanese waiter.

They were dancing between courses when Dallas said suddenly:

"You know, I counted up the other night and it's nine years since we knew each other in England. It seems another world ago."

Does it, Dallas? To me, it seems like yesterday!

"It was really strange running into you again . . . brought back so many memories of my flying days. I got quite nostalgic thinking about our squadron and the times we had."

But not about me! Scilla thought, feeling that every word was like a knife in her heart.

"I suppose the 'drome is non-existent now?"

"They ploughed over it. Nothing's left but the runways and they are slowly crumbling away." How many times had she driven herself over that 'drome and haunted the wheatfields that had been Dallas' airfield!

"It's rather sad to think of that. I suppose one should be glad the war's over and that kind of life over and done with. But we were very happy!"

You and I, Dallas? Or you and the other boys in your squadron?

"Yes!" she said.

"Time marches on! However trite the remark, it's none the less true!" Dallas said. "I know I'm not the same person I was in those days . . . we all change, I suppose!"

But not me, Dallas. I've never changed!

"Tell me about your work here!" she said, unable to bear the trend of conversation any longer.

He spoke for a little while about the F.A.O., explaining that it was part of a U.N.O. plan to help backward countries . . . that he felt it was a worthwhile job since he had spent so many years destroying land . . . a kind of recompense for his conscience. It was also in a way, a 'last fling' for him before he went back to Australia to settle down.

Was Nancy Harold part of the plan? As if in answer to her thoughts, he went on:

"I'd like to get married when I go back . . . have a family . . . start thinking a bit about the future. That's one of the things about planning what you're going to do . . . you feel you need to be doing it for a generation ahead of yourself. It's the building up that's fun but only if it's for someone. I'd like to get married."

There was no qualifying remark about 'if there's a girl who'll have me'. But of course, Dallas knew that Nancy was his for the taking. But he might not find it so easy to acquire a son, she thought, remembering Nancy's views on children.

He took her back to the table and they resumed their meal. Scilla had lost her appetite and was now wishing she had not come. Dallas, however, seemed unaware of her quietness.

"You know," he was saying, "sitting here with you makes me feel a kid again. I'd be quite capable of doing a Maori dance for you in the middle of the floor. Maybe I'm a bit tight."

"Do you . . . ever wish you were a kid again?" She could not prevent the words passing her lips. He considered it a moment and shook his head.

"No! Being young has some compensations but, generally speaking, I think growing up a painful process that must, perforce, be endured. When you chucked me over, Scilla, I was pretty badly shaken. It was a nasty blow to my pride. It took me a hell of a long time to realise that my pride was my main consideration. Well, we all make mistakes. The pity of it is that we don't realise them sooner. If it had not been for my pride . . . oh, well, *malishe*, to use the local expression for 'what's it matter, anyway'! Let's dance again, Scilla."

It never occurred to Scilla that there were two interpretations to his last revealing remark. Because she had already made up her mind that he was in love with Nancy Harold and not the slightest bit interested in her, she automatically assumed that all that remained to him of their romance was a blow to his pride. That was all he remembered, all he had really cared about . . . not losing her, but being jilted by her. If she had hurt him then, he had by those words delivered a mortal blow in return.

But there was another interpretation which, had she considered it, would have revealed the true state of his mind and heart. Dallas Poulten still loved her . . . still regretted that she had not become his wife; he blamed himself bitterly for having been too proud to give her a little time. He had, in his youthful eagerness and more mature longing, expected from a completely inexperienced seventeen-year-old girl a certainty of herself that was entirely unnatural in the circumstances. But not knowing this at the time, and knowing all too well how her family were set against such a marriage and doing their best to influence her, he had stood on his pride and delivered an ultimatum that was stupid and drastic. Because of it, he had lost her. If he had become secretly engaged to her . . . written to her . . . she might have gone on loving him . . . married him a short while after, despite her parents' objections.

But as Scilla was now misjudging him, so had he once again misjudged Scilla. He believed that she was in love with Bill, and, fostered by suitable remarks to this effect from Nancy, intended to marry him. Neither was prepared to let the other see what this reunion meant to them. Neither would ever, if they could help it, infer by word or deed what the sight and sound and touch of the other did to their minds and senses. In fact, they were both still young enough, hurt enough by the past and present, to pretend that they had long ago ceased to love; that their attentions were engaged in another direction.

So they danced again, casually, without intimacy but with a dreadful awareness that was unbearable to them both. Soon afterwards, Scilla pleaded tiredness and Dallas, depressed and hopeless, drove her home. He did not try to restrain her when she held out her hand at her front door, thanking him politely for a nice evening. She did not suggest that he come in although it was still early. Presently, the door closed between them and in the thoughts of each, unbearably lovely, unforgettable, was a memory of other nights when a dance ended in Dallas' car and their arms and lips pressed together in a passionate embrace.

# Four

"That you, Dallas?"

Nancy's rather deep-throated voice startled him as he climbed the stairs to his flat. He had been so lost in thoughts of Scilla and of the mess he had made of his life . . . of his love affair with her, that he had not noticed the shadowy figure outside his door.

"You!" he said, barely concealing his surprise. It must be well past eleven o'clock and he could not think what could have brought her to his flat at such an hour . . . unless . . .

"Expecting someone else?" Her eyes were laughing at him in the dull light of the landing but there was a harsh undertone to her words which, fortunately for her, escaped the man.

"Of course not, Nancy. You startled me. Anything wrong?"

He unlocked the door and closed it behind them as he spoke.

"Only a fearfully dull evening. It became so boring I pleaded a headache and thought I'd come round for a night-cap with you. I'd just arrived when I heard your footsteps coming upstairs."

This was not strictly true for she had been waiting nearly twenty minutes, irritated, anxious, but none the less determined to see him alone that evening. She had been thinking a good deal about her relationship with Dallas Poulten and was not entirely satisfied that it was progressing as speedily as she had planned. And now that old flame of his had appeared on the scene, she was worried. She had long since made up her mind that Dallas would marry her, Nancy. She considered him by far the most attractive man she had met . . . attractive to her in every way. He had money . . . a great deal of it.

She knew that however trying she might find life as a sheep grazier's wife, plenty of money would amply compensate for such drawbacks. If she became bored with the other farmers' wives, she could always nip over to Europe for a few weeks' holiday. But she did not fancy she would be bored so long as Dallas was dancing attendance on her.

The trouble was, he had never really done quite that. He had 'dated' her of course, far more often and more regularly than any other woman or girl in the place. He had kissed her once or twice on the way home from parties and there was a comfortable intimacy between them. She had every intention of developing it. But Dallas for some odd reason of his own had never shown himself willing for a *liaison* . . . the kind of love affair she had so frequently visualised for them and which, in her plans, would merge into marriage.

Nancy Harold had begun to get worried. It was six months since her divorce and it was clearly only a short time before she would be completely free of the husband she had never cared for. Yet Dallas' attitude to her was still no more than that of a man mildly attracted by her, mildly interested in her. Seeing to what lengths she had gone . . . and never before had she had to do so much to draw a man to her, she knew that she had so far failed to rouse him to the pitch she desired. She wanted him . . . and come what may, she intended to have him. She was, of course, far too experienced in the ways of men to let him know how she really felt about him. Dallas would, like most men, she expected, turn and run if he guessed he was being chased. So she had had to wait for him to make the running and her patience was wearing thin. Moreover, she was a little afraid that Dallas might, after all, be merely whiling away the time with her. This nocturnal visit was, on the surface, a casual plan that had occurred to her at a moment's notice. In fact, she had resolved during the afternoon to play one of her trump cards and try to pin Dallas down.

"Whisky?" Dallas asked, knowing by now that Nancy could drink any man under the table and yet remain sober. It was one of the facets of her character that he did not care for very much.

He poured out the two drinks and sat down in an armchair beside the empty grate. Nancy went across the room and flung open the french windows, standing outlined for a few moments against the bright moonlight. She knew it would silhouette her figure admirably. Then she turned and walking back to him, perched herself on the arm of his chair.

"This is rather fun!" she said casually.

It might have been . . . at any other time, Dallas thought ruefully. He quite liked Nancy and she attracted him in a purely physical way. He wondered suddenly why he had not taken advantage in these past months of what he knew instinctively she could offer him . . . was willing to offer him. Odd that he had not done so. Now that he had met Scilla again, he knew that he no longer desired this woman, however much he could appreciate the fact that she was eminently desirable. His thoughts were of the young girl . . . his girl . . . the only girl he had ever really fallen head over heels in love with and who had hurt him so desperately by refusing to marry him. Scilla couldn't know, of course, that she had only to lift her little finger to have him back . . . that without doing so, he was caught again in the old snare of her innocence and femininity and charm and loveliness. But she would not be interested in his reactions. She was all but engaged to Bill . . . and judging by the way she had avoided him, Dallas, he guessed she would have preferred not to run across him again in this strange fashion.

Dallas felt a moment of hopelessness. He believed Scilla to be out of his reach and yet in spite of that, he would have preferred to sit here alone thinking about her to sharing a nightcap with Nancy Harold.

"Sorry your party was so dull!" he said for lack of any other appropriate remark.

"I suppose yours was about as boring?"

The question caught him unawares. He guessed that Nancy would be none too pleased to learn he had broken his engagements and taken Scilla out to dinner instead. Still, she'd find out sooner or later. In a place like Benghazi everyone knew what everyone else was doing and discussed it freely! He told her briefly that he had been dinner-dancing at the Officers' Club with Scilla.

Nancy concealed her jealousy and irritation fairly well. Had Dallas not realised that she would willingly have broken *her* dull party to go out with him if he had suggested it? Spitefully, she said:

"Aren't you back rather early?"

"Scilla was tired. I daresay that ducking I gave her was partly responsible."

"I think it was rather a song and dance about nothing!" Nancy said with a short laugh. "You said yourself she was only under water a few seconds."

"Scilla isn't the type to play-act!" Dallas said curtly. "I've never known her do it in the past!"

"That was a long time ago . . . nine years, wasn't it? People change. I daresay you've changed a lot since those days, my dear."

Dallas considered it a moment. Had he changed? Physically, of course, he had grown older. He had grown wiser, too. But fundamentally he was the same man at thirty-three as he had been at twenty-four. The main difference, he supposed, was that he had learned not to reveal that fact. He was just as dare-devil, just as impulsive . . . witness his invitation to Scilla tonight! But he had learned to control his ideas and to simulate when necessary.

"I don't know that human nature does change!" he said, choosing his words carefully. "We may lose a little, or gain a little, but I think, underneath the exterior we choose to present to the world, we remain fundamentally much the same people all our lives."

She might have asked whether he believed Scilla was the

same girl he had loved years ago. But she preferred not to risk the answer. Instead, she remarked casually:

"You know, I love discussing life with you, Dallas. You never agree just for the sake of agreeing. I admire a man who sticks to his own opinion every time. In fact, I admire you as a person a good deal!"

"That's rot!" Dallas said, unmoved by the compliment. "Take it from me, Nancy, I'm a pretty poor type at heart. And I'd be damned difficult to live with."

"Would you?"

He felt rather than saw her quizzical glance at him; he knew then that if he chose to make love to Nancy tonight, she would be willing to have him. Her words were as near an invitation as they could be without being too obvious. To cover his uncertainty, he stood up and walked past her to the window. The night air was cool on his face and, away from the close proximity of the woman's sensuousness, he no longer felt any particle of desire for her. He said:

"I may be going home soon . . . to Australia. As you know, I'd expected to be out here at least another year. But I rather doubt I will stay on now."

He heard the shock in her voice as she said:

"But surely you've signed a contract, Dallas?"

"Optional break every six months. They could always replace me, you know. The truth is, I've a hankering to get home."

He never had before . . . before that girl came! Nancy thought desperately. She was stung to taunt him:

"Running away?"

She saw the slight movement of his head and then regretted the remark. He might think she meant running away from her!

He turned and came back to stand looking down at her. He knew that the moment had come for him to be honest about his feelings. He said:

"Perhaps I am, Nancy. You see, I guess I'm just a bachelor

at heart . . . always have been since . . . since Scilla threw me over. Maybe this sounds daft but I just don't seem able to fall in love again."

She stared downwards into her empty glass. She knew this was the brush-off and yet she could not . . . would not accept it as such. Dallas had been interested in her until Scilla arrived on the scene. He might be so again if that wretched girl went away and left them in peace. So long as Dallas didn't go first! She'd fight for him somehow. Her mind raced with plans, suggestions, ideas. Finally she said:

"I'd have thought you were far too proud a person to let a girl know she still meant anything to you after all this time."

Dallas flushed a little beneath his tan.

"Maybe . . . maybe not! I don't count so much on pride as I used to. If I'd not been so darned proud, I might not have lost her all those years ago."

You could win her now, Nancy thought with a moment's panic. Unless she was very wrong in her judgment of human behaviour, Scilla still loved Dallas. If either should get to know that the other still cared, she, Nancy, would have lost the most important thing in her life.

"She'll be going soon. Bill was saying the other day he expects a posting to Egypt or Cyprus. That will bring things to a head. I imagine they'll use the leave he gets on posting to get married."

"But they aren't even engaged . . ." the words were all but wrung from Dallas.

"*Sous entendu*, all the same," Nancy said calmly. "I'm terribly sorry, Dallas. I think the girl's a fool . . . she must be to have jilted you in the first instance and certainly to do so a second time." Somehow that made it seem even more definite that Scilla had no time for Dallas. "You'd be a fool to regret it too much, Dallas. As you say, you've grown used to a bachelor existence and I'm sure you'll be the first to agree that such a state of freedom is very agreeable. I'm having a taste of it myself at the moment and revelling in it. Free to

come and go as I please . . . free to go out and about with
whom I please . . . no one to nag because I shall be late back!
No one to nag you because you're sitting here talking to me
at midnight alone in your flat!"

In a way, she's right, Dallas thought suddenly. I have
enjoyed my freedom even while I've been darned lonely at
times. I don't say I wouldn't throw it all away like that . . .
he mentally snapped his fingers . . . if marriage meant Scilla
. . . but since that's hopeless, I may as well make the best of
what's left to me.

He looked round and saw Nancy watching him, a half-smile
on her face, her dark eyes smouldering. There were a hundred
men he knew who would give a great deal to be in his shoes
. . . here in this room alone with Nancy Harold.

She held out her hand and her fingertips touched his lightly,
sufficient for him to feel the tenseness of her body. She was like
a magnificent tawny lioness, teasing him, tempting him . . .

"Dallas?"

A moment later she was in his arms. He kissed her not
tenderly but savagely, bruising her lips and her bare arms
where he held her gripped tightly against him. She seemed
not to care that he hurt her. Her eyes, surprisingly, remained
open, smiling like dark pools into his. Her whole body was an
invitation to him and he knew in that second, before his senses
took an upper hand, that he hated her . . . hated and desired
her. And as if guessing his thoughts, she laughed huskily deep
in her throat and twined her arm about his neck.

Scilla sat on the grass amongst the wild flowers that were
still not yet withered by the hot sun. Spring was nearly over,
but on the Tocra Pass, the gateway to the Jebel, the green
remained all the year round, and up here there was always
a faint fresh breeze that was welcome after the hot hazy days
on the coast.

It was Sunday afternoon and Bill, off duty, had driven them
the fifty odd kilometres to this pleasantly deserted spot for a

picnic. She had accepted his invitation eagerly . . . feeling an intense longing to be away from everybody. She would, in fact, have preferred to be here quite alone, but in this country it was not safe for a woman to be out by herself in the comparative wilderness of the sparsely inhabited Barce Plain.

She had had a deep and severe shock during the morning . . . a shock that had dealt her a pretty terrible blow. She had taken Paul and Dina to the Sailing Club for a swim, and while lying on the warm sand, watching them, she had overheard a conversation that she would have given a good deal never to have heard. Behind her, two women whom she did not know were discussing various friends and acquaintances. At first their voices had been low, but perhaps imagining Scilla to be out of earshot, or asleep, their voices had risen. Although she was not in fact listening, her stricken ears had caught the following conversation.

"My dear, you know Betty . . . Betty Shepherd . . . she was telling me on the phone this morning that Jack Christie . . . yes, you know . . . the nice G.P. . . . made an awful ass of himself last night. His wife told Betty, so it's authentic. It appears Jack was called out in the early hours . . . fourish or so, to Mrs Jones, the one who's having a baby. She's had it now, of course! Anyway, he was driving to her flat when he passed that Australian's flat . . . Poulten, I think his name is. Apparently he and Nancy Harold were just getting into his car. Jack, the idiot, immediately jumped to the conclusion that there'd been an accident or something . . . at any rate, he stopped and asked if anything was wrong. Nancy Harold laughed in his face, more or less, and indicated that quite to the contrary everything was fine. I believe the Australian was rather embarrassed, but small wonder, really. I mean, suppose you'd had a night of it with some woman and were caught in the act of driving her home at dawn!"

"How frightfully funny! Typical of old Jack . . . innocent as they come!"

"Typical of Nancy, too. She's been chasing that Aussie for

some time. I suppose she'll flaunt him in our faces now she's got him. The only thing you can say for her is that at least she doesn't pretend to any morals. I'll say that for her."

"And better that Australian than a married man. She's really rather stunning . . . you have to admit it . . ."

Scilla had heard no more. Only the complete paralysis brought on by shock as the sense of the words had slowly penetrated her mind had prevented her moving before. She had run down to the water and, passing the surprised children paddling at the edge, had plunged straight into the sea. Had it not been for the fact that she was responsible for Dina and Paul, she might have swum out for miles to put as much distance as she could between her and the horrible gossip she had overheard. As it was, she had had to swim within a limited orbit until she was so cold that she was forced out again.

She was still trying to put distance between herself and the words she kept hearing over and over again, when she had driven out here with Bill.

He was watching her now, a puzzled expression on his usually cheerful face.

"Scilla, I wish you looked happier. You look positively miserable and I can't think of a thing to say or do that might cheer you up!"

His anxiety for her touched an emotion that brought her near to the tears she had so far been unable to weep.

"Oh, Bill!" she said rather pathetically. "I wish I'd never come out here . . . I wish I could hop on a plane and go home!"

"And I wish you didn't feel like that!" he said. "After all, if you did go home, I'd lose you. Scilla, can't you tell me what it is that's making you so unhappy? It isn't anything I've done or said, is it?"

"No!" she whispered. "You've been sweet to me. If you really want to know, Bill, I'll tell you. It's all over now . . . so it probably doesn't matter."

"Something to do with that chap you used to know?"

She nodded, barely trusting her voice.

"I met him again out here . . . I suppose you can guess now who he is. We used to be very much in love. A long time ago, I was going to marry him . . . but I was only seventeen and I didn't want to rush into a war-time marriage. He didn't want to wait so he went back to Australia without me. I was a fool . . . but . . . well, that's what happened."

Bill listened in genuine amazement. It had never for an instant occurred to him that Scilla had been in love with Dallas Poulten.

"When we met again here," Scilla went on in that broken whisper, "I knew it was all over. I couldn't have expected that he should still feel anything for me after all these years. I . . . I thought I still loved him. Anyway, it's finished now . . . for always . . ."

"But he's not married!" Bill offered the only comfort he could think of, forgetting his own hopes in his anxiety to help her. "Maybe in time he will fall in love with you again."

"No!" she interrupted him fiercely. "No! He and Nancy Harold . . . oh, I can't talk about it, Bill. I hate him now. I never want to see him again. That's why I want to go home . . . away from here. If it weren't for Kathie . . ." Her voice broke and impulsively Bill put his arm around her. She turned her face to him then and giving way to all the pent-up emotions that she had so far controlled, she wept into his shoulder.

Tenderly, Bill stroked her hair. He felt deeply perturbed by what she had told him. He had never realised just how much he was up against. It was one thing to set out to fight an old romantic memory . . . quite another to be rivalling a living man; moreover a handsome, charming fellow like Dallas Poulten. Bill liked him . . . had liked him since their first meeting. He thought him a thoroughly decent chap and admired him, too. The Australian had brains as well as charm, and Bill could see why a girl like Scilla should fall for such a man. Now she had said that Dallas and Nancy were making a go of it. Well, that was far from being a permanent state of affairs. Nancy was well known to have had one man after another in tow, even in the days when she'd been a married woman. Surely if Dallas knew that Scilla still loved him, he could not in his right senses prefer Nancy. But Scilla had said she didn't love him any more . . . though naturally a girl as sweet as Scilla could never sit back and watch an affair like that going on and still love the man. Whatever chance Dallas had once had with her, if it was true that he was carrying on with Nancy, he'd lost Scilla now.

"Are you sure of your facts?" he asked quietly.

Scilla dried her eyes and took the cigarette Bill had offered her. She nodded her head.

"Don't let's talk about it any more, Bill, it's finished. You've been sweet to listen to me and I'm grateful. I'd have been miserable without you."

He grinned at her somewhat ruefully.

"I wish you felt more than gratitude for a shoulder to weep on. Maybe, though, you'll turn to me on the rebound. Do you think that's possible, Scilla?"

She smiled in spite of herself.

"You're far too nice for anything so second-rate!" she said genuinely. "Don't fall in love with me, Bill. I'll only make you unhappy and there's no point in two of us feeling that way."

"Well, perhaps we could be less miserable together!" Bill replied cheerfully. "Why don't you marry me, Scilla? We've lots of things in common . . . we'd get along, wouldn't we? As friends, I mean."

"Yes, I think we would!" Scilla agreed truthfully. "But marriage isn't for two people who are just 'friends', Bill."

"Well, I know that's all you feel for me now, but maybe you'd learn to care. Maybe I could make you love me a little bit if I tried hard enough. Even if you were just fond of me, that would be enough for me."

"But it wouldn't, Bill, it wouldn't!" Scilla said with conviction. "If you really loved me, you'd be miserable. I nearly married a man I was fond of once but I couldn't go through with it. He wanted, and deserved, far more affection than I felt for him. He thought when we were first engaged, that it would be enough. But I knew . . . and in the end he admitted . . . that it wouldn't work. If it's any comfort, Bill, I'd marry you tomorrow if I thought you'd be happy."

"You really mean that?" Bill asked.

"Yes!" Scilla said. And it was true. Maybe to turn her thoughts towards loving someone else would be the best possible way to forget the past. To be genuinely fond of someone as dear and lovable as Bill, and spend one's life trying to make them happy, was perhaps the only way to forget one's own unhappiness; to kill once and for all those childish dreams. But she would not take a chance on Bill's future . . . his happiness. She might risk her own but not his. Falteringly, she tried to explain a little of this to him.

"Then you don't think that loving is as important as being in love? I always rather looked on the happily married couples I know as being very close, very intimate friends. I think that the 'in love' starry-eyed state wears off . . . or so it seems to me. The couples I know don't sit and hold hands every five minutes. They grow out of that stage into a happy, companionable 'loving' stage. They have children and the 'honeymoon' phase is over."

"Yes, I know. But Bill, they have been 'in love'. Their closeness, as you put it, has probably grown from that earlier hand-holding stage."

"But it is only a stage!" Bill argued hotly. "You admit that it does wear off. I suppose very rarely you do run into a real old Darby and Joan who sit and look into each other's eyes from their rocking-chairs! But not often. The majority are perfectly content with the second stage and I believe one could reach that without the first."

"You say that now because you want to believe it!" Scilla said hesitantly. After all, he could be right. One could fall in and out of love but it was much harder to break that close intimate friendship which grew up between happily married

60

men and women. She had seen for herself that this was so. Could she and Bill find happiness together?

Her mind flew back to Dallas and she gave an involuntary shudder. The mere thought of him now brought instantly to mind the voluptuous, colourful, hated vision of Nancy Harold. She never for one instant considered the fact that the gossip she had heard might not be the truth. She had seen Nancy Harold looking at Dallas, heard her proprietary tone of voice, known that she meant to have him. It had not surprised her, even while Dallas' part in it had shocked her, to learn that Nancy had achieved her aim. Now, since her own feelings for Dallas were completely dead or numbed, she could at least contemplate the thought of marriage with another man . . . especially since that man was Bill. He was so much Dallas' opposite, so much the kindly, sympathetic 'brother' to her, that it was impossible for her to feel repulsed by him. Her own feelings for him were affectionate and tender. She liked him so much . . . particularly these last few weeks, and she wanted to make him happy. Could she really do so by marrying him?

Scilla could not know that her whole being was parched with the need for comfort . . . for love. At a time when she was bitterly hurt, humiliated, mortified, Bill's love for her was as the rain must be to the dry land around her. She had no thought of using him . . . yet his offer of marriage, coming at such a time, offering mental and even physical escape from Dallas, swayed her clear thinking along the channels of acceptance. Nor did she realise that part of her longed to strike back a blow . . . to be able to say casually, 'I'm marrying Bill next week' . . . to show Nancy Harold *and Dallas* that she was not concerned with them.

But such emotions were buried in her subconscious and she did not realise them now. She only knew her need for Bill, which was an entirely new thing to her . . . born in the last few minutes. She had loved a memory for so long that now it must die she had to have someone else to love and cherish.

There was a strong maternal element in Scilla's make-up as well as a normal woman's desire to love and be loved. She was twenty-seven, young, attractive and desperately lonely. She wanted children. These needs had been unsatisfied for nine long years while she sought to attain for a second time the rapture of her first and only love affair. And now she truly believed herself free of the past.

Yet in spite of everything, she would not rush into saying a word that might end in tragedy for Bill. There was a strong streak of common sense that years ago had forbidden her to make a war-time marriage at the age of seventeen.

"Give me a little time!" she said at last. "Let me think about it a bit, Bill. Give me time!"

He was so elated by the thought that she might really consent to marry him that he eagerly agreed to do so. With a tact that was surprising in so relatively inexperienced a man, he did not try to kiss her but changed the conversation and in a little while suggested a walk. He put himself out to distract her attention, amuse her, make her laugh. To her delight, they found a tortoise sunning himself beneath a rock and Bill gave it to Scilla to take home for the children. Then he helped her to pick some of the great clumps of mimosa that hung from the wild bushes. He was rewarded to see the colour come back to her cheeks, the smile to her eyes. Once she even laughed gaily, saying:

"This is fun, Bill. Let's come here again soon!"

But as they drove home in the last hour before the sun set, he knew her spirits had drooped again and that she dreaded returning to civilisation.

"You must let me take you and Kathie and the whole family, if they like it, to Cyrene on my next leave. You'd love it there, Scilla. So would the children."

But even while she nodded her head in agreement, she remembered Nancy talking about a trip to Cyrene with Dallas . . . saw in her mind the two of them walking through the fir forests and ruins she knew to be there, their hands and arms entwined, and involuntarily she shuddered. Bill, noticing the shiver and supposing her to be cold, solicitously covered her knees with the navy blazer he had removed in the heat of the day. Then he held her hand as he steered with the other one until, laughing again, she placed it firmly back on the wheel as he nearly knocked over a camel laden with barley, to the curses of the Arab leading the animal.

When they reached Benghazi, Scilla invited Bill to stay and have supper with them. She knew Kathie would not mind . . . in fact would be pleased to have Bill there. Everyone liked him. He was always welcome and Scilla knew that fundamentally Bill well deserved his popularity. Surely, she told herself again, it should not be hard to love a man with such a disposition? Surely she could be happy with him . . . could make *him* happy? If only she had not loved Dallas so much and for so long! Even now she had to remind herself that it was in the past . . . that she no longer loved but hated him.

She shivered uncontrollably and was glad to have Bill's arm linked in hers as they climbed up the stairs to Kathie's flat.

# Five

"I don't know that I should necessarily believe that kind of gossip!" Kathie remarked carefully.

The two sisters were having a late night cup of tea together in Scilla's room . . . a half hour when they exchanged confidences, had discussions about the children or made plans for the next day. Both loved these moments and as Kathie's husband liked to lie in bed reading for an hour or so before he fell asleep, the fact that the girls were 'nattering', as he put it, did not bother him in the least. He liked Scilla . . . felt a little sorry for her, too, and shared Kathie's hopes that this 'holiday' in Libya might find her happily married off to some pleasant young man with whom she could settle down. It was dashed unfortunate that that Australian fellow should have been out here, too . . . and worse than bad luck that he was dating that woman, Nancy Harold. Kathie had told him about it earlier and he had guessed this was probably the topic of conversation between his wife and her young sister tonight.

"Does it make any difference whether or not it is true?" Scilla asked her sister rather bitterly. "It's quite clear he's in love with her."

With one part of her mind, Kathie was thinking how ridiculously young Scilla looked, sitting up in bed in a pair of palest blue nylon pyjamas, her thin bare arms stretched around her hunched knees. She might still be seventeen . . . when love had been hers for the taking. The other half of Kathie's mind considered the problem of Scilla now. She felt herself inadequate to deal with the situation. If she fostered Scilla's new-found dislike of Dallas, maybe the girl would turn to Bill. But would that necessarily be a good thing? She feared that it might not. So she had resolved at least to tell Scilla the truth, as she knew it.

"I suppose it may not make any difference, but the fact is Dallas can't have been taking Nancy home at four in the morning."

"Why not?" Scilla asked sharply.

"Because Mrs Jones' baby happened to be born at four. I heard that today and it's quite authentic. Since Dr Christie was on his way to see her when he passed Dallas' flat, it must have been several hours earlier. Babies, especially first babies, don't arrive in five minutes. As you yourself weren't home till eleven-thirty, Dallas couldn't have got back much before midnight, and by my reckoning, Nancy and he left soon after."

Scilla was silent a moment, considering this new aspect to the question. She had blindly accepted the gossip she had overheard because she believed that Dallas was in love with Nancy; and she had no illusions as to Nancy's feelings or her morals. But even if they were not true, it still could not alter the fact that there was nothing left between herself and Dallas; the old love they had once had for each other was long since forgotten . . . by him. And he had still been seeing Nancy late at night . . . after taking *her* out to dine and dance. How had Nancy known he would be home so early? There must have been some kind of assignation and it must have been made by Dallas, since Nancy could not have guessed what time she, Scilla, would ask to be taken home. Maybe she had been sitting in the flat waiting for him! Maybe she had a key and just let herself in and sat there waiting for him to come back. Maybe . . .

"I don't want to think about it . . . about him, any more!" she cried, feeling herself tortured by her own thoughts and suspicions. "He doesn't love *me*, Kathie, and that's all that really matters. I don't blame him. I sent him away all those years ago. I couldn't expect him to have gone on caring all that time just because I was stupid enough to do so.

It's all over now . . . finished. I'm seriously thinking of marrying Bill."

"Not really?" Kathie said anxiously, convinced now that this was no solution to the problem. "You wouldn't really do that, Scilla, would you?"

"I thought you liked Bill so much. In fact, correct me if I'm wrong, but didn't you and Pete choose him with that idea in mind?"

"Well, yes!" Kathie admitted with a half-smile. "But I never realised you were still so deeply in love with Dallas!"

"I'm not . . . I'm *not*!" Scilla cried childishly. Then in a quieter tone of voice, she added unexpectedly: "I wasn't really . . . not desperately . . . after all that time. But seeing him again . . . oh, Kathie! I know it's crazy after so long but I do still love him. I never really stopped loving him and regretting what I did. I tried hard to make a fresh start . . . to find someone else . . . to fall in love again. I never could. Then one look at Dallas and the past might have been yesterday."

"We made a dreadful mistake preventing your marriage," Kathie admitted softly. She herself had not really taken an active part in persuading Scilla to the action that finally broke her engagement. None the less, she was acutely conscious now of the pressure her parents had put on a very young girl . . . and how drastic had been the results. Dallas had been to blame, too. If he had waited a little while, Scilla might have married him despite everything. But they'd never heard another word from him.

"This Nancy Harold stage may pass, Scilla dear. You've waited so long, can't you wait a little longer? If you still love him isn't he worth waiting for?"

"Another woman's left-overs?" Scilla said harshly. "No, Kathie! I still have some pride left. As long as I live I shall never let him see how I feel . . . have felt."

"Perhaps you're right!" Kathie said doubtfully. "But don't marry Bill just to spite Dallas, Scilla. It wouldn't be fair to

Bill for one thing and you'd end up utterly miserable yourself. That's no basis for a happy marriage."

"Yes, I know!" Scilla whispered. "I wouldn't do it for that, Kathie. You know I wouldn't. I'm terribly fond of Bill . . . I like him better than anyone I've ever known. And he loves me in his way. I don't think it's a terribly deep way, he hasn't that kind of nature. Because he's so nice in himself, he'd do anything in the world for me, but I don't think he would feel that his world had come to an end because the girl he cared about had refused him. He's too easy-going . . . too casual. I don't think he'd ask a lot because he isn't a demanding or exacting person. He doesn't need the height and depth of love. He just wants affection . . . and a happy home, and children. I could give him those things. I want them myself, Kathie. I need them desperately . . . far more than Bill does."

Kathie felt her heart ache for the loneliness in Scilla's voice. Maybe Scilla was right . . . maybe she *could* be happy with Bill. Maybe it would be better for her than to go on, lonely and bitter and living in the past. If only she could be sure how best to advise her for her good. She felt wretchedly inadequate. Hers was not Scilla's highly-strung, deeply emotional temperament. She was far more placid, more simple in character, and things had gone so easily for her in her life. She had fallen in love with a man who was already in love with her and they had married with the approval of both their parents and been calmly and satisfactorily happy ever since. Scilla's life had been the antithesis of her own. No one could judge what would be best for Scilla except someone who had suffered and loved as Scilla had done. And what worried Kathie more than anything was that she felt Scilla might not be the best judge of herself.

"Well, don't act hurriedly!" she begged her. "Marriage is . . . or should be, for always. Don't forget that, Scilla dear."

"I know!" Scilla said quietly. "If I married Bill, however much I might live to regret it, I'd never let him know."

"You might not find it so easy to simulate feeling you don't have!" Kathie remarked sagely. There had been one occasion when Pete had been worried over his work and at the same time she had been none too well. It was during the time she was carrying Dina, and she had resolved to keep her own state of mind to herself and not bother Pete with her worries on top of his own. But he had seen through her false gaiety and her efforts to be bright and full of life. People who were in love were not easily deceived.

"I'd never have to simulate affection for Bill. I'm sure of that. I really am fond of him, Kathie!"

"My dear, I believe that. But marriage does mean more than 'affection'. To put it at its most obvious angle, it means living together as man and wife . . . desiring one another and conceiving children. Suppose that side of your marriage to Bill became distasteful to you?"

"Why should it?" Scilla cried, almost defensively. "I'm as much a woman as you are, Kathie. Am I to do without any woman's birthright because I was once in love with Dallas Poulten? All right . . ." she corrected herself with a rueful smile " . . . because I know in my heart that I can never love any man as I loved him?"

"No, darling, of course not!" Kathie agreed. "But emotions are strange things, Scilla, and sex is far more complicated than you might imagine. As an example, I know of one woman who was passionately attracted to her husband . . . that side of their marriage was quite perfect. But after the birth of her first baby, she no longer wanted him . . . desired him. Her doctor explained to her that women very often felt a perfectly normal subconscious desire to have children which gave them a conscious desire for a normal married life. But when they had achieved their subconscious wish for a baby, they ceased to have any interest in that side of marriage. That could be true of you. You love children and I know you long to have babies of your own. Scilla, don't think I'm trying to put you off marriage . . . far from it. I think it's a wonderful state of being, provided you love one another. But I can imagine it might be hell otherwise. That's the only reason I'm afraid for you."

"I'm not going to be afraid a second time . . . and have life pass me by completely!" Scilla said with a violence of emotion that surprised even herself. "I was afraid to marry Dallas . . . I'm not going to be afraid again."

"If you're quite convinced you would not be making a mistake, then I wholeheartedly agree with you marrying Bill," Kathie agreed. *"But not if you are still in love with Dallas.* Are you, Scilla?"

Scilla remained silent, her eyes on her hands. That question was almost impossible for her to answer. She both hated and yet still loved the Australian. It was not just that loving him had become a habit with her in her secret heart . . . not just that somewhere deep down inside her she had gone on hoping they might find each other again. There was a strange, unaccountable knowledge that she belonged to him . . . that she had been put here on this earth to meet and fall in love with and marry Dallas, bear his children.

Yet love must have something to feed upon if it is to endure indefinitely. She could no longer treasure memories of the old Dallas for they had been replaced by the new man . . . the reality rather than the image. And the new man she did not love. He was carrying on a sordid affair with a woman Scilla despised and, most bitter pill of all to swallow, had not the slightest feeling left for her, unless it were of indifference. She would never marry him now . . . she knew that. What had been beautiful and fresh and perfect about their love so many years ago was trampled in the dust and dirt now. Nothing could replace it on its pedestal of perfection. She would not want Dallas when Nancy Harold had finished with him, however much he might beg her to marry him. So what was the use in thinking about him, worrying about what had once happened? There was no going back, and because her life had stood still for nine years, she felt that it was time she went forward and started to take the controls into her hands instead of drifting along with the tide.

And Bill loved her, needed her, wanted her. He had been

on the scene at the psychological moment. Part of her was aware of this fact but could find no reasons to ignore it. It was nothing more than coincidence, good fortune, that someone as nice as Bill should happen to turn up at the moment her life was broken for a second time into hopeless pieces.

"I won't do anything in a hurry," she said finally. "But I've made up my mind to marry Bill, Kathie . . . sooner or later, if he still wants me. I shall be honest with him about my feelings and if he still wishes to go through with it, then I shall do everything in my power to love him and make him happy."

"If only it lay in one's power to do just that!" Kathie remarked as she stood up to take the tea-tray back to the kitchen. "Somehow I am not so sure one can, Scilla. But by all means, if it means your happiness, have a try."

Scilla pondered the question long into the dark hours of the night and only fell asleep exhausted with the dawn.

# Six

It was very hot in the back of the car in spite of the fact that all the windows were open and theoretically it was still only spring! None the less, the sun was hotter than they ever knew it at home in midsummer and a haze of dust lay motionless in the air around them.

Kathie sat beside Pete, and Scilla and the two children were in the back. They had a large basket of soft drinks and fruit to keep the children quiet during the four-and-a-half-hour journey to Cyrene, or, as the Arabs called the little village, *Sharat*. They had booked rooms at the Officers' Leave Centre, the one and only British hotel, for ten days. Pete had got weekend leave to bring them out and would be going back on Tuesday after a four-day holiday. Bill was coming out the following weekend and would drive them home. They would be three days on their own, but as Kathie said, this was one of the many occasions when she felt so lucky to have Scilla out here with her . . . she would not be lonely if Pete was away.

Scilla, who had already driven with Bill along the scrubby flat uninspiring road as far as the Tocra Pass, cheered them up during the first hour telling them of the pleasant green hills that would soon be coming into sight and of the breeze they would encounter as they climbed spirally up the road to the Pass. At the top, they stopped to let the children stretch their legs and have a drink and then climbed back into the car for the drive over the Barce Plain. Here and there they could see the results of the Italian colonisation scheme. Pete explained a little of the history to them as they drove. The country had first been colonised by the Greeks in the fifth century B.C. and was later occupied by the Romans. The ruins they were so looking

71

forward to seeing at Cyrene were of the great city that had once existed under these rulers. By the end of the third century A.D. the country of Cyrenaica had come under the Eastern Roman (Byzantine) Empire. Various wars were fought with invading Jews and Berber tribes, and in the next century by the ruthless and fanatical Bedouin tribes, and gradually the country lost its importance. In 1517, it became part of the Turkish Ottoman Empire and much later, in 1911, the Italians attacked and by 1912 had been ceded the country by the Turks. By 1939, there were twenty-one thousand Italian colonists in Cyrenaica. These colonists, financed by their mother country, were given small farms and areas of agricultural land on which by hard work and considerable industry they had managed to produce crops that the Arab population had never conceived possible. Some of these farms, derelict now since the Italians had been forced out of the country by the British in the last world war, could be seen on either side of the road for mile upon mile, the white stone villa-type farmhouses, all uniform in pattern and design, still bearing their foot-high inscriptions IL DUCE on the faded, weathered paint.

"It seems a fantastic waste that so much the Italians did here is now all but back to nature again," Scilla said thoughtfully. "I can't believe that the Arabs are grateful to us for throwing out the people who had started to cultivate all this land for them . . . and by all accounts, made an excellent job of it!"

"But the Italians did not do it for the Arab population!" Pete explained. "They did it for themselves and their own country. They treated the Arabs as slaves and gave them none of the benefits of the enormous output of production. The Cyrenaicans were delighted to be rid of them. I agree, however, that it was a pity the British could not do more to help them during their occupation at the end of the war. However, the Libyans must stand on their own feet now they are an independent nation."

"Are they able to do so?" Kathie asked.

"Well, they are getting a certain amount of assistance from

organizations like UNO. I believe that your Australian friend is sent by them and this is more his line of country than mine! Then there is LATAS, American technical assistance, and of course the British are paying three million a year under the Treaty of Friendship and Alliance."

The two sisters sat in silence for a while, considering this strange country they had come to. So much of it was wild desert which could produce nothing. Only the coastal belt and the Jebel could be cultivated . . . so different from tiny England where the green fields stretched like a patchwork quilt of farmland for mile upon mile. This was a hard rugged desert land which had to struggle to survive at all.

They drove downhill again towards the Waddi Kuf, a valley between the hills which rushed with water in the torrential rains but was now dry and green with growth that was refreshing to their eyes after the parched sandy land of the coastal belt in which Benghazi was situated. They began to climb again, great jagged rock faces hundreds of feet high towering on either side of them. High up these rocks could be seen enormous caves where, Pete told the delighted children, it was reputed the cave men had actually lived.

There was not one single soul in sight. The sun blazed down fiercely and when they stopped the car again to admire the view and stretch their legs, Scilla was struck by the silence and the loneliness of these mountains. Yet they appealed to her, too. Something primitive responded in her to the magnificence of nature, untouched by civilisation. She could imagine those cave-dwellers, herself among them, hunting their food amongst the wild animals, cooking in primitive pots on a spit over a fire of wood gathered from the trees that grew everywhere, even from between great jagged rocks. She could imagine lying here in the sunshine, Dallas beside her, listening to the bees and the sound of the leaves rustling on the bushes and trees. She could imagine bright moonlit nights such as she had encountered in Benghazi, lighting up this fantastic scene and a million stars high above their heads. Perhaps in another life, she and Dallas

. . . She broke off her imaginings at that point and turned her attention to the present. She was suddenly chilled and glad to hear the children calling each other, to see Kathie's broad back in her light flowered summer frock, to hear the civilised hum of the engine as Pete restarted the car.

They continued climbing until the land levelled out and they reached the tiny village of Bada where the Libyan king had his summer residence. Bare-footed, sparsely clothed Arab children played in the dusty streets and watched the car go by without undue interest. Some wore remnants of army uniforms and here, as everywhere in this country, there were the ugly remains of war . . . old petrol cans, scrap iron, old tyres. Nothing was wasted. Walls of Arab dwellings had been made from petrol cans filled with stones or cement. Scilla had seem them often in Benghazi and realised the ingenuity that was born of dire poverty and need.

A few kilometres beyond Bada, they turned off the road to Tobruk and were soon entering the little village of Sharat. Both Scilla and Kathie, who had heard so much about the beauty of Cyrene, were a little disappointed in the ramshackle, untidy street that was typical of a million other Arab habitations. There were a few shops, a little market, and only the fact that it was more or less untouched by modern times made it attractive. With only this one road for communication with its nearest big towns, Benghazi and Tobruk, each at least two hundred miles away, the little village remained as it must have done for thousands of years.

But beyond it, the glorious view that came upon them as they rounded a bend in the road took their breath away. Far below stretched the green coastal plain that surrounded Apollonia, and there, against the green, shone the brilliant, sparkling blue of the Mediterranean.

Pete turned the car into a road running between a small wood of fir trees and they were at the hotel. The children scrambled out excited, eager to explore. Kathie and Scilla stretched their stiff legs and resolved to try to bath and shower before lunch if there were time. Pete, directing the unloading of their suitcases, was momentarily interested only in a cool drink in the bar!

Calling the children, they went into the comparative cool of the hall and were told their room numbers. They went upstairs and surveyed their rooms appreciatively. They were all side by side, Kathie and Pete next to Dina and Paul, and in a single room, Scilla. The double rooms each had their own private bathrooms.

"It's going to be fun!" Kathie said, her cheerful face glowing. "I am glad we came!"

Scilla, too, felt a lifting of her spirits that was not entirely due to the cooler, fresher air of the higher elevation of Cyrene, which was some two thousand feet above sea level. She had not realised until now how greatly she had missed the country. Now she was immensely glad to be able to look out of her window and see the fir trees and the green grass and here and there the wild flowers.

By the time they had unpacked, washed and changed, the gong had sounded for lunch, and collecting Pete from the bar they went into the dining-room. As she passed through the swing doors, Scilla felt her heart jolt and every breath of elation leave her body. There, at a table by the window directly facing her and staring at her with equal surprise, was Dallas.

Even Kathie was halted momentarily in her tracks and it was Pete who observed social etiquette sufficiently to half wave his hand in greeting. His movement seemed to release the others from their stunned surprise and dismay and, white as was possible beneath her tan, Scilla followed Kathie to a table as far removed from Dallas' table as possible. He must have remarked their avoidance of him for although he finished his meal a few moments later, he made no move to come over to their table to say hello and he walked out of the room without glancing at them again.

Kathie shot an anxious glance at Scilla but she was looking down at her soup plate. It was impossible to discuss this latest development with the children present and, in any case, Kathie had the feeling that Scilla would not be in the mood to talk about it. It seemed appalling bad luck. In the three weeks since Scilla had told her that she had all but made up her mind to marry Bill, they had none of them seen Dallas Poulten. Bill had been a frequent visitor and there had been much to discuss when they resolved on this plan to come to Cyrene. Scilla had seemed happier, less strained, more her old self, and Kathie had begun to hope that perhaps after all she was 'getting over' Dallas . . . was really a little in love with Bill. He, too, must have thought so for he had said to Kathie one evening when Scilla was out of the room, 'If she'll have me, Kathie, you won't mind?' She had assured him that he had her blessing as, indeed, he would have. Bill was a dear!

It had not escaped her thoughts that Bill might be hoping this holiday in Cyrene, most romantic of places, would bring things to a head. She had herself felt that Scilla needed only a slight push to persuade her to accept Bill's proposal; that she might purposefully be awaiting the right moment to say 'yes'.

Now . . . now they had found Dallas Poulten here . . . in the hotel. Angrily, she told herself that he was a civilian and had no right here in an Army-run establishment. But she knew that that was nonsense since civilians could always book rooms provided there were vacancies, which usually there were. But what could have brought the man here . . . by himself? What brought him now . . . this same day they had come? Fate seemed to have it in for poor Scilla in no uncertain terms. In a small, family hotel such as this, there would be no avoiding the man.

They ate their meal in a flurry of forced conversation that was entirely different from their earlier mood. Kathie, anxious and apprehensive, talked too much; Scilla said nothing; Pete made a lot of very stupid remarks. Only the two children, unaware of what was going on over their heads, chattered excitedly and ate a meal worthy of their appetites.

As if by mutual consent, they had coffee in the dining-room

instead of the lounge and afterwards arranged to set off immediately to explore the ruins. For the next few hours at least they could avoid the Australian, and as to the evening . . . well, that problem lay ahead.

With a sigh of relief, they left the hotel and walked slowly down through the trees that led to the past.

# Seven

Dallas sat in the lounge holding but not reading a three-day-old paper. He had seen Scilla and the others come out of the dining-room and, without coming near the lounge where he sat, go quickly out into the garden. He knew then what he had suspected in the dining-room – that they were going to try to avoid him. He was angry, hurt, disappointed and yet not altogether surprised. He knew of the gossip that had been circulating Benghazi about himself and Nancy and supposed that it had long since reached Scilla's ears. Her behaviour was understandable under the circumstances. For the hundredth time, he mentally swore at Nancy. Gone now were his hopes of patching things up with Scilla . . . or rather of trying to win her back again. True though it might be that she intended eventually to marry Bill, she was not yet engaged to the fellow and all was fair in love and war. So much he had resolved the night he had rejected Nancy and all she had to offer him.

There had been a brief moment when he had thought himself lost . . . powerless to resist the temptation she threw at him. Holding her in his arms, he had felt his senses weakening and only the curious little cry of satisfaction that she had given as he drew her into his arms had broken the spell of that moment of desire. He had known then that she had deliberately set out to seduce him . . . and that she thought she had won. It challenged his innermost pride to think that any woman . . . especially a woman like Nancy, could plan such an act like a campaign and he be the mere pawn in the game. Desire had died and he had released her with a gentleness he was far from feeling. The expression on her face as she realised that he had refused her was oddly pathetic to him.

"I'm sorry, Nancy," he said at last, to break the silence and the astonishment in her eyes. Her expression had turned then to anger and for a brief instant he had almost felt afraid. Then suddenly she laughed.

"Oh, but there's nothing to be sorry about, Dallas. I really don't see why you should be apologising to me."

He could not believe that she could be so obtuse and it occurred to him instantly that she was salving her own pride by pretending that she had expected nothing more than a few kisses from him. He was willing to play the game that way if she chose.

"I was afraid I was being rather a dull companion," he said briefly. "I'm on edge, Nancy, nervy, can't settle. I suppose I'm tired."

"It's past midnight!" she replied lightly, drawing out a vanity case and touching up her lips. "I'm tired, too. It's an enervating climate, I think. Perhaps you'd ring for a taxi, Dallas?"

"Oh, but I'll run you back, of course!" Dallas offered swiftly. That was the least he could do now.

Then as he was helping Nancy into his car, that stupid ass of a doctor had had to stop and ask if anything was wrong. He supposed now that it was inevitable that word would go round that Nancy was leaving his flat late at night and he was not in the least surprised by the story, greatly exaggerated, when it reached his ears again a week later. He might have laughed at the 'taking her home at dawn' if it had not been that he feared his real friends – and Scilla, might have heard this version.

Now he was practically certain that she had. If he had ever had a chance of winning her love again, he knew he'd lost it now . . . unless she did still care a little bit. Then she might listen to his explanation . . . the true story. But if she was in love with Bill, then she wouldn't be interested.

Dallas felt hopeless and utterly miserable. While he had not actually remained passionately and desperately in love all these years, he had never ceased to think about Scilla; had never stopped regretting his folly. Once or twice he had thought of writing to her but his pride had always forbidden it. He could never forget that her family did not think he was good enough for her; that Scilla, herself, had doubted him and his love; had not had sufficient faith in him to trust their future together. So he had not written and yet he had not fallen in love again or ever wished to marry. He had thrown himself heart and soul into his work and derived some bitter satisfaction from achieving what he had only been able to promise Scilla that he might achieve.

Successful, wealthy, socially acceptable everywhere, popular and, as he could not fail to know, attractive to women, he had nonetheless felt little pleasure in his achievements. There had been no one to share in the glory . . . and he was desperately alone. He sought sometimes to alleviate that loneliness of his very spirit by going to parties, by flirting with women like Nancy, by drinking a little too much at the bar with the fellows. He was not happy. Yet he had not fully realised until he had met Scilla again that it was because of her . . . or the lack of her, that he could never feel radiant with joy, and success was bitter in his mouth.

Meeting her had been a shock. She was so much more beautiful than he remembered her. The childish immaturity of the seventeen-year-old had gone and she was now a woman. His heart had taken the same plunge seeing her as it had the day they first met. Stupidly, perhaps, he had felt he could not bear to have her know it. That same stupid pride . . . recalling all too easily that she had thrown him over once long ago, had made him speak on that occasion with a sharpness, a curtness he was far from feeling. Afraid that he might betray himself if he remained, he had risen abruptly and left her sitting there with Robert Hendry, not knowing what the sight and sound of her had done to him.

To be in love at thirty-three, Dallas had since discovered, was a far more painful experience than at twenty-four. One had learned a different set of values and he had known, discovering Scilla anew, that she alone of all the women he had ever met, was worthy of love; that she was sweet, good, kind, innocent, maternal . . . that to be with her was to be with the very essence of untouched womanhood. He had felt himself both hopeless and helpless and unworthy of her. Nevertheless, if it had not been for the fact that Nancy had told him Scilla was soon to marry Bill, he might have fought for her.

He wondered what had brought Scilla and her sister and family to Cyrene this particular weekend. He, himself, had come out to have a look at the agricultural development around Barce Plain and had decided to combine business with pleasure . . . to drive on to Cyrene and stay the weekend and see the ruins he had heard so much about. He had welcomed the thought of a few days away from all the people he knew in Benghazi and their now typical remarks, such as: 'Where's Nancy tonight? Not dancing?' 'Where's Nancy . . . not golfing?' Always the link between his name and Nancy's that he could not deny outright except to his more intimate friends. He merely laughed and said he was not Nancy's keeper, but they clearly thought otherwise.

In point of fact, he had tried not to be alone with Nancy since that night in his flat. Whenever he had seen her, it was with a party of others. Unfortunately for him, they were now automatically asked out together; well-meaning friends said, 'Oh, yes, we'll ask Dallas and Nancy, too!' The only real consolation Dallas had was that he had put in for a transfer back to Australia and would be gone in a couple of months. Until then he would have to put up with suggestions that had been so nearly justified.

Now he knew he had to deny them. He could not bear that Scilla should remember him with this nasty bit of gossip attached to his name. That is, if she thought about him at all. He wondered how he might engineer a few hours alone with her . . . to talk to her. Perhaps she would give him a chance to explain, not only about Nancy but how he felt about her.

He could at least make one last attempt before going back to Australia. Judging by Scilla's attitude to him he had not much hope but he knew, at last, that pride ceased to matter when what lay in the balance was losing her . . . or perhaps winning her.

Maybe I should speak to Kathie first, Dallas thought uncertainly. Kathie could tell him how much truth lay in the rumour that Scilla was in love with Bill. Kathie could tell him what Scilla's attitude was to him, Dallas . . . whether he stood a chance. But on the other hand, he felt that this was a coward's way of going about things. He preferred to go direct to Scilla . . . or at least, fabricate a suitable moment and then tell her outright that he still loved her, that he had never loved any other woman . . . that there was no truth in the gossip about himself and Nancy. He would stake everything on one direct approach to her . . . and at least he would have the certainty of a direct refusal or the shadow of hope.

He did not, however, see Scilla again until dinner-time. He had been at the bar watching the hall which led to the stairs where she must come down. Pete joined him a little before eight and they stood each other a round of drinks while Pete told him about their visit to the ruins and that the two girls were putting the excited children to bed.

It was nearly nine when at last Kathie and Scilla appeared, changed into short dinner frocks and looking fresh and attractive. Dallas, watching Scilla closely, saw her eyes meet his gaze and then drop directly as she moved away from him to stand beside her brother-in-law. Kathie looked a trifle anxious, Dallas considered, but at least she spoke to him, whereas Scilla immediately started a discussion with Pete on the ancient history of Cyrene. Dallas, acutely sensitive, was aware she had intended to exclude him.

Pete, however, invited him to share their table for dinner, and Dallas accepted promptly, still hoping for a word with Scilla . . . a moment in which he could tell her that he particularly wanted to speak to her alone.

All through the meal, Scilla maintained the merest fringe of polite conversation with him as was necessary for good manners. During the coffee that followed in the lounge, Dallas was beginning to feel the strain and had all but given up hope of his project when Kathie suddenly disappeared upstairs because she thought she heard one of the children call out, and simultaneously, Pete went out to the bar to get some more cigarettes.

"Scilla!" Dallas said quickly. "I know you've been trying to avoid me. I think I can guess the reason. But for the sake of . . . of old times, will you give me a few moments alone . . . to talk to you?"

She appeared surprised and a little unnerved by this sudden request, spoken in a hurried undertone. He saw her eyelashes sweep down to veil her expression and noticed that the slim, sunburnt hand was gripping the tiny coffee cup as if it had been a ton weight.

"Scilla, please! What can you be afraid of? Come out for a short walk in the garden with me . . . now. Please, Scilla! It isn't much to ask!"

Because Dallas' request was so utterly unexpected, because she had felt a strange electric atmosphere surrounding him the whole dinner, Scilla was off guard and unprepared with a ready refusal. She could not know what it was Dallas wished to discuss with her alone . . . and yet something . . . something about him and the way when she had glanced up continuously always to find his eyes on her, had confused her, and in spite of her determination, caused her nerves to tauten like violin strings. She was afraid . . . and yet she was not sure what she feared. She longed . . . and yet did not really believe . . . that Dallas could be about to tell her that he still cared about her. It was a crazy thought . . . without any foundation on fact, and yet something deep in her heart had told her these last few hours that it *was* so.

"All right!" she whispered. "I'll come!"

Neither Pete nor Kathie had returned as the two stood up and walked in silence to the door, through it on to the tiled patio with the large flight of steps leading down into the garden. A bright moon flooded everywhere with a silver light. The air was cool but not cold . . . like a midsummer's night at home. In the distance, Scilla could hear the barking of the pye-dogs . . . wild dogs that roamed the desert. She could hear, too, the chirrup of the crickets in the grass.

Dallas put a hand lightly beneath her arm and steered her down the second flight of steps that led to the tiny fir forest below. Then, as they reached the bottom steps, he turned suddenly to face her, and holding both her arms tightly in his two hands said:

"Scilla, Scilla!"

The tone of his voice told her what in words he had been unable to express. She felt her body tremble and a sweet fire rush through her veins as her heart answered that call. Every fibre of her being responded with the love she knew he was asking for, and yet, even as she raised her face to receive his kiss, she remembered Nancy and she drew back.

His face shone white in the moonlight and she saw the bitter hurt in his eyes. Then his face softened and he said:

"So you believe what you heard about me . . . and a certain woman in Benghazi?"

He had released his hold on her arm and weakly she sat down on the steps.

"I . . . yes, I suppose I do!" she said at last.

"But it isn't true. I swear it isn't true!" Dallas cried. "Let me explain, Scilla. Please let me tell you what happened."

"But I don't want to know," she cried. "It doesn't concern me, Dallas. You've no need to explain to me."

"But I want you to hear the truth. Scilla. If it weren't for that, would you . . . could you still feel anything at all for me? Anything of the love you once bore me? Just now . . . I thought maybe, after all, there was a little hope for me. Tell me I wasn't wrong, Scilla."

She felt herself torn in two conflicting directions. All her instincts, all her emotions, soared with the glorious utterly unexpected knowledge that *Dallas still cared*; that her own love was not unanswered. But at the same time, reason and her new-found scorn for Dallas' behaviour, her resolve to forget him, made her cautious and proud and she knew that however much she might love him, she could not bear to have Dallas kiss her if he had in fact come from the arms of that other woman.

"What did happen?" she asked at last, her voice nearly inaudible.

He told her falteringly what had occurred. He tried to spare Nancy, which under the circumstances was a little difficult, so that his words lacked the conviction they might otherwise have had.

"You must believe me, Scilla! I wouldn't dream of lying to you about a thing like this. And if it had happened, I wouldn't be here, talking to you, telling you how desperately in love with you I am. You must believe me!"

She wanted desperately to do so. Somewhere in the back of her mind, she felt that Dallas' story was not a very likely one; that Nancy would not have come to his flat late at night wanting nothing but a night-cap. Nevertheless, it was credible. Kathie herself had said that Nancy must have left soon after midnight and nowhere near as late as four in the morning. Not that times were so important. What mattered was how Dallas felt about Nancy. He had at least convinced her that he was no longer in the slightest bit interested in the woman . . . that he had never felt anything but a mild attraction to her because she was amusing and good company and he had been lonely.

He stood in silence, looking away from her down the mountainside where, faint and sparkling in the moonlight a mile or two far below them, sparkled the sea. He was unconsciously silhouetted against the light sky and horizon and, looking up, Scilla felt a sharp pang of remembrance of the long face, the straight nose, the clean line of jaw. Everything about this man was magnetic to her . . . and it was not just a physical reaction of her body to his. Memory recalled as well the delight of his quick smile, the tenderness of his touch, the sympathy of a mind that had once been so closely in tune with her own.

"Oh, Dallas!" she whispered, rising softly to her feet and moving the few steps forward till her head was level with his shoulder. "I want so much to believe it. I—"

But he allowed her no further words for he turned quickly and drew her into his arms, silencing her lips with kisses that made her forget the existence of anyone else in the world but the two of them.

"I love you! I love you!" he said against the soft fragrance of her hair. "Scilla darling, darling girl. We were crazy young fools to allow anyone to separate us all those years ago. We belong together . . . you and I. Say you believe that, too."

"Yes, we belong together!" Scilla breathed the only words of which she was completely certain.

Triumphantly, he kissed her again and the bright fire of their desire mounted swiftly until at last, suddenly tender, he said:

"Dearest . . . darling . . . my lovely girl. I'm going to take you in . . . before your fond sister comes looking for you and finds you compromised by me. I'm going to take care of you now . . . and always."

Scilla felt dazed by the overwhelming swiftness of her varying emotions. Fear, doubt, anxiety, had been swept aside in the glory of their reunion . . . the rediscovered love in each other. She held his hand in a fierce possessive grip because she needed by this physical contact its reassurance that this was not a dream . . . had really happened. Her heart was too full for words . . . they would come later. She had not, as yet, told Dallas how she felt about him although he must have guessed! Tomorrow . . . and on all the tomorrows, she would tell him how much she loved him . . . how she had always loved him . . . all through the years. Now, each was content just to hold the other's hand and to know that the future once more stretched brightly in front of them. And Dallas, deeply touched by the girl's sweetness and fundamental innocence, was curbing the impatience he felt to make her all his own. Had he been able, he would have wished to marry her tonight . . . to put the deed between any possibility of misunderstanding or mishap in the future that might prevent him making her his wife.

But he would not rush her; would not prejudice his great happiness by any action that might make her doubt the real quality of his love for her. Above all, he did not wish her to think that it was based only on a physical desire. He loved her too much for that to be more than a tiny part of the whole.

"Don't say anything about us to the others!" Scilla said as they climbed the stairs that led back to the hotel. "Tomorrow we'll tell them. Tonight I want to be quite alone with my thoughts. I don't want them to know tonight!"

"You will not be alone, dearest, for I shall be sharing the same thoughts!" the man said softly. "But I know how you feel. It's too wonderful to talk about yet. I still can't believe that I've found you again . . ."

She turned her face towards him and with a sweet gesture lifted her hand to touch his cheek gently with her fingertips. He caught the hand and pressed his lips against the soft palm.

"I love you, so much!" he said. "To think that had you refused to talk to me alone, we might never have known the other still cared. We would have gone our own separate paths and might never have seen each other again."

She shivered suddenly, but mistaking her strange fear for cold, Dallas said solicitously:

"You go in, darling, I'll follow later. There's no need to say you've been with me, no one saw us come out. I'll see you tomorrow."

But she could not leave him yet and with a little cry she held out her arms to him again and was drawn back into the safety and the warmth, the wonder of his embrace.

"Dallas!" she said at last. "Kathie is sure to guess. It must show in my face! No one could feel as I do and it not show. I shall tell her if she asks."

"Let's tell everyone!" Dallas cried eagerly. "I want to proclaim it to the whole world."

"No!" she said, although she could understand his feelings. "Let's have one day just to ourselves. Let's spend the whole of tomorrow alone together. I'll talk to Kathie tonight . . . tell her I'm going off with you for the day. We could get a picnic packed up so we need not come back to lunch. Remember the picnics we used to have at home, Dallas?"

"I remember!" he said instantly. "The long sunny days, the hayfields, that farm where we had bacon and eggs on our way home and the farmer's wife was so nice to us."

"She knew we were in love!" Scilla smiled. "I recall, too, that you deserted me to talk sheep with the farmer. One day we must go back and see them."

"Let's start off early tomorrow!" Dallas said eagerly, reminding her poignantly of the eager boy who had so often planned in just that voice one of his day's leaves.

"We can't get breakfast before eight!" Scilla laughed.

"I'll fix that!" Dallas said firmly. "Let's be off before anyone else is up. Is six-thirty too early?"

"No!" Scilla agreed. For every moment of this day would be precious and she knew that the night between would be far too long since it must mean parting from him.

"We could see the ruins together. I've not been over them yet. Would it bore you to go over them again?" Dallas asked. She shook her head, for she had observed very little of them this afternoon. Could it have been only this afternoon? . . . when her mind had ached with unhappiness and despair. How little had she imagined those few short hours ago that she would now be here in Dallas' arms, planning a day together alone, in love . . . loving . . . being loved. For surely she could not doubt Dallas' love any more? He had given his word that nothing had happened with Nancy that she could object to. Everything he said, did, proved that he loved her. He had not forgotten those precious moments in the past. If he had ceased long ago to care about her, he would not have those memories fresh in his mind. She must not doubt him . . . ever again.

"Say it . . . say it!" Dallas was whispering against her hair as he had used to do long ago. She smiled from pure joy and suddenly wildly happy, she broke free of his arms and laughing softly to him in the darkness, said:

"Tomorrow I'll say it!" For she knew he wanted her to tell him she loved him. He must know it, of course, and he was only as eager to hear her say those words as she had been to hear them from him. But because they had been so near to her lips for so many long years, she would not say them now. She would make him wait a little longer to hear them . . . until tomorrow.

"Good night, darling!" she called as she ran from him up the steps. "I'll be ready at half-past six!"

Kathie looked worried when Scilla went back through the lounge but seeing Scilla's face, she knew that something momentous must have happened and that Scilla could not speak of it now. With a glance at Pete, she followed Scilla upstairs to her bedroom. Scilla, radiant, flung herself on the bed and smiled with all the joy in her heart.

"He loves me! He loves me!" she told Kathie exultantly. "Kathie, you're not to tell anyone yet . . . not even Pete. It's so wonderful we want to keep it to ourselves . . . just for a day. We're going to spend the whole day together . . . I'm to be ready at six-thirty. Oh, Kathie, I could shout I'm so happy."

Gradually, Kathie made sense from Scilla's broken sentences and her own kindly round face beamed.

"I'm so glad . . . so glad!" she said happily. "The only thing that worries me a little is Bill."

Scilla put her hands to her face.

"I . . . I'd forgotten," she said at last. "Kathie, Pete will have to take a letter to him when he goes on Tuesday. It wouldn't be fair to let Bill come here perhaps expecting that I . . . oh, Kathie, how terrible that I should have to do this to him . . .

89

hurt him. I'm so fond of him, I can't bear the thought of his disappointment."

"But it will have to be done!" Kathie said firmly. "Don't think about it now, darling. Just go on being happy. I haven't seen you like this in years. Scilla, you're sure . . . no doubts at all?"

For a second, she saw a shadow pass over Scilla's revealing face. Almost admitting that the doubt existed, she said:

"Dallas swears there was nothing between himself and Nancy. I have no reason to doubt his word, Kathie. You yourself thought it was nasty gossip."

"Of course!" Kathie soothed her. "I trust Dallas myself and I'm sure he wouldn't lie about a thing like that."

"Only if . . . if he loved me so much that he knew the truth would keep us apart. No, that isn't what I really feel . . . I do trust him, Kathie. I think he might have been attracted to Nancy . . . but that's all. It's only—" She broke off, her face showing her inner uncertainty.

"Only what?" Kathie asked.

"It's silly really and such a little thing. I just can't understand what Nancy was doing at Dallas' flat that night. Dallas said she was waiting on the top landing for him outside his flat when he returned home after leaving me. I suppose that makes sense and yet . . . well, Kathie, would you go round to a man's flat at that time of night and just hang around on the landing waiting for him?"

"No, I wouldn't!" Kathie admitted. "But Nancy might. She'd be capable of anything."

"But it doesn't sound like her . . . to wait unless she thought there were something to wait for!" Scilla persisted, voicing the doubts that she had not considered when she was with Dallas, listening to his explanations.

"Maybe she thought there *was* something to wait for and was disappointed!" Kathie said, coming nearer to the truth than either at the time believed possible.

"Dallas admitted that he had been carrying on a mild

flirtation with her . . . but nothing more. He said it meant nothing to him except that it helped to pass the time and he had been lonely and rather bored here in Benghazi until she had 'taken him up' and started introducing him to people. Because he had been more or less 'under her wing', to use his own words, they had been asked out frequently together since many of his friends were the ones she had introduced him to in the first place; that he found her attractive in a rather flashy way. But that was all."

"Isn't that all believable?" Kathie asked. "I think he has told you the truth about Nancy, Scilla."

"Yes, so do I! But I *still* can't understand what she was doing outside his flat that night. He said they had had no prearrangement to meet . . . that she must have turned up on a sudden impulse. He says she had only just got there on her way back from her party when he turned up."

Kathie was silent a few moments thinking. Then she said sensibly:

"I think you're making too much of a small incident. If you love Dallas, you have to trust him. Even if he had been flirting a bit with Nancy before he found you again, surely that's perfectly natural? She is attractive . . . in her own way. Dallas was lonely, bored. What man would have been disinterested?"

"I suppose I feel like this because of the way she talked to him in front of other people . . . as if they belonged together. It was 'darling' every other word . . . and 'Dallas and I', and I suppose I took it for granted that they were in love. Now I find it hard to reconcile my ideas."

"Nancy may well have acted in a proprietary fashion without any real grounds for doing so. Maybe she hoped she would marry him; maybe she was just trying to get him accustomed to the idea in her own way. Men can be very obtuse, Scilla, and he probably didn't even consider that she was in love with him . . . scheming to marry him. If he wasn't thinking in those terms himself, it probably never occurred to him that she might be getting serious."

91

"I think you are right!" Scilla said.

She sat up and brushed the curls from her forehead. Her eyes were bright again and she seemed to Kathie to have flung off with sudden resolution any last doubts she had maintained. She was glowing and vital and a little drunk with sheer happiness as she told Kathie of their plans for tomorrow.

"I'll never be able to sleep, I'm so happy!" she cried.

But as soon as her head touched the pillow, she was lost in a deep, dreamless, untroubled sleep such as she had not had in years. When she awoke to the knock on her door at six o'clock the next morning, she felt fresh and wide-awake, and her heart was still singing with joy.

Dallas was waiting for her at the foot of the stairs when she went down twenty minutes later. She had pulled on a cardigan over her dress . . . a yellow and white check gingham with a fresh muslin collar which made her, to Dallas' eyes, look seventeen again.

There was no one else about in the hotel and as he held out his arms to her, she jumped the last two steps and was caught and held against his heart.

"Oh, Dallas . . . at six-thirty in the morning!" she laughed as the quick, impulsive kiss ended.

"Breakfast!" Dallas replied, taking her hand and running with her along the passage to the dining-room. They had bacon and eggs, fried by one of the *gaffirs* who smiled at their good spirits and was clearly enjoying his small part in their happiness.

They left the hotel as the first guests were stirring and ran down into the fir woods where they behaved like schoolchildren, chasing one another down the steep banks, throwing fir cones, stopping to pick bunches of wild flowers. They stopped for a rest on a fallen log and smoked cigarettes and talked. On his back, Dallas had slung a small rucksack containing their picnic sandwiches, a couple of bottles of beer and fruit. They ate an apple now and counted the pips to play 'This Year, Next Year, Sometime, Never'. It was 'This Year' for each of them and they laughed again and believed in the magic that had made the apple pips tell them the truth. For they would be married this year, Dallas said happily. This week, if he could have his way.

Then, together, they read the romantic Legend of Cyrene from the book Dallas had bought the night before in the hotel.

*The city owes its name to the nymph Cyrene. The legend of her marriage to the god Apollo, who pursued and brought her from Greece to Libya, is beautifully descibed in one of the odes of the great Greek poet Pindar (522–443 B.C.)*

*Cyrene was a girl of great beauty and unconventional tastes. "She was not one who loved the pacings to and fro before the loom, neither the delights of feasting with her friends within the house, but with bronze javelins and sword she fought against and slew wild beasts of prey and gave great peace and quiet to her father's herds, letting her sweet bedfellow, Sleep, brush her eyes but briefly before dawn.*

*"Once, as she struggled alone, without spear, against a terrible lion, Apollo found her. He was very much struck by her beauty and at once called the centaur Cheiron to ask advice. 'Is it lawful openly to put forth my hand to her, or rather on a bridal-bed to pluck the sweet flower?'*

*"Cheiron replied that Apollo being a god knew the answer, but – 'To wed this damsel camest thou into this glen, and thou art destined to bear her beyond the sea to a chosen garden of Zeus, where thou shalt make her a city's queen, when thou hast gathered together an island people to a hill in the midst of a plain. And then shall queenly Libya of broad meadowlands be well pleased to receive within a golden house thy glorious bride, and there make gift to her a portion of the land, to dwell there lacking neither the fruit of*

*all kinds of plants, nor acquaintance with the beasts of the chase.'*

*"And swift the acts and short the ways of gods who are eager to an end. That same day accomplished he the matter and in a golden chamber of Libya they lay together; where now she habiteth a city excellent in beauty and glorious in games."*

"It's beautiful!" Scilla said. "I'm so glad I've come to see the ruins again today . . . with you, Dallas. Yesterday they were nothing but a jumbled mass of stones in a rather beautiful setting. Today I shall see it as 'a city excellent in beauty and glorious in games' and feel that I am walking where Cyrene and Apollo walked all those thousands of years ago."

They took no guide with them as they wandered into the Sanctuary of Apollo. They preferred to discover alone its beauty and to try to imagine for themselves how it must have been when Cyrene and Apollo lived there.

One of the most fascinating things they found were the continuous springs which so long ago had supplied that once great city with water, and today splashed unceasingly into the Roman Bath. Above the Sanctuary of Apollo with its altar and fountain, where pilgrims had come from ancient Greece to worship, they found the remains of the city of Cyrene itself . . . no doubt a city worthy of modern times with its big square, its town hall and public buildings, its theatres, law courts and shops.

With the help of a map of the city, they discovered the many domestic buildings that covered the whole area, some with marble and fine mosaic floors still wonderfully preserved. Further afield, they saw the great temple of Zeus, Apollo's father, the Circus where horse races were held, and the great water tanks.

Dallas was particularly fascinated to learn from his book that much of the city was still unexplored and that the little museum where they saw bronze statues, pottery and other such replicas, probably held only a tiny proportion of what lay buried beneath their feet as they walked.

Scilla, womanlike, was lost in the romance of another world. Here, in the hot sun, she could half-close her eyes and see the inhabitants, perhaps taking their baths, or sitting in the theatre; imagine the pilgrims bathing their feet in the rows of troughs built for this purpose near the Temple, or the more elect pilgrims being fully initiated in the subterranean grottoes and cult caves which she had just seen with Dallas. She identified herself with the nymph Cyrene and transformed Dallas into her god, Apollo, and wondered if Dallas or Apollo loved her the more! Whether Cyrene's future lived 'in a city excellent in beauty and glorious in games' had been happier than hers would be living in present times with Dallas.

At last, a little bemused by so much legend and sightseeing, they left the ruins and wandered off hand in hand to find a place to picnic. Because the sun was hot, they elected to stay beneath the shade of the fir woods rather than go back to the hotel for the car and drive down to Apollonia, the port of Cyrene.

"We can go there tomorrow!" Dallas said happily. "We'll take another picnic and spend the day at the sea. Isn't life wonderful, darling? I'm so terribly happy!"

Lying in his arms for the lazy hour after their meal, Scilla felt almost too great a happiness to be borne. She could find no words to tell Dallas how she felt . . . it was still too new . . . too overwhelming to put in mere words. She returned his kisses with her heart overflowing with love for him and only the arrival of three inquisitive young Arab boys trying to sell them Roman coins broke them away from each other's arms and momentarily ended the hour of rapture in each other.

"Let's go to Derna!" Dallas suggested suddenly as they walked off among the trees in the direction of the hotel. "It's only an hour and a half in the car and we can have tea there in the Derna Officers' Club. One of the chaps told me to go to Derna if I could if only to see the approach road from the top of the Jebel escarpment. Would you like to, darling?"

Scilla was immediately in agreement with this plan. She had forgotten how impulsive Dallas could be and how her own temperament fitted her moods so well to his. He told her to wait by the drive while he slipped back for the car. Neither wanted to run into anyone they knew for they had planned to have this day quite alone together.

Dallas drove slowly for there was no hurry and they had a better chance to see the scenery. As Dallas had promised, the descent into Derna was breathtaking. They wound their way down perilous hairpin bends with the flat coastal belt hundreds of feet below them.

Scilla was glad of the tea they had at the Club. They saw no one there they knew and they stayed on in the lounge, talking softly and hearing the strange Arab music coming in through the open windows from the square. It was after seven when at last Dallas said they should have a meal and start back.

"There are at least two hours of daylight left," he told her. "Shall we go back along the little-used coast road? I'm told it is even more breathtaking than the one we came in by."

Scilla had implicit faith in Dallas' driving and knew, as they climbed up the sides of the steep cliffs, the road badly fenced in places with sheer drops down to the sea, a brilliant blue beneath them, that she would not have missed this awe-inspiring and frightening experience for the world.

It was nearly ten when she recognised in the car's headlights the turn into the drive to the hotel at Cyrene. It had been a wonderful day . . . unforgettable and quite perfect. As Dallas switched off the engine and turned to ask her if she had enjoyed it, she could find no words to express her happiness or her gratitude. Instead, she held out her arms to him and in the moonlit shadows of the car, their lips met as they clung to each other.

Most wonderful of all to realise at the end of this day was that tomorrow there could be another just as perfect. It was not just the activities . . . seeing the ruins, the picnic, the drive to Derna and back, that had made it so ideal. It was as much their joy and happiness in each other . . . in their desire to do the same thing; their ability to enjoy the simple and the supreme as one mind, one heart. Most of all because they were in love.

"Tomorrow we'll go to Apollonia!" Dallas promised as she drew away from him, knowing that the time had come when they must go indoors. "Shall we make another early start?"

"Yes!" Scilla agreed, for she knew the same longing to avoid people . . . to escape from the world . . . to be quite alone in it but for Dallas. "I'll go straight to bed now."

"I love you, darling . . . so very much!" he whispered.

"I'm going to say good night to you here!" Scilla told him softly. "Now . . . while we are alone."

She flung her arms round his neck and kissed him with a childish impulsiveness that brought back the past to Dallas as nothing else had done. She was still the same girl he had fallen in love with so long ago . . . his sweet, sweet girl.

Then she was gone, and as if in sympathy, the moon slipped quietly behind a cloud and everywhere was dark. Wonderfully content, he sat down on the stone wall to smoke a cigarette.

Five minutes later, Scilla, leaning out of her bedroom window, saw the bright spark of the cigarette-end as he flicked it away and stood up. Her heart leapt, as it must always do, at the sight of him. A smile curved her lips and she waited for him to turn towards the house before lifting her hand to wave to him. She felt unbearably happy . . . so filled with it that she had had to leave Dallas because she felt unable to support any more emotion without crying . . . weeping. For so long she had dreamed of just this miracle . . . of finding him again and of hearing him tell her he still loved her. Now, at last, it had all come right and nothing . . . *no one should ever separate them again.* She would marry Dallas just as soon as he wished to marry her and she would go back to Australia with him and spend the rest of her life loving him. The future stretched ahead of her like a long, shining path.

She thought of Kathie, who had worried so. Now she, too,

would be happy and if Scilla were to be married here, in Libya, Kathie could be matron of honour and Pete give her away. The two children could be bridesmaid and page. Scilla's heart glowed with plans as they swept across her mind in the brief seconds that she stood on the balcony above him, watching Dallas throw his cigarette into the darkness.

Then, as she lifted her hand to wave, he paused, his head turned suddenly in the direction of the drive. Then she heard the sound which had arrested him and saw a car's headlights coming through the trees towards the hotel. It drew up with a screech of brakes and a cloud of gravel dust.

Bad driving! Scilla thought, then her heart stood still for she had recognised the car . . . a bright saffron yellow sports coupé that belonged to Nancy Harold.

The woman climbed out of the driver's seat, slammed the door, forgetting to switch off the lights, and started to walk, stiffly it seemed to the watching girl, towards the hotel steps. She paused as she saw the man standing watching her and Scilla heard her low, husky laugh.

"Nishly timed, darling! Made it in three hoursh. Not bad, eh?"

Scilla heard Dallas' low reply:

"Nancy! What on earth are you doing here?"

"Well, what d'you think, darling? I came to shee you!"

Scilla drew in her breath.

"You're tight!"

Again that throaty laugh.

"Sho what? Been to a cocktail party. Shomeone said you were staying here so I deshided to come and find you. Aren't you pleased to see me?"

"The hotel's full, Nancy. You're mad to drive out here like that! And in your state . . . that road . . . good heavens, woman . . . are you crazy!"

"Crazy about you, Dallas, my pet! I've come to see you!"

"There's no room available!" Dallas' tone was harsh. "I'm sorry, Nancy, but—"

"I'll share yours, my sweet," she broke in obstinately. "Ugh! I need a drink. Long drive . . . that. I'm stiff!"

"Nancy, you'll have to go back. *You can't stay here.* I tell you, the hotel's full."

"Too tired to go back. Anyway, I want to be with you. I'm crazy about you, Dallas. Say you still love me a little bit? Just a little tiny, teeny bit?"

"No!"

"Because of what happened the other night? Thash not fair, Dallas. Thash not fair! I can't help loving you."

Scilla felt she could not bear to hear another word. With an enormous effort, she released her body from its numbed position and stumbled back into the room. Tears coursed down her cheeks although no sound came from between the lips except one word which she cried over and over again: "No! No, no!"

She lay down on her bed fully clothed and buried her face in the pillow, her hands over her ears as if she could in such a way shut out the words that kept repeating in her mind. She would not have believed that so much transcending happiness could be wiped out in one ghastly moment! If only she had not gone to the window . . . stayed downstairs a little longer . . . or that Dallas had come in with her. But that would have left her in a fool's paradise. She had believed Dallas . . . believed him because she wanted so desperately to do so. He had told her that Nancy had come to his flat for a drink . . . nothing more; that she had left a half hour later. His story had been credible for everyone knew that Nancy Harold cared not a jot for her reputation and might quite well have done such a thing. And Dallas had sworn he was not interested in her . . . had never loved her. Yet Nancy herself, unaware that she was being overheard, so with no possible motive, had said, '*Because of what happened the other night?*' And when Dallas had told her the hotel was full, she had remarked, quite casually, that she would share his room! No wonder Dallas was eager to get rid of Nancy . . . so eager that in spite of the fact that the woman was not in a fit state to drive, he had still told her she would have to go back to Benghazi. If Nancy stayed, she, Scilla, would be sure to see through his deception; sure to learn the truth.

Then why had he lied to her? If he loved Nancy Harold, what need had he of her, Scilla? Almost immediately she knew the answer. Dallas did not love Nancy, but had nonetheless been willing to have an affair with her and, at the same time, he had hoped for a love affair with Scilla. He had not loved her either . . . or if he did, his way of loving was far removed from hers. Oh, how she hated and despised him now! Never again would she feel sentimental about the past. Never again would she regret that she had refused to marry him so long ago. Had she done so, she would no doubt have learned by now to her cost that he had been repeatedly unfaithful to her with every attractive woman who came his way. She had escaped . . . and nothing would ever again bring her within the poisoned magic of his spell.

I hate him! she cried in her thoughts, the pain seeming to cut her heart with an actual physical torture. Dallas, how could you? *How could you?*

Suddenly she jumped up and hurried to her suitcase. Feverishly she sought for a writing-pad and her fountain pen. Then she sat down on the edge of the bed and began to write furiously.

*Dear Dallas,*

*I am afraid I owe you an apology which I do not feel able to make in person. I should have told you today that I am engaged to Bill . . . and shall soon be marrying him. As it was, memories of the past rather took me off guard and I realise now that it was rather naughty of me to have allowed you to kiss me as I know Bill would object. I hope you won't bear any grudge, because I know I did lead you up the garden path a little and encourage you to say all those nice things to me. I'm very sorry . . . and*

*can only say by way of recompense that I enjoyed our
little flirtation while it lasted, and hope you did, too. I
realised, naturally, that you didn't mean much of what
you said but I ought not to have let you think I was taking
you seriously.*

*Please forgive a repentant
Scilla.*

*P.S. – I do hope you will come to our wedding in due
course and I shall expect an elaborate present from you
for 'old time's sake'.*

She read it through once and then hurriedly folded it and put
it in an envelope. A few moments later, she had slipped out of
her room, and praying that no one would be about (if they were,
she would slip into one of the public bathrooms) she ran down
to the end of the corridor where she had heard Dallas tell Pete
he had the end room. Then she pushed the envelope beneath
his door, and breathing quickly with nervous apprehension and
suppressed emotion, she ran back to her own room and stood
panting with her back against the locked door.

Dallas would find that note when he came up to bed. He
would not know that *she* knew Nancy Harold had arrived. She
therefore had this advantage of him, for on reading it he would
see no other cause for the sentiments expressed except that they
were in fact how she felt. For this part of her pride that she had
been able to salvage, she felt a little better. And there was a
savage satisfaction in knowing that Dallas would be hurt. He
had always hated to be made a fool of . . . and from her letter,
he must certainly look a fool. Tomorrow she would have to
play a part . . . to be gay, amusing, very mildly flirtatious,
and without any enmity towards Nancy Harold. Dallas would
never, never learn what that note had cost her; what a terrible
blow he had dealt her tonight when in one moment she had lost
for the second time all the world's happiness she had believed
to be hers.

So she did not cry. She lay dry-eyed on her pillow, staring

into the darkness, her hands clenched, and her body rigid. At last, unable to bear her thoughts any longer, she took fifteen grains of aspirin, the only sleeping drug she had available to her, and in another half hour was in a deep drugged sleep.

But her ordeal was not yet over. In the morning, as she stepped out of her bedroom, she felt a hand grip hold of her arm and knew without turning her head that it was Dallas.

Uncaring of the publicity of the corridor, he said:

"Scilla! It's not true, is it? You didn't mean it?"

She raised her eyebrows and looked at him with feigned misunderstanding.

"But I explained in my note that I didn't mean a thing I said yesterday, Dallas. Didn't you get it?"

His grip on her arm tightened as she tried to release herself. Fortunately no one else was in the corridor.

"Scilla, for goodness' sake stop play-acting. You can't mean what you said in that letter. *I refuse to believe it.*"

"It's true nonetheless. I'm sorry, Dallas. I have already apologised in writing. Now please let me go."

"I won't . . . not like that. You *couldn't* have pretended the things you said and did. For some reason, you're playing a game with me."

"But I'm not, Dallas. Believe me, I am sorry about it, I know it was very wrong of me. Bill would be furious if he knew. Naturally, I never thought you'd take me seriously!"

Not knowing what the words . . . the casual tone of voice was costing her, he kept her from moving away from him. He was desperate. He had lain awake all night, trying to fathom out the truth of that note. He could not believe that Scilla had been playing a nasty little game with him. Every instinct told him that she was still in love with him. She could not have feigned the tenderness, those emotions, however well she might act.

"Look, Scilla, whatever your reason may have been for writing that note, and I can't guess, then at least think of this on its own merits. I meant every word I have said this last twenty-four hours. I'm desperately in love with you. I've never been in love with any other woman but you. I asked you to marry me and I ask you again now. Don't let anything come between us, I beg you – not if you have any feeling at all for me."

She was hit through her carefully prepared armour because she had never believed that Dallas, always so proud, would ever plead with her. And he sounded so desperately sincere. For a second, she hesitated, then a door slammed and broke the spell and she said:

"I'm sorry, Dallas. I never realised you were serious. As I said in my letter, I'm shortly going to marry Bill."

"Then you never loved me?"

"Well, once, yes! But that was a long time ago, Dallas. We've grown up since then . . . grown apart. We haven't much in common any more."

"How can you say that after yesterday? I can't understand you, Scilla. I can't believe that this is *you*! What has happened to change you since yesterday?"

He sounded desperately puzzled, hurt, yet still he pleaded with her.

"Scilla, you're *sure* you mean all this? We might never meet again . . . after this. We have been given another chance but I doubt it will happen a third time. Do you really want this to be goodbye?"

She knew it was her last chance . . . knew that this really was the end. His words tore what was left of her heart to pieces. Yet her whole body recoiled from his touch even while her heart answered his call. She would not have a man who lied to her, who could make love to one woman and a few days later hold her, Scilla, and kiss her passionately and speak in the same breath about love. That was not love . . . not as she believed it to be . . . not a decent, pure emotion. He desired her now as he had a little while ago desired Nancy, and he might reject her proffered affection just as he had last night rejected Nancy once his passion was satisfied and he had achieved his aim.

She might have liked him better if he had stood by the woman he had seduced. She despised him now . . . even while she still loved him and longed to be able to throw herself back into his arms.

"If you're going to be so serious, Dallas, I think we had better stop seeing each other altogether!" she said, shaking her arm free. "In any case, Bill arrives next weekend so maybe it's the best idea all round. I'm sorry, Dallas. Now, if you'll excuse me, I must go and see what the children are doing."

"Scilla . . ." He would have spoken again, but at that moment Nancy Harold came down the passage towards them. He heard Scilla's surprised voice saying: "Oh, hullo, Mrs Harold. I didn't know you were staying here. When did you arrive?"

Up to that moment, he had nursed the faint hope that maybe Scilla had learned of Nancy's late arrival last night and, misunderstanding, had written him that shocking letter. Now the hope died and what words he might have spoken died with it on his lips. He saw Scilla turn into another room; heard as if in a dream, Nancy's voice saying: ". . . afraid I was shockingly tight last night, Dallas. Hope I didn't embarrass you!" Heard his own non-committal reply, then with some excuse he hurried as quickly as he could out of the hotel.

He would go back to Benghazi today . . . put as much distance as he could between himself and the woman he loved, who, after all, had turned out to be a casual flirt. He would send an urgent signal to his H.Q. trying to hurry his transfer. He could no longer bear to stay in this country, where both his pride and his love had been trampled in the dust.

# Eight

"Is she all right?" Kathie asked the young army doctor as he closed Scilla's bedroom door behind him. The M.O. nodded.

"Just nerves. I believe most young women are subject to a few tears on their wedding eve. I shouldn't be over-concerned, Mrs Henshaw. I've given her a sleeping draught and it's my guess she'll be radiant when she walks up the aisle tomorrow!"

"I hope so!" Kathie agreed doubtfully as she opened the flat door for him. "You're absolutely certain she isn't sickening for something?"

"No one can ever be a hundred per cent certain, but she has no symptoms of any kind . . . not even a temperature. In fact, it is subnormal. I really think you need not worry, Mrs Henshaw."

"Thank you, Doctor!" Kathie said.

But she was not grateful. She would have preferred to hear that Scilla had sunstroke, or 'flu or measles . . . anything that might serve to put off the wedding tomorrow. No matter what Scilla had said to the contrary, Kathie was convinced that she did not really want to marry Bill.

Calling in the M.O. had been her own idea. She had heard Scilla weeping into the early hours of the morning and during the day her young sister had been listless and shadowed beneath the eyes. Yet when Kathie addressed her, she had answered in a brittle tone of voice that was quite out of keeping with her appearance.

The telephone rang and lifting the receiver Kathie heard Bill's voice.

105

"Can I speak to Scilla, Kathie?"

Scilla, who had gone to bed soon after tea, had told Kathie earlier that she did not wish to speak to anyone who might ring up . . . anyone at all.

"I think she's asleep, Bill. She had a bit of a headache and the M.O. gave her a sleeping draught. I think it better not to disturb her unless it's urgent."

"No, of course not. I just wanted to tell her . . . how much I love her. You can tell her for me. She's not ill, Kathie?"

"No! Just over-tired. I suppose you're having a stag party tonight, Bill?"

She heard his pleasant laugh as he agreed that he was going to have 'a few drinks with the chaps'. That was why he had telephoned Scilla now.

Poor Bill! Kathie reflected as she put down the telephone. He was so pleased . . . so proud . . . so desperately fond of Scilla. No one had ever thought that the placid, charming young man could have succumbed so helplessly to Cupid's darts. Secretly, Kathie believed that Scilla had been both surprised and a little frightened by so much affection and ardour from the man she had agreed to marry.

She went into the sitting-room and in a few words brought Pete up to date with the latest developments. Pete was, in his usual masculine way, attentive but not really worried and could not see why Kathie should be making such a fuss.

"Scilla isn't a child any more, my dear. She's twenty-seven and quite old enough to know her own mind. You admit that she has never once changed her mind since that day in Cyrene when she told Bill she'd marry him. She has not once mentioned Dallas Poulten's name. You have no facts at all to substantiate your theory that she'd back out of this wedding tomorrow if she could."

"I know," Kathie said quietly. "Nevertheless, I am quite convinced that she would. She doesn't love Bill . . . she never did love him. Why, two months ago she was going to marry

Dallas! No, she just wants to be married and have children and be happy."

"Isn't that what most women want of marriage?" Pete replied calmly. "Because Scilla isn't raving about Bill like a love-sick schoolgirl, it doesn't necessarily mean that she is not very fond of him. I think they stand an excellent chance of being very happy together. Bill adores the ground she walks on and he's a delightful fellow. You know how fond I am of Scilla . . . what a wonderful girl I think she is. Well, I think Bill is just as nice a chap as she could hope for."

"But she doesn't love him, Pete!"

"What is love?" Pete countered, putting his arm affectionately round his wife's shoulder. "You can't define it for yourself, Kathie, my sweet. Nor could I give it a name. So how can you know what Scilla feels for Bill?"

"I don't know . . . I admit that. But I did know she was in love with Dallas . . . there was no doubting *that* fact."

"But there are so many different kinds of love," Pete said to reassure his wife. "That mad passionate adoration she had for the Australian was probably a much less real emotion than the affection she has for Bill. Probably just one of these biological attractions."

Kathie was silent. She had said all these things to herself, trying to believe that they were true. But ever since their trip to Cyrene, Scilla had been unapproachable. Apart from telling Kathie she had changed her mind about Dallas and it was all off, she no longer confided in her. On the contrary, she spent their half-hour-before-bed 'gossips' trying to elude Kathie's questions. After Pete had gone back to Benghazi and the day before Bill was due to arrive, Scilla had announced quietly that if Bill asked her to marry him again, she was going to say 'yes'. None of Kathie's searching questions had produced anything but the one sentence: '*Yes, I'm quite sure I know what I'm doing!*'

Now two months had gone by . . . two hectic months during which time Scilla had been rushing around Benghazi in much the same way as she had rushed round London so many years ago when Dallas had gone back to Australia without her. She stayed out till the early hours . . . with Bill, of course, or otherwise Kathie might have said something to stop it; she attended every invitation, every dance, every function that came their way. Bill, clearly loving the chance this afforded him to show her off, was in complete accord with the mad pace Scilla set. He did not seem to suspect, as Kathie did, that Scilla was always hugging the places where there were a lot of other people . . . that she might be doing this to avoid being alone with Bill.

I'll make one last effort to talk to Scilla . . . to get near her again! Kathie thought. Tomorrow will be too late. We could put the wedding off . . . even now.

She went into Scilla's bedroom without knocking and found Scilla weeping into the pillow. In her hand she clutched a crumpled piece of notepaper.

"Scilla, darling!" Kathie sat down on the bed and put her arms round the shaking shoulders. "You must stop this, Scilla. You'll be a wreck tomorrow if you don't!"

Her words seemed to arrest the storm of tears and in a moment or two Scilla lifted a white face, patchy and swollen with weeping.

"Yes! I'm better now. Sorry, Kathie!"

Kathie drew in her breath sharply.

"Scilla, I have to say this. If you have even the slightest doubt that you are doing the right thing, then it isn't too late to put off the wedding. Bill knows the M.O. was here. We could give it out that you were ill and no one would suspect anything. Even if they did, it would be better than ruining your life . . . or Bill's."

For what seemed an interminable time to Kathie, Scilla made no reply. Then she said:

"No, I can't do that to him, Kathie. He loves me. I can't let him down now."

Kathie's heart sank. So she was not very far from the truth

after all when she had supposed that Scilla might have broken this engagement had she a loophole.

"You don't love Bill?"

"Yes, yes I do! I really do, Kathie. It . . . it isn't . . . the same way I loved Dallas . . . nothing could ever be the same. But I'm terribly fond of him. His happiness means a lot more to me now than my own."

"That's stupid!" Kathie said sharply. "In a successful marriage the two are synonymous."

"Yes, in a way. But I shall be happy making Bill happy."

"Then why the tears?" Kathie asked with a directness she had never used with Scilla before. She had always awaited the confidences . . . never forced them.

Simply, Scilla held out the crumpled paper in her hand. It was a letter from Dallas Poulten. Kathie read it.

*Darling Scilla,*

*As you may know, I have not been able to get back to Australia after all and I have to remain here for a further six months. I can assure you that had the terms of my contract provided me with a loophole I would have left last week.*

*I received the invitation to your wedding but I shall not be there. I cannot believe that you would want me there, in spite of what you once said. Scilla, I may be making the biggest mistake of my life but I'll risk sounding a fool when such vital matters are at stake. I have thought unceasingly about Cyrene. I cannot bring myself to believe that you were playing a game with me. Something MUST HAVE HAPPENED to make you change your mind. Whatever it was, I can only repeat what I said to you at the hotel . . . I have never been in love with any other woman but you. There was nothing you could have objected to between Nancy and myself. I have never to my knowledge done anything that could warrant you hurting me so certainly.*

*I could have understood if, when I spoke to you first in the garden, you had told me you no longer felt anything for me then. I had not expected that you could still care after all those years. When you agreed with me that we always had and always would belong together, I was the most surprised and certainly the happiest man in the world. It is not vanity that makes me say I am convinced you meant what you said. On the contrary, I know that I would have been hellishly lucky to win the love of so wonderful a girl. But you convinced me even more next day that you did care, by your tone of voice, your gestures, your words, your kisses.*

*If you meant it then, Scilla, why not now? It is not too late to come to me. This time, if necessary, I will wait another ten years while you reassure yourself as to my character . . . if that is what you doubt. I am not too proud now to say that. And I believe that you would not lack the courage to make an eleventh-hour break if you wished to do so. Scilla, I love you, with heart and soul and mind. If you love me, I beg of you not to marry Bill tomorrow. You will ruin the happiness of three people if you do.*

*If, as I cannot believe, you are about to tear up this letter and throw it away with a laugh at my conceit, then I humbly apologise. If not, then I can only repeat that I love you . . . now and always.*

*Dallas.*

Kathie drew in her breath sharply.

"Well?" she said. "I see you have not thrown it away and are not laughing!"

Scilla bit her lip.

"No, I'm not laughing. But it has come too late, Kathie. Maybe Dallas means what he writes . . . maybe he does love me. But it's too late."

"In what way? Because of the wedding arrangements tomorrow?"

Scilla shook her head nervously.

"No! Because I can't hurt Bill . . . and because I could never really trust Dallas again. He may love me, but he has not told me the truth about Nancy. Why didn't he say anything the night he took me to the dinner-dance at the Officers' Club? We were alone. I was hoping desperately that he might give me some indication of his feelings. But he did not. And that same night, Nancy was in his flat. He swore to me that nothing happened . . . that she had come unexpectedly; but it never did make sense to me that Nancy would wait around outside his flat not knowing what time he would return. Not unless she had a key, and that makes it worse. I've thought about it for hours on end, Kathie. I can't believe there was nothing between them. I never told you the details of what happened that night at Cyrene, after I had spent the day with Dallas. It was not a quarrel as I led you to believe. I heard Nancy Harold arrive in her car . . . heard what she said to him. I know you think she tried from the first to make me jealous . . . to try and keep Dallas and me apart, *but she could not have known that night that I was upstairs on the balcony listening.* In any case, she was tight. She just said what came into her head. I cannot forget those words, Kathie. She asked him if he still loved her and he denied it. Then she said: 'Because of what happened that night, Dallas? That's not fair!' There is only one explanation to that remark, Kathie. He had made love to her that night in his flat, but later . . . because of me . . . he was no longer interested in her. I hated her before but I felt sorry for her then. Oh, Kathie, I think if he'd told me the truth, admitted he'd been playing around with Nancy, that he'd been lonely and she'd been around, I should have understood. Dallas wasn't to know we were going to meet again . . . that I still loved him. I know men do these things and it isn't the same for them as it would be for a girl. He was free to do what he wanted. If he'd been honest, I would have understood and forgiven him. But he lied to me. And he continues to do so!" She indicated the letter. "I know he hasn't been seeing Nancy since then . . . everyone is remarking on it and anyway, Nancy is going around with some Greek and cuts Dallas dead. But so would I, if he had treated me like that. He took what she offered him and then turned his back on her because he thought he was on to something better. No, Kathie, I can't love a man like that. He isn't the Dallas I used to know and love. At least the man I used to know was always honest and decent and . . . and worthy of my respect."

Kathie tried to gather her scattered thoughts. In one long speech, Scilla had revealed so much of what had kept Kathie puzzled. She had known nothing of Nancy's arrival at Cyrene. After Scilla had gone up to bed, Dallas had come in with Nancy Harold, who was noisy and difficult and managed to have everyone in the hotel lounge hear her argument with the man in the reception office about a room being available for her.

In the end, Dallas had given up his room and gone down to one of the dormitories, a large room that led off the lounge, which he had to share with four junior army officers. Next day, Nancy Harold had left alone after breakfast and Kathie, at any rate, had forgotten the incident, except to suppose that Dallas and Scilla had probably quarelled on Nancy's account.

She still held the letter in her hand and she glanced down again at the closely written words. Somehow they rang true . . . they gave one a feeling of being the impulsive sentences of a man desperately in love and as bewildered as she, Kathie, had been as to the reason for Scilla's behaviour.

Scilla explained the note she had written Dallas and put under his hotel room door. Apparently he had received it before he packed his belongings and moved down to the dormitory. Maybe it would have been better if Nancy Harold had received it . . . and yet in the end that would have made little difference. Scilla was convinced that Dallas had lied to her and there was, too, the knowledge that Dallas had been able to do such a thing even after he had met Scilla again. She could have forgiven such a happening if it had occurred before they met. In a way, Kathie could understand that. She would never have opened her arms to Pete if she had known *he* had come straight from the arms of another woman.

"So it's the end?" she asked at last.

Scilla nodded. Two tears coursed slowly down her cheeks and they distressed Kathie terribly.

"And the beginning, too . . . of a new life," she tried to comfort Scilla. "Darling, don't marry Bill . . . don't marry him. You know in your heart that you still love Dallas, even though you can't marry him now. Don't make an unhappy marriage because of it."

"No . . . not because of it. In spite of it!" Scilla said fiercely. "I will be happy, Kathie, I will. I want to make Bill happy. He loves me and I'm terribly fond of him . . . I respect him and . . . I need his love. Don't worry about me, Kathie dear. I'll be happy . . . I promise!"

She was getting sleepy now and Kathie knew that the drug was taking effect. There was nothing more that she could do anyway. Scilla had made up her mind and would not go back on her promise. Tomorrow she would become Bill's wife and all Kathie could do now was to pray for their happiness.

She kissed her young sister tenderly and turned off the light. Then she went back to her husband, and despite her intentions to the contrary, gave way to a pleasant, relieving weep.

"Oh, well!" said Pete as he held her hand. "I suppose I must resign myself to the fact that I have an old worry for a wife. I dread to think what you'll be like the night before Dina gets married. You just can't interfere in things like this, Kathie. People must make or mar their own lives. It's up to Scilla now . . . and Bill. Still, I'm sorry for Dallas . . . looks as if he's fallen between two stools. Poor devil. Or maybe he's better off a bachelor."

As he had hoped, his last remark brought a smile to Kathie's face and she stopped her tears to tell him in mock anger that he'd eat those words before she had done with him.

"Maybe the 'for better or for worse' isn't far off the mark!" Pete agreed. "I'll put up with you, Kathie mine."

She nestled contentedly against his shoulder and for a moment forgot the wedding next day.

# Nine

Scilla lay awake listening to the regular breathing of the man at her side. She, herself, felt curiously light-headed and drained of emotion. She could not sleep, tired as she was, for the noise of the traffic beneath their hotel window.

This was the second night of their honeymoon. They had been married in the army church in Benghazi at three in the afternoon. Afterwards they had held a reception for the wedding guests in the Officers' Club and since it was Saturday night many had stayed on to dine and dance later. She and Bill had booked passages on the night plane to London because it was Bill's wish to spend their honeymoon there.

She had not questioned his reasons for going home to England. It crossed her mind that he had considered other places . . . Cyprus, Cairo, Italy. Yet he had chosen London and since she had told him many weeks before that she preferred to leave the decision to him, she had been quite satisfied when he announced that he was taking her home.

It was barely four months since she had flown out to Libya, and she had certainly not expected to be back in England so soon. But then she had never expected to be married within that time . . . never expected so many of the things which had happened to her.

She believed now that there were two reasons why Bill had brought her home . . . one of them was to meet her parents, because at heart he was very conventional and a home-loving man who respected his own family, and also to have her meet his mother and father. They were going to keep two of the four weekends of their holiday free to make trips to each of their homes. The other reason was that Bill had wanted her to

115

have everything in the world that he thought she might want, and he knew that in London he could give it to her. First there had been the luxurious comfort of the hotel. Their room had been filled with flowers and on entering it she had found a parcel lying on her pillow containing a beautiful old diamond necklace. It was his mother's and there was a charming little note with it saying that she wished Bill's wife to have it as a wedding gift and knew that Bill wanted her to have it, too.

She had been very touched, and had felt a little upset that they had not after all waited to come home to be married so that both their parents could have been there. Bill's people and her own mother and father might have flown out to Benghazi but had not done so since they knew the couple were leaving the same day for England. But Bill had wanted his army friends round him at his wedding and Scilla had felt a greater need for Kathie than for her mother and father from whom she had become estranged since her girlhood. Now she felt she and Bill had been a little selfish. Her own father had sent her a very large cheque which he wished her to spend on a trousseau, and although Scilla had had many new clothes to take to Libya, she nevertheless had spent that first day in London buying the kind of clothes she thought Bill would like her to wear. He had been delightfully and boyishly happy shopping with her and the day had been so busy that there had been no time to think.

They had dined in the hotel and danced for a little while, but Bill was not a very good dancer, and since they had both been travelling all the night before and had hardly been alone together for five minutes since their wedding, they had retired early to their room.

Remembering the hours which had followed, able to look back now with that cold vision of complete emotionlessness, Scilla could see two things – first that she had known Bill would be like this . . . gentle, loving, considerate, carefully controlled in his love-making; and secondly, that she was not in the least in love with him.

It seemed wrong to her that she should feel this so strongly at a time when Bill had been his most likeable self. The things he had given her had been the things she needed, and yet, as she lay there in his arms, she could feel no answering response to him . . . only an acquiescence that was an answer to gentleness. She had always known that beneath the surface she was a woman with violent and passionate emotions. Had Bill been able, he might have swept her off her feet in the tide of his own feelings. But he had not. The calm sweetness that had attracted her to him as a husband had failed her in this moment. She had needed no time to think . . . no time to remember . . . no time to wish herself in another man's arms. As it was, her only conscious desire had been that she should not fail to make Bill's wedding night all that he hoped for.

He had seemed suddenly to be very young and any love she bore for him was protective and maternal. She had thought that this overriding wish to make him happy would result in her own happiness, and yet she lay beside him now knowing that she had not failed him as his bride and at the same time terribly afraid that she would fail him as a wife. Try as she might, she had not been able to keep the desperate longings for Dallas out of her mind as Bill's hands held her. She knew that, after all, her strength of will had not been able to keep her as faithful in mind as in body to the man she had married. On her wedding night, she had betrayed him . . . and in a way betrayed herself.

She was too fine a person to be filled now with self-pity. Her only concern was for Bill. Nevertheless, she could not prevent the thought that had she and Bill anticipated their marriage and spent a night together as lovers, she would never have married him. Not because he had failed her, but because she had learned that she herself had failed . . . failed to forget the man she still longed for in spite of knowing the kind of person he had become.

Her thoughts flew back to Kathie's warnings when she tried to prevent her from marrying on the rebound. Kathie had told her that she might not find it easy to reciprocate love just because the desire to do so was there. Kathie had told her again and again that she would be responsible for Bill's happiness as well as her own if she married him knowing in her heart that she was not in love with him; that fondness was not always enough.

But it can be . . . it must be! Scilla cried silently into the darkness. I'll do anything for Bill . . . anything.

She did love him in a way; knew that she had far greater cause to respect him than ever she would have to respect a man like Dallas Poulten. She could trust Bill . . . admire him . . . be fond of him. Weren't those sufficient grounds, if the will was there, to make their marriage a happy one? In time, she *must* forget Dallas. In time, she would grow used to Bill's arms around her and his kisses . . . his sweetness and gentleness.

Slowly, Scilla began to convince herself that all she had ever felt for Dallas was a passion of the senses; that there had been nothing more between them than physical desire. If she could only rid herself of the belief that she belonged to him heart and soul, then the desire would leave her and she could really give herself completely and utterly to Bill.

Wordlessly, Scilla began to pray. In the army church in Benghazi, she had been so nervous that she had barely heard the words of the marriage service. She had never been particularly religious but she had attended church fairly regularly and she had a calm, steady faith. If she prayed now, maybe strength would come to her to do what she had promised. She recalled the solemn vows she had made and repeated them slowly. But, instead of comforting her, they frightened her. 'Until death us do part' . . . 'let no man put asunder'. Life could go on for fifty years or more, and she must spend all that life with Bill . . . keep herself unto him only, bearing his children . . . caring for and loving him. She could never as long as she lived lie in Dallas' arms . . .

Tears suddenly stung her eyes and brimming over, rolled down her cheeks. Still they were not tears of self-pity but of regret . . . regret that Dallas had not been the man she had believed him. She had never lost her idealism . . . the high standards that she applied to herself as well as to others. When she had met and fallen in love with Dallas at seventeen, he had more than qualified as her ideal. He had been brave, as many of his squadron had told her, truthful, perfectly mannered and his behaviour to her . . . a young innocent girl awakening for the first time to love, had been, she now knew, wonderfully chivalrous. Many men might have taken advantage of her in little ways which she had been too ignorant to realise at the time. She thought now of some of the glorious hours she had lain in Dallas' arms . . . on a hot summer's day in the hayfields, on a cool starry night in the back of Dallas' car . . . on a wet misty afternoon in the attic of her house. She had not known then how eager her responses to his restrained love-making must have tried that restraint. During the long moments when his body had seemed to become one with her own, so tightly did they press against one another, he must have used an iron control not to give way to the desire to which she was only half-awakened herself. She had been perfectly and wonderfully content with his kisses, the gentle touch of his hands, the hot words of love, the wonder of her own contentment. She had not realised the will-power he had had to exert to prevent himself from harming her. But when she had been in his arms in the sunshine and in the moonlight at Cyrene she had known what it meant not to give way to such powerful emotions. She had grown from girlhood to womanhood and her own physical emotions were as deeply aroused as his had been.

She wondered suddenly why he had not taken advantage of that moment of her weakness. After all, he had long ago ceased to be a man to whom moral behaviour meant anything. That must be so since he behaved as he had done with Nancy. Perhaps she, Scilla, had ceased to tempt him now that he had a woman like Nancy to do with as he wished. Perhaps that explained what must otherwise be inexplicable. She could not doubt that Dallas, the boy she had loved, had changed into a man she could no longer respect. He had lied to her . . . and he had lacked the courage to tell her the truth. If he had done so, she might have forgiven that moral weakening. She *would* have forgiven that moral weakening. She knew now that if Dallas had told her then at Cyrene that he regretted what he had done, she would not have had the strength to resist him. Only his lies and his underhand dealings with both Nancy and herself had given her the strength to go against her heart. She could never marry a man she could not respect.

The tears on her cheeks had dried now and in the darkness, her face was both sad and bitter. Her mouth twisted a little with pain as she remembered that last letter Dallas had written her. Even then he had persisted in denying there had been anything between him and Nancy. Even then he had lied. Perhaps even then it would not have been too late. Suppose that he had suddenly confessed in that letter . . . begged her to forgive . . . to have faith in him, would she have put off her wedding? Would she have had the courage to deal Bill such a blow at that eleventh hour?

Her thoughts swung back to the man beside her and she knew a moment of self-loathing. What kind of bride was she who lay on their wedding night imagining what happiness she could have had with another man?

She shuddered, afraid, with a cool chill on her spine, of the insidious power of love. It might make men and women great but it could also make them weak and horrible. It could make them betray those who loved them best. It could undermine all that was best in them.

"I will be strong!" Scilla whispered. "Never, never again will I remember Dallas. He's dead to me now . . . dead, dead. I'm Bill's wife . . . Bill's wife."

Her teeth bit against the palm of her hand as she tried with all her will-power to banish the ghost which haunted her. She might close her eyes, but against the dark shadows of her lids it was Dallas who reposed there. She might give her body to the man she had married . . . but her heart-beat quickened only to that other man's touch. She might give her life to Bill . . . but Dallas possessed her soul.

Made desperate by her thoughts, Scilla reached out and touched Bill's arm. He stirred slowly and, waking, spoke her name.

"Hold me!" she whispered. "Tell me you love me! Tell me again that I belong to you!"

Not understanding what lay behind her cry, he smiled tenderly and repeated her words.

"I love you!" she said. And only she knew the depth of that lie.

"Bill's like the cat who caught the canary!" Kathie said to Pete. "He looks positively radiant!"

"Which is more than you do!" her husband replied, knowing from his wife's expression that something was wrong. She had been round at her younger sister's flat 'seeing them into their new home' after meeting them at Benina airport. Pete had been on duty and unable to go.

Kathie took the drink that Pete held out to her and stared at the ice cube which was melting quickly in the tepid water.

"Scilla?" Pete prompted.

"She's radiant too!" Kathie said flatly.

Pete knew his wife and sat down to wait until she was ready to tell him what worried her. He knew how devoted the two sisters were and was never jealous of the love and attention Kathie gave the younger girl. He was fond of Scilla himself, although he had thought her very stupid to marry young Bill on the rebound. He had feared all along that it might not work out although he knew better than to say so since he could not have altered Scilla's decision. And he had had no desire to make Kathie more worried than she was already.

"It's not like Scilla to be so 'jubilant'!" Kathie said at last, choosing the word with difficulty.

"Scilla hasn't been married before. Maybe she really is happy!" Pete suggested hopefully.

"You don't understand!" Kathie replied. "I've seen Scilla happy, really happy . . . in the days when she was engaged to Dallas. Unlike me, she goes quiet. It's a kind of inner radiance that shines all over her face . . . a sort of breathlessness . . . a radiance. But silent. And I've seen her 'jubilant' before, too. That was after she knew Dallas had gone back to Australia and wouldn't be coming back for her. We took a flat in town and she went 'madly gay' . . . dancing, singing around the house, talking four times as much as she usually did, out every night with this man and that. Well, that's how she was today. She was chattering like a magpie from the moment they stepped off the plane. 'It's lovely to feel the sun again, isn't it, darling? I'm so looking forward to seeing our flat . . . you're a dear to have met us, Kathie . . . how are the children? How's Pete?' and so on. Neither Bill nor I could get a word in edgeways. She was like an excited kid on a Sunday-school treat . . . only it wasn't Scilla."

"She could have changed, Kathie."

"No! Marriage couldn't change a person in three weeks. In some ways, perhaps, but not fundamentally. I've seen plenty of starry-eyed brides back from their honeymoons. I've been one myself! This was a cover-up, Bill. She was afraid of what I might see. I know she was. She avoided any chance of talking to me alone. She hung on to Bill's arm as if he were a straw and she the drowning man. She was avoiding me . . . and she never once met my eyes."

"Perhaps she's just shy, Kathie. Don't let your imagination run away with you."

"But I'm not imaginative, Pete. You know that. I'm placid and steady and rather dull! Scilla's the one who day-dreams and has strange flights of fancy. But she isn't day-dreaming now. I think she has woken up to the hard facts of life."

"Marriage isn't a hard fact of life!" Pete said half seriously, half teasing. "I'm going to resent that!"

Kathie's frown gave way to a smile and she reached for and held his hand for a moment.

"It could be . . . if it was to the wrong person!" she said at last. "You know that's true, too, Pete. We've seen it so often in other couples and felt ourselves blessed because we made the right choice."

"I know," Pete agreed softly. "All the same, I like young Bill and I can't believe he'd make Scilla unhappy."

"No, I didn't mean he had. She has made herself unhappy, Pete."

"Well, there's no going back on it now . . . or at least not without a lot of unpleasantness all round. Anyway, I don't believe Scilla is the kind to take the easy way out."

"Divorce? No!" Kathie said firmly. "I'm quite quite sure that however desperate she was, Scilla would never go back on her vows; she'd never let Bill down. She told me that."

"Then, darling, give them a chance to settle down," Pete said sagely. "There's a world of time ahead of them. In any case, a happy marriage grows – it isn't made on a honeymoon. They could grow close. And then when the first kid comes along, Scilla will be busy with all that side to married life and she'll settle down."

There was every reason to hope that Pete was right. And Kathie wanted to believe it. She felt a little cheered. It might not be easy for Scilla at first, but if she kept trying she could find happiness. She loved children and a few babies would help to mend those scars on her heart.

In her new flat, Scilla busied herself unpacking while Bill shifted the furniture around to the way he had been planning it on the plane coming here. He was perfectly and completely happy. He had always loved his chosen career . . . and he felt an even greater affection for the army at the moment for making everything so simple for him. Here he was, provided with a married quarter, reasonable furniture, a decent allowance, a paid leave on which to have his honeymoon. His future was secure . . . as long as he didn't do anything silly like appropriating army funds for his own use! . . . and he had Scilla!

He paused in the doorway of the kitchen and surveyed his young wife with adoring eyes. She turned and gave him a smile.

Immediately encouraged, he put down the chair he was holding and moving across the room put his arms round her in a boyish hug. If her muscles stiffened, he was not aware of it.

"Gosh, I'm happy!" he said, and told her what had been passing through his mind. "I must be the happiest man in the world!" he ended his little soliloquy.

"I'm so glad, darling!" She released herself gently from his encircling arms and added:

"It's hot after London. I think I'll have a shower and leave the rest of this till tomorrow."

"Good idea!" Bill agreed immediately as he always did with anything she might suggest. He was not a man of very violent opinions and had always been ready to fall in with the wish of the majority. This was not weakness but merely that he was easily contented and quite happy to do what everyone else wanted. As far as Scilla was concerned, he was always instantly ready to please her. After the three brief weeks of marriage, he was convinced he had the most perfect and wonderful wife any chap could have. Even now he found himself stopping to wonder how it had all happened. A few months ago he had been plodding along quite content with life as a bachelor, a fact which now seemed incredible when he knew what heaven married life could be. Not for one instant did he imagine any other marriage was as perfect as his . . . any other wife one part as adorable, as unselfish, as thoughtful, as considerate, as beautiful, as perfect as Scilla! That she should have married him was still an unbelievable fact.

He was fully aware that not so long ago she had been in love with Dallas Poulten. He could understand that. Dallas was in every way more attractive than he considered himself to be. Not only was he exceptionally handsome but he had a fine nature and a great brain and Bill respected him. What he failed to understand was that Dallas had not wanted Scilla! He thought of it sometimes and wondered how any fellow in his right mind could fail to believe Scilla the most attractive and desirable wife a man could have.

But he did not worry about the why's and wherefore's for long. It was not in his nature to be introspective nor to probe too deeply into the feelings of others. He was happy enough to accept life and people as he found them and his own life seemed to him so completely perfect that he had no wish to question it. Quite simply, he knew that Scilla was his happiness, and that was enough to have made him her complete slave.

He remembered how sweet she had been with his parents. Any opposition they had had to his sudden marriage abroad had melted completely in a matter of hours. His father, a retired brigadier, had clapped Bill on the back at the end of that weekend and told him that he thought he had been a sensible chap.

"Must admit when we got your letter telling us you were to be married out there, your mother and I were a bit worried. Thought you were rather rushing things . . . and yes, I admit it, we were a bit hurt, too. Now we both understand why. Couldn't let a girl like Scilla slip through your fingers to some other fellow, eh? If I'd been in your shoes I'd have done the same thing. We'll be looking forward to visiting you next year."

Scilla, in her charming way, had persuaded them to come out for a long holiday next Easter. His mother, too, had been delighted with his choice. And Scilla had liked them both, simple, unpretentious folk as she knew them to be. Bill hadn't cared for her family quite so much but maybe that was because Scilla herself seemed so remote from them. He didn't fully understand why, as they appeared more than pleased to see her and were obviously quite satisfied with him as a son-in-law. They'd done everything to make them welcome, but somehow Scilla was never quite herself with them the way she had been with his parents. It was almost as if an invisible barrier were between them and he hadn't understood it.

125

But it had not worried him long for they were only there for a weekend and then they were back in London, doing all the shows, going to night-clubs, or driving in a hired car to spend a day at the races or on the river.

It had been a perfect and exciting honeymoon, and at the end of every day when night fell he had Scilla to hold in his arms and the chance to tell her how happy he was and how dearly he loved her. Her quietness at such moments seemed perfectly natural to him. He knew that she had come to him inexperienced and innocent and her quiet acceptance of his love-making seemed to him to be in keeping with her youth and sweetness and femininity. He wanted nothing more from her. To him, she was perfect just as she was. If sometimes she seemed to elude him in a strange way to which he could not have put a name, he put that down to his own inexperience of women and supposed that all girls liked to stay a little bit of a mystery to the men they had married. It made them elusive and even more attractive. And her modesty he respected and also thought natural.

He had learned already that she preferred to keep any intimacy to the quiet moments of darkness. Now, when he might have liked to go into their bedroom and take her in his arms, rosy and warm from her bath and adorable to touch beneath the great turkish towelling she had wrapped around her to dart across the hallway, he refrained from doing so because he knew that she would stiffen at his touch and that if he could wait until her long slender finger had turned off the bedside lamp, she would open her arms to him in the darkness.

He smiled to himself as he went to take his own bath before changing for dinner. They were meeting Kathie and Pete at the Officers' Club at eight-thirty and he was feeling a very happy man.

Hearing the bathroom door close and the water running from the shower, Scilla felt her whole body relax. She leant forward on her arms on the dressing-table, littered and untidy now with her half-unpacked bottles and lotions and brush and comb. In the glass, her white face stared back at her. Her eyes were ringed with violet and she felt deathly tired. If only they could avoid going to the Club! But it had never occurred to anyone that she might not want to go. After that long journey in the plane and the unpacking, it had been the obvious way to avoid cooking an evening meal. They might have dined with Kathie but Pete apparently had expressed a wish to treat them to dinner by way of a welcome home, and Bill had accepted for them both.

She knew that there was no alternative without drawing suspicion of her reasons for avoiding something or someone! Kathie must not know . . . or even if *she* guessed, never, never should Bill know how much courage she needed to come back to Benghazi with him. *If only Dallas had gone back to Australia.* Once she had prayed that something . . . anything would happen to prevent him returning to his homeland. This last week, she had prayed equally hard that they would return to find him gone.

She drew in her breath wearily. What point was there in avoiding the Club tonight? If Dallas were in Benghazi, and she had not dared ask Kathie if he were, then she would be bound to run into him sooner or later. If only she could think of some good reason why Bill should put in for a posting. But he loved it here and he supposed that she liked to be near Kathie. Bill considered Benghazi to be an excellent station. He could sail, hunt, fish, swim, play golf and tennis, and the climate was near perfect. They had a very nice quarter, and above all, she could be with him here. The situation in Egypt, for instance, was none too good and if he were posted there conditions would be incomparably worse and she might even be separated from him. How could she then make him think that it was above all essential to leave Benghazi? She could see no way to do so.

"Coward!" she told her reflection fiercely. "The way to kill a ghost is to face up to it. When I meet Dallas, I shall look him straight in the eye and see for myself that he isn't worth a single thought, let alone this agony."

She began to dress slowly and carefully. Before putting on one of the new dresses she had bought with Bill in London, she made up her face carefully, removing any trace of tiredness or anxiety and adding the necessary colour to her cheeks. She was fastening the diamond necklace Bill's mother had given her round her throat when Bill came into the room, a towel wrapped round his waist. He completed the job for her.

"You look stunning, darling!" he said, giving her a boyish grin and a brief hug. "I'm so proud of my lovely wife."

Scilla's face softened.

"I'm so glad, Bill. I hope you never feel differently."

"As if that were possible!" Bill said, rummaging through a suitcase for the tie he wanted. "I can't wait to show you off tonight. Wonder who'll be there?"

"I . . . I expect much the same faces we saw three weeks ago."

"Daresay! Darling, what say we give a house-warming as soon as we're straightened out and you think you can cope? Ask all our friends!"

"You're like a small boy wanting to show off his new cricket bat to the other small boys!" she said gently. "The trouble is, half of them have got cricket bats just as nice as yours."

"Impossible!" Bill grinned at her. He found the tie and gave a whoop of sheer delight. "I feel as if I'd drunk a whole bottle of champagne . . . on top of the world!" he told her. "You know, darling, dozens of the chaps warned me that I'd find it stiff coming back here after three weeks' heaven in England. But do you know, I'm jolly glad to be here. I like this place, don't you, darling?"

She avoided a reply by telling him that it was after eight and Kathie and Pete would be calling for them at any moment. Then she left him to dress and went out on to the balcony and stared out across the tops of the trees towards the east. One could not see the hills from here . . . the shadow across the horizon that broke the infinite flatness of the coastal plain. But she knew they were there. In that direction lay the Tocra Pass and the Jebel and, beyond, Cyrene . . .

She turned her face suddenly to the bright sun that still lingered above the harbour. Not for her the twilight shadow of the hills . . . the dark memories of the past. She had started a new life . . . a bright, happy marriage that must be full of sunlight and without regrets. Then the doorbell rang and composing her face she turned and went back into the room.

# Ten

Dallas Poulten was not at the Club that night. Nor did Scilla see him at the Sailing Club where she joined Kathie and the children in the morning. Despite all her resolutions, her thoughts kept turning back to him; wondering with a mixture of fear, dread and longing to see him, whether she would run into him that day, the next or the next. She asked herself whether he could, after all, have returned to Australia as he had desired. But she could not ask anyone . . . even Kathie, and no one mentioned his name.

Her self-loathing became more acute as her longing to see Dallas increased with every passing day. Whenever she caught herself slipping into these day-dreams, she would feel a wretched disgust with herself and determine once again that she would not think of him. She would remind herself that she was now a married woman, no longer free to live in a world of dreams; that with every thought of Dallas, she was being unfaithful to the man who was the most perfect husband in the world to her.

Bill had started work again and she had known another moment of self-dislike when relief had flooded through her at the thought that from eight in the morning until two-thirty in the afternoon she could be alone. It was not that she did not enjoy Bill's company . . . only that she found the necessity for continually playing a part such a strain. When Bill was with her, she must always have a smile in her eyes, a gaiety in her voice, which she was often far from feeling. And most difficult of all, she must always be on her guard against her betraying body which so often shrank from Bill's caresses. Only with an enormous concentration of will-power could she bring herself to return Bill's kisses or the touch of his hand. That effort alone tired her and made her welcome the mornings that were free of strain. Shopping in the market, tidying the house, giving orders to her Arab boy and preparing the lunch, occupied the hours easily enough, and only occasionally did her mind stray away to forbidden fields. She would feel refreshed by the time Bill returned; sufficiently so to manage to be the wife to him that she had resolved on, and she could at least feel comforted by the thought that so far in the two months of their married life he had not had cause to regret what he had done.

Scilla guessed that Kathie had seen through the part she was playing. Kathie, who knew her so terribly well, was the hardest of all to deceive. Even while Scilla knew she could have confided in her sister without harm to anyone, she felt that such a confidence would in itself be a disloyalty to Bill and she could not do it.

Then one morning, five weeks after her return to Benghazi, Scilla found herself confronted by Nancy Harold. Had it for one moment occurred to her that Aly, her house boy, was answering the door to Nancy, she would have fled to her bedroom and locked herself in, telling Aly through the door to inform Mrs Harold that she was ill and could see no one. But not suspecting a visitor, she continued with her weekly letter to Bill's parents and, looking up as the door opened, saw the older woman coming towards her.

The colour drained from her face as she jumped to her feet. There was no escape and without being openly rude there was nothing she could do but ask Nancy to sit down.

"I'm afraid I'm rather belated with my congratulations!" Nancy said calmly as the boy closed the door behind her, leaving them alone. "Unfortunately, I wasn't able to come round any sooner as I've been in hospital with jaundice. Now I'm teetotal . . . absolute hell!"

"I'm sorry about the jaundice," Scilla said flatly, recovering a little of her composure and wondering what had brought this woman to see her. She could not believe that it was just a friendly call. Except for the man who had linked them, they were virtually strangers. "Aly will be making coffee," she added.

"Thanks!"

Nancy stood up and moved around the room for a moment or two. It was almost as though she herself were not entirely happy being here. She seemed on edge. "I must congratulate you on this room, too. It's charming. You obviously have taste. I've seen lots of army flats and they haven't made anything like so elegant a room with their furniture."

"Thank you," Scilla said flatly. She could think of no topic of conversation and wisely decided to leave it to the woman, who must have called here for some purpose. Nancy lit a cigarette and returned to her chair. "How was London?" she asked without much interest.

Scilla mentioned the shows they had seen and was glad when Aly came in with the coffee. She wondered if Nancy would go and what hint she could drop that she was busy and would be glad for this visit to end. But now that there was not much chance of a further interruption, Nancy began to edge round to the topic she had come to discuss . . . Dallas.

"You could have knocked me down with the proverbial feather when I heard you and Bill were really going to be married," she said, speaking a little too fast. Scilla's silence was not helping her. "I used to tell Dallas you were about to announce your engagement but I never really believed it."

"Then you had no right to talk about it!" Scilla was stung to reply.

Nancy gave a low, deep laugh.

"Oh, but my dear, I had every right. You see I was desperately in love with Dallas. All's fair in love and war . . . and I looked on you as a serious rival."

Scilla felt her hands trembling in her lap.

"Is there much point our discussing all this . . . now?"

Nancy raised her eyebrows.

"Not for you, perhaps . . . but for me. I don't take defeat

easily. And I hate being in the dark. It makes it so much harder to play your hand when you don't know your opponent's trumps, doesn't it?"

"I don't understand what you are talking about!" Scilla replied, nervously twisting her handkerchief.

"But my dear, it's perfectly simple. I was crazy about Dallas . . . in fact, I still am. But for some reason, he hasn't any interest in me. I could understand that when I thought he was in love with you. But apparently he wasn't after all. Or did *you* turn *him* down?"

"Would that surprise you?" Scilla said swiftly. "In view of all you know about Dallas, I should have thought you would have been the first person to understand why I didn't want him."

Nancy leant forward in her chair, her face intent and vaguely evil.

"So you did throw him over a second time? You must be mad! I would have sworn you were in love with him, too."

I can't stand any more of this, Scilla thought. I'll tell her to go. I can't listen to this.

She stood up, her hands trembling.

"If you don't mind my being rather rude, Mrs Harold, I was writing letters when you came in. I want to finish them in time to catch the post."

Nancy remained seated and a curious smile played about her lips as she watched the younger girl.

"Have I offended you? You know, I can't see why you should object to discussing something that's all over and done with . . . *for ever*," she underlined the last words ". . . as far as you are concerned."

"My personal feelings are my affair and no business of yours! Would you please go?"

Again ignoring Scilla's request, Nancy leant back in her chair and said calmly:

"Of course, you're still in love with Dallas. Otherwise it wouldn't worry you to talk about him. Have you been wondering where he was . . . why you haven't see him around? He left here, you know, the day before you and Bill were due back from England. He's been in Cairo, drowning his sorrows and avoiding you. But he'll be back . . . this afternoon."

She was watching Scilla's face closely and was rewarded to see the colour flood into the girl's white face as she took in this information. Now she was certain that Scilla loved Dallas.

"You must have been out of your mind to marry Bill . . . feeling the way you do about Dallas. I've been married for years to a man I didn't love . . . it's hell. Tell me, *why* did you do it?"

Scilla's eyes stared at her companion. There was an evil fascination in that insolent voice saying things she had believed unknown to anyone but herself. This woman alone in the world but for Dallas . . . knew why she, Scilla, had refused to marry him, yet she could ask her reasons. Anger replaced her caution and she cried out:

"You know why I couldn't marry him. *You* know . . . and you dare to come here and ask me . . ." Her voice broke and she turned and went quickly across to the window, afraid for her self-control.

"But I don't know! That's just why I've come here . . . to find out. Did you suppose he was in love with *me*? Were you so feeble that you were prepared to lose him without a fight?"

"Fight? For the man who'd just left your bed? Never!"

For a brief second, silence held the room. With that bitter accusation, anger had left Scilla and she felt ashamed. The other woman was taken aback with sheer surprise. Then she laughed . . . and the laughter was horrible. Scilla clenched her hands to refrain from striking that lovely curved mouth.

"Oh, but my dear, how wrong you are! To think that the night of my defeat should have ended in Dallas' defeat, too. How absurdly funny that is! How just the retribution. I can't wait to tell him . . . but of course, you will have done so? Didn't he deny it? Surely he must have done!"

"Yes, he denied it!" Scilla said, feeling her whole body

tremble now with shock. 'The night of my defeat!' That could mean several things . . . but she knew in her heart that there was only one true meaning. Dallas had spoken the truth . . . he had rejected all that Nancy offered him. Gossip, rumour . . . her own conclusions had been false . . . quite false. Dallas had not lied to her.

She sat down weakly in the chair and caring nothing now for the other woman's opinion of her, said:

"Since I've told you, so much, will you tell *me* about that night?"

"But willingly. After all, you are hardly likely to discuss it with others, are you? And in any case, you are safely out of the running now with Dallas. It rather amuses me to show you what a silly little fool you have been. Yes, a fool! I went round to Dallas' flat that night determined that he should make love to me. I thought that once I was his mistress, I could make him marry me. But he was only concerned with you. He was bitterly jealous of Bill. I fed that pill to him as often as I could, and he believed you meant to marry Bill. I thought that my chance had come then . . . because if you were lost to him, why not take what I could offer him instead? But no! He calmly and firmly told me to go home. Oh, my God! How damn glad I am that that fool of a doctor saw us! That has paid Dallas back in full."

A woman scorned! Scilla thought, suddenly understanding now why Nancy should be laughing and enjoying this. Revenge was sweet and Dallas had indeed had to pay back in full for scorning Nancy's charms. Dallas . . . Dallas . . . Scilla's heart wept long bitter tears. The ache was insupportable and again she stood up, this time quite firmly, and said:

"Aly will show you out. I'm going to my room!"

"He'll marry me in the end . . . you'll see!" she heard Nancy's deep voice follow her into the passage. Then, as she reached for the kitchen door, she heard the front door slam and knew that Nancy had no more to say; she had learned what she had come to learn, and inadvertently taught

Scilla a terrible, unforgettable, irredeemable lesson. Now she was gone.

Scilla ran into her bedroom and locked her door. Then she flung herself down on her bed and lay there, inert, her face white with shock.

She had been so sure . . . so absolutely sure that Dallas was lying to her. She had believed rumour . . . believed a few words overheard in the dark, and thereby doubted a man who had never given her cause to doubt him before. What madness had possessed her? What chain of coincidences had driven her to the state of mind where she had offered no resistance to that evil thought? How was it possible that she could have been so certain about something that had never happened?

She tried to remember . . . to recall the events which had led up to that mistaken knowledge. Her first meeting . . . no, even before she had met Nancy, she had heard someone say that Dallas was keen about her. Then when she did meet Nancy on the beach, it had been clear that Nancy was in love with him. So the worm of suspicion had been seeded in her mind and grown, fed by gossip . . . fed by her belief that whatever love had existed in Dallas' heart for her, Scilla, had long ago been supplanted by Nancy. Then, at Cyrene, Nancy herself had endorsed that lie, talking loosely to Dallas about sharing his bed because she was drunk and because that was all she had been thinking about. But not Dallas. Not Dallas . . .

Kathie, calling in on her way back from the Naafi, found Scilla in her room. This time, her young sister had no strength to resist the desire to unburden her heart. The load had become too heavy and the words were rushing from her incoherently until Kathie calmed her and made her tell slowly and quietly what had distressed her so terribly. When at last she understood, she was aghast. How must this affect Scilla . . . and Bill? It had been hard enough for Scilla to play a part when with all her heart she longed to make a success of her marriage; when her one desire had been to forget Dallas. Now that she knew she had done Dallas a terrible injustice;

that she could have been married not to Bill but to the man she loved had she not rushed into marrying on the rebound. How much harder it was going to be for her! Had she considered that yet? Or was she still too deeply shocked for anything but emotion?

"What about Bill?" Kathie asked gently.

Bill! Scilla remembered with a sudden pang that so far she had not once considered Bill. She had thought only of herself . . . of the terrible mistake she had made . . . of the love which overflowed in her heart for Dallas and the love he had, after all, borne her. Bill . . . the man she had married! The boy who was her husband loving her in his own way as much as she loved another man.

"He'll never know anything about it!" she said wildly. "I promise that, Kathie. I promise you . . . on my life. Give me a little time, just a few hours, and I'll be able to carry on. Only now I can't think of him . . . I can't. He has the whole of my future. Oh, Kathie, it's Dallas I'm thinking of . . . poor Dallas! How bitter he must be . . . how he must be hating me!"

"Yet he went to Cairo because he could not bear to see you return triumphantly from your honeymoon with Bill!"

Kathie regretted the words immediately. They had been too spontaneous for forethought. Now she could see that it might have been better to let Scilla believe that Dallas' love had turned through bitterness to hate. Maybe it had. Maybe he had gone to Cairo for other reasons.

Scilla was crying quietly.

"I've made such a ghastly mess of things. All my life I've taken the wrong turning. I should never, never have let Dallas go away without me all those years ago. I was a coward then. And I'm still a coward. I married Bill because I wanted love and a home and children . . . because I was afraid to be *alone*. I was out of my mind. Don't you see, Kathie? I was afraid of my own love for Dallas even then? Marrying Bill was running away from temptation. If I'd not done so, I might not have been able to hold out against Dallas. And I hated him so much

137

for what I thought he had done. I despised myself for loving him and I thought by marrying Bill I could forget him. I was wrong . . . terribly wrong. You told me not to do it, Kathie, and I wouldn't listen because the last time I took other people's advice, I lost Dallas. I swore then that I'd use my own judgment next time . . . and it has proved no better . . . even worse than my parents'. Oh, Kathie, what a fool . . . what a blind, silly fool I've been! And this time, there is no second chance."

There was nothing Kathie could think of to say to comfort Scilla. She had taken an irrevocable step when she became Bill's wife, never realizing that she might wish so soon afterwards to revoke that step. And in her heart, Kathie believed that except for Dallas, no man could have come between Scilla and Bill. They might have been happy . . . might still be happy if only Scilla could find a way through this present moment of regret. Bill, of course, might agree to divorce her if he knew what had happened. But somehow Kathie felt that no matter what happened, Scilla would never make Bill pay for her mistakes. Nor did she believe that Dallas would do so.

"I'd like to write and tell Dallas . . . how sorry I am!" Scilla said in a whisper. "But I think that would only make him more bitter than ever. Perhaps if I saw him, I could explain, but I dare not do that. I could not trust myself. Kathie, is there nothing I can do to make amends?"

"Darling, I don't see that there is!" Kathie said gently. "I don't know that I altogether agree that the truth would make Dallas more bitter and unhappy. Somehow I feel that if I were in his shoes, I could bear the thought that I'd lost you so long as I knew I had lost you fairly. Believing that you played a game with him at Cyrene and that letter you wrote and those things you said, must have hurt him desperately. I suppose Nancy won't lose much time telling him the truth. If you tell him . . . write to him . . . then he can hear it from you and I think that is kinder. She might so easily tell him only half the truth . . . that you believed him to have had an affair with her . . . but not that you loved him . . . still love him."

"I want to tell him what really happened, but I can't do anything that might hurt Bill. Suppose through some frightful mishap he ever saw that letter?"

"Then go and see him if you don't want to write. Tell him. When it's done, you can say goodbye and try to start life again, Scilla. You have to do that. Life can't end now . . . however much you may be wanting it to. And you know, darling, there are other ways of loving people and being happy. I think you told me that yourself. You know that there can never be anything now between you and Dallas, but you can at least now respect his memory. Can't you learn to think of him as someone who died in the past? Many women were widowed in the war and made second marriages which were, in the end, just as happy."

"I could try." Scilla spoke so inaudibly that Kathie only just heard the words. "For Bill's sake, I'll try, Kathie. I've done him as much harm as I've done Dallas . . . and myself. I know that now. I can't give him all of myself. I've tried so hard. I think he believes that I do love him. He hasn't guessed how hard it has sometimes been for me."

"Perhaps if you don't try quite so hard, Scilla. Just let yourself drift along. You're so intense, so emotional. If you could teach yourself to take life more calmly . . . to be more placid like I am."

"Oh, Kathie, I'd give everything to be you . . . everything! You have Pete and the children and you're happy. Am I never to find happiness? Is it always to elude me? Must I always make everything I touch go wrong?"

"You mustn't blame yourself!" Kathie said gently. "You have never really been to blame, Scilla. You were so very young and inexperienced when you first met Dallas. You couldn't have known that what you felt then was the real thing. You were just unlucky that you met Dallas in the circumstances that existed. And later, everything conspired to keep you apart. I blame Nancy Harold, not you.

"But marrying Bill?" Scilla stated harshly. "You cannot lay

139

that at anyone else's door. I was old enough to know better and I acted with my eyes open."

"Not quite open . . . because you believed that Dallas had failed you. But you can put right that mistake, Scilla. I know it can't seem easy . . . or even possible. But I'm sure you and Bill could be happy together in time. If you don't believe that, then you should let him divorce you now. That would be kinder than to let him grow slowly more and more unhappy and become gradually more and more disillusioned."

"No . . . no!" Scilla cried. "I won't fail him, Kathie. I promise you that. Since happiness is out of my reach now. I can be free to devote my life to Bill. I have done so since we were married and he is happy."

"Yes," Kathie agreed quietly. "But you'll have to find something in marriage for yourself, too, Scilla. Bill may not be very introspective but the time will come when he will begin to see through your façade. He'll get to know you better and see, as I have done, that you are playing a part . . . forcing yourself to be responsive and affectionate for his sake."

"He'll be home soon!" Scilla cried desperately. "How am I going to pretend that everything is all right? I can't, Kathie, and yet I know I must."

"Then tell him part of the truth," Kathie suggested. "Say that Nancy Harold was here and upset you and that you'd prefer never to have to see her again. Then, in future, he'll avoid her for your sake, as far as it is possible in this place to avoid anyone."

"If only we could be posted!" Scilla cried. "Dallas has tried to get back to Australia, but can't. How can either of us continue to live here, in this small town, wondering when we shall next see each other, knowing the other is never more than a few miles away? Dallas' flat is only a stone's throw from here. How can I begin to forget?"

"Can't Bill get a posting elsewhere?"

"He could, I expect. But he likes it here and I can't tell him why I want to go. He thinks I'm glad to be here near you, which is true, of course. But even you wouldn't keep me from running away from Dallas if I could!"

"Then find some other reason . . . health, for instance. People do get sinus trouble here. You could develop headaches and I'm sure Bill would pretty soon suggest a change of his own accord."

"More lies . . . more pretence!" Scilla whispered. "Sometimes I wish I could talk to Bill openly, throw myself on his mercy! But that's being cowardly again. It's asking him to share my burden, my unhappiness."

"Yet you told him when you first met about Dallas?"

"Yes! It's strange that he never mentions it. I think he must believe that I got over it long ago. Of course, he didn't know about Dallas and me in Cyrene. He knew only what I had told him earlier when I believed it true myself . . . that Dallas was in love with Nancy. But Bill isn't the jealous type and I don't think it has occurred to him that I might still have any feeling left for Dallas. He believes that I love him, Kathie. At least I've played my part well enough for that. And in a way, I do love Bill. One just can't help it . . . the way one loves a charming little boy. He is a boy at heart, so pleased with little things . . . so impulsive and generous and endearing. When he has done something nice to surprise me, and he often did on our honeymoon, he waits watching my face just as Paul watched yours when you opened the present he'd chosen for you for Christmas. The love I have for Bill is a maternal one . . . protective. Maybe that's why I can't hurt him. One just can't hurt a child."

So Kathie learned that Scilla was herself no longer a child. She had grown up and the growing pains had been bitter ones for her. But at least now she had Scilla's confidence again, Kathie would do whatever she could to help her. She decided now to telephone her flat and tell the new nanny to give Pete and the children lunch . . . then stay and lunch with Scilla and Bill. It would be easier for Scilla to appear normal if she, Kathie, were there to make idle conversation.

Scilla was grateful and pulled herself together sufficiently to wash her face and put on fresh make-up. Half an hour later, there was little trace of the emotional upheaval she had undergone, and at Kathie's advice she announced at lunch that she had had a bad headache. Bill was instantly solicitous and told Scilla she was to lie down and rest that afternoon and keep out of the sun. He would put off his golf foursome and stay with her.

Between them, the sisters persuaded him to go alone and so, without difficulty, Scilla was free to go round that very afternoon if she wished to see Dallas. Kathie was anxious that if this meeting were to take place, it should be soon . . . for she knew that Scilla would think of little else until it was off her mind. With a promise to be back at tea-time she left Scilla alone in the flat, hiding her trepidation. All the way home she worried about what she had herself encouraged. Away from Scilla, it no longer seemed such a good idea that her young sister should see Dallas. It might be putting an impossible strain on them both. At best, it would be a heartbreaking revelation for Dallas and a terrible afternoon of agony for Scilla.

Pete, hearing the story while they rested with the shutters down against the sultry heat of early afternoon, told her she had been wrong to interfere. Whatever happened now she would be partly responsible, he told her.

"But I'm that anyway," Kathie cried. "I can never forget that I once helped Scilla lose Dallas. I know I didn't play much of a part in those days, but I agreed in mind and spirit with Mother and Father and Scilla knew it. Since then, her unhappiness has been mine, too, in a lesser degree. Pete, at least seeing Dallas can't make matters any worse."

"I suppose not!" Pete agreed. "I feel sorry for all three of them. What a menace that Harold woman is!"

"I suppose we can blame her . . . since it helps to put the blame on someone!" Kathie agreed with a wan smile. "Oh, Pete, I wonder what's happening . . . if Scilla found Dallas in. It's probably a crazy idea to go to his flat anyway. Some busybody may see her and start gossip about her."

"Hardly . . . at three in the afternoon. In any case, she might be visiting anyone in that block. Try and relax, Kathie. It's too hot to worry!"

It was to Scilla unbearably hot as she climbed out of the gharry and paid the driver. Too hot to have walked the brief distance between her block and Dallas'. Now she was here, she wished that she hadn't come and in the same instant was terribly afraid that Dallas might not have come back yet; or not come to his flat from the airport. She was not sure what time the Cairo plane came in and Nancy had told her only that he would be back today. Nancy might have been wrong and she might herself be here. This fresh worry assailed Scilla and she nearly turned round to recall the gharry. But some inner instinct drew her on up the cool stairs to the flat she knew was Dallas'. Some inner compulsion made her put her finger on the bell and while her body trembled with fear and longing and a desperate anxiety, she heard footsteps on the tiled floor and knew he was coming to answer her ring.

# Eleven

Dallas opened the door. The widening of his grey eyes and an audible intake of breath betrayed his surprise at seeing her. Then he said calmly:

"Come in, Scilla!"

It made her feel almost as if he had been expecting her. Her heart was beating violently and she felt beyond speech. Relief was uppermost . . . that she should have found him in; and nervousness was beneath the relief, as she wondered how she could begin to tell him all that was in her heart and yet use the necessary constraint.

Glancing around the hall as she followed him across it to the living-room, she saw his half-opened suitcase and realised that he had probably only just arrived back. He must have been searching through it in true masculine untidiness for the clean shirt he was wearing. Against the white silk, his skin looked browner than ever. The fair hair, cut short, nevertheless still curled over his head like a sculpture of a Greek god of whom he invariably reminded her. She felt the same inevitable magnetic pull of her whole body towards his as she had done so many years ago when they had been introduced for the first time. In that instant she had lost her heart, never to regain it.

"Come and sit down here!" Dallas said, leading her by the arm to a chair. He seemed aware of the weakness in her legs and his tone of voice was gentle . . . unnervingly so, for she had expected him to rebuff her or at least be cool and distant. Instead, he was the Dallas of long ago . . . the Dallas of Cyrene . . . the man who had always known so well how she was feeling and so intuitively known just what to do and say to meet the occasion.

144

"I only got back half an hour ago. I've been in Cairo."

"Yes, I know!" Scilla spoke for the first time. She saw Dallas glance up at her. Then briefly, his eyes went down to the ring on her finger, and he looked away as if the sight hurt him.

"Dallas! I came . . . to apologise!"

"No, no!" The words were low and now the grey eyes were once more fastened on hers. "Don't do that, kid. It wasn't your fault. Anyone would have believed the same . . . everyone did."

"But Dallas . . . it wasn't just the rumour . . . I overheard the things Nancy said to you when she arrived late that night at Cyrene. I was on the balcony. I . . . I jumped to conclusions . . . wrong conclusions . . ." Her voice broke on the last words and trailed into a stifled silence.

Opposite her, the man sat still on the arm of the chair, his hands clenched in his lap. The moment he had seen Scilla in the doorway, he had realised at least part of what had occurred. Deep in his heart, he had never been able to believe the girl he loved to have changed into the woman she had afterwards made herself out to be in Cyrene. Hour upon hour, day upon day, he had tried to imagine what might have caused that change in her. Eventually, he had written that letter to her, feeling that somehow or other he had failed to convince her that nothing had passed between himself and Nancy Harold and that he must at least make this one last attempt to attain justice for himself . . . and for her. Now, as he thought of that fatal night in Cyrene, remembered Nancy's careless, loose conversation, he could understand. And he knew, too, that Scilla had meant, after all, all the things she had said to him earlier that day . . . that she had loved him then . . . and *still* did. And on her finger lay another man's ring! Only that prevented him from moving to claim her for his own.

"I have felt all along that there must be some easy explanation for . . . for the letter you wrote to me!" he said, his voice harsh as he strove to keep the tone level. "I could never believe that you were pretending that day in Cyrene. Oh, Scilla, why didn't you wait a little? Why didn't you ask me the next morning about Nancy? Why didn't you trust me? I don't know how you discovered the truth but surely you could have waited a little longer?" The words were wrung from his heart despite his intentions to say nothing to reprove or upset her.

He saw the small white teeth bite into her lower lip; saw the fingertips crush the soft palms of her hands, and knew how hard it was for her, too, to control her emotions.

"I know I should have done all those things, Dallas. But it's too late to go back on it now. We both know that. I came only because I . . . I had to tell you how . . . how sorry I am!"

"Sorry!" he echoed the word bitterly, knowing its inadequacy and yet understanding the fullest implications of what she had said. "Scilla, don't you see what has happened? We've lost each other for always this time. For always!"

"Don't!" she broke in wildly. "I know it, Dallas. I've thought of nothing else since Nancy told me this morning what really happened." The tone of her voice lowered and was soft and helpless and hopeless as she breathed the words: "I loved you for so long, Dallas. For nine long years I went on loving you. You were never out of my thoughts . . . my dreams. Even now you haunt me, waking or sleeping. But I have to try to forget you . . . forget my love for you. And I'm afraid, Dallas, afraid!"

No longer able to prevent himself, Dallas had dropped to the floor beside her chair and his arms were round her waist, his face lying against her lap. He felt her hand lightly on his head and remembered, as she was doing, how often they had sat in silent communion in just this position in the long years ago when they had been young and free and in love.

"Scilla, Scilla! If we could only go back to those days! What a fool I was. I should have made you come to Australia with me. I should have stayed in England . . . gone on trying to persuade you to become my wife."

"If you'd only written . . . one word . . . I would have

come," Scilla said. "I knew the day after I'd let Kathie give you my letter that I had been mad to let you go without me. But I was too proud to go back on the things I had written. I waited and waited for you to phone . . . watched the post and nearly went crazy when I heard you were leaving England. I even went down to the port to see your ship go. My heart went with it, Dallas . . . with you."

"Oh, darling! If I'd only known! I thought you really meant it and I was so hurt that I almost hated you. Yet time and again I nearly telephoned you. I had someone write to you to say we were really off . . . giving the name of the ship. I, in turn, was hoping you might still get in touch with me. I, too, was too proud to ask you again. But I never forgot you, Scilla. I never met a girl I wanted to marry . . . or that I could love even a little bit. Then seeing you again, I could hardly bear it. You had grown so incredibly beautiful . . . so infinitely more desirable with the years. Nancy told me that you were going to marry Bill and I presumed that you had, after all, never really been in love with me and that you had long ago ceased even to think about me with any affection. Nancy made a nice fool of me . . . when I was not making a fool of myself. That night we went to the Club I nearly told you how I felt . . . so nearly. But that wretched pride of mine came between us. Never as long as I live will I be proud again, Scilla. I've learned my lesson now."

"But you did speak, Dallas . . . at Cyrene. Mine was the ultimate fault . . . the only one that really counts now. If I'd only had faith in you and in the dictates of my heart . . . we might—"

"Yes, we might!" Dallas stopped the sentence neither could bear to hear in words.

"Forgive me, forgive me!" Scilla whispered, the tears pouring down her face. He clung to her hands, not daring to look into those tear-filled eyes for fear that he would lose the control he had imposed on himself and kiss her, hold her, protect her, love her. He had known in the long nights of agony that had followed her marriage, that she was forever lost to him . . . beyond his reach.

"I'm . . . glad . . . I know what really happened," Dallas said hesitantly. The pain of such knowledge was bitter sweet, but at least it was preferable to believing that he had loved all these years a girl who had turned into a cold, casual flirt; who could have deliberately stirred him to propose to her a second time only to turn round next day and laugh in his face. He had not believed it, not deep down inside himself. He knew that they belonged together; belonged in the way that they had been born to meet and fall in love and marry. That conviction had been his from the moment he first met her, so young, so innocent, so incredibly sweet. It had been strengthened when they had come together for that brief idyll in Cyrene. Now he knew that if the whole world were to try to part them a third time, they could not succeed. Yet they must part now . . . for always. The thought sent a shiver of unutterable loneliness through his body. He tried again to imagine a life without her as he had tried so hard in Cairo. He had lived through nine years without much joy but without too great a difficulty. Surely he could pick up those threads of his bachelor life again?

"I tried so hard to forget you in Cairo!" he said aloud. "I tried in every way man can think of to drown a memory. Yet I could not do so. It was too late this time, Scilla. If we hadn't met again in Cyrene, I suppose I could have gone on living, always hoping deep in my heart that one day I should find you again. But when it happened, I knew what had made my life so empty, so meaningless; that you were, and have always been, my only reason for living."

"Don't!" Scilla cried desperately. "I can't bear it, Dallas. I cannot endure my own pain and yours hurts me even more deeply."

"Scilla, why? Tell me why?"

He was looking now into her eyes, his own puzzled and striving to learn the truth. She knew what his question meant.

"I married Bill because I was lonely and bitter and because

my life had no meaning. For nine years I had lived only in my memories of you. When we met again I believed that you had changed . . . had grown from the boy I loved into a man I could love still but never respect. I hated and yet I still loved you, Dallas. In my heart, you were lost to me because the man I loved was, so I believed, gone for ever. I had nothing to live for . . . not even the memories on which I'd lived in the past. Bill loved me . . . wanted me to be his wife. I thought perhaps I could make him happy and that he might help me to forget you. I made a terrible mistake. I know now that it is criminally wrong to marry a man when you are still in love with someone else. I lie in his arms and pretend I am in yours. Only when it is dark can I bear him near me for then I can believe that it is you. Dallas, I am afraid . . . afraid that one day he'll discover the wrong I have done him. He's so terribly good and kind and sweet to me. I'd die rather than hurt him. That's why . . . why . . ."

"Why we can't even think about divorce!" Dallas said. "It's all right, darling, I understand. I like Bill and I'd never come between any man and his wife whatever the circumstances . . . not wittingly, anyway."

"I ought not to be here now!" Scilla whispered. "It would be hard explaining to Bill what I was doing. I'm supposed to be in bed with a headache. I'll have to go soon."

"Not yet!"

The cry touched her heart and weakened her as she had feared might happen. She knew a moment's terrible, wild desire to give way to that weakness; to slip into Dallas' arms and let him do as he wished with her. At least she would have this one hour of belonging to him, body, heart and soul, to remember in the lonely years to come. She could give him that memory, too.

Dallas, thinking the same, was equally close to breaking the strongest of his beliefs, the most rigid of his moral standards. He knew that if he chose, he could take Scilla now. But he knew in the same instant that he did not want a brief hour of

149

love, not when afterwards she would regret such behaviour; when he would himself feel ashamed and have to bear the knowledge that he had smeared what otherwise remained the one true, pure love of his life. Nor could he bear to think that the day would follow when, for the first time in his life, he would be unable to meet another man's eyes. No, it was not for him nor for Scilla. He would be content to know that he had her heart forever in his. Let the man who had won only her body at least have that compensation unsullied. It was Bill and not himself who in the end was the loser.

Yet he knew that was not quite true. The thought that when he returned to Australia he would in all probability never see her again, filled him with acute anguish. This last moment when they would ever be alone together was nearly gone . . . and it became so violently charged with their joint misery, their joint desperation and love, that without a word spoken, both stood up and Scilla moved silently into his arms.

He did not kiss her, just held her close against him in a terrible awareness of his loss. She clung to him weakly and he could feel by the shaking of her body that she was weeping. Tenderly, he wiped the tears from her cheeks and tried to smile.

"I shall love you . . . always!" he told her, as thousand upon thousand of past lovers must have said on parting. "I shall never marry, Scilla, and if ever the time comes when you are free, no matter how far into the future, how old we may be, then come to me. I'll give you my address in Australia, an address that will always find me. If ever things become too hard or you are ill or you need me . . . or if ever you are free, then you have only to let me know. Never fear that I'll change . . . that I might not come. Promise me that, darling!"

"I promise!" Scilla said.

Very gently, he took his arms away from her and tried once more to bring a smile back into those eyes staring at him so desperately. She looked unbearably young and helpless and lonely. Then she turned her face away from him and he heard her voice say:

"I'm going now, Dallas. It would be a lie to pretend that I shall not think of you . . . often . . . always. For Bill's sake I must try not to do so but I know that it will happen. Will you promise me one thing, too?"

"Anything!" Dallas cried hoarsely. "Anything!"

"If you are ever very ill and need me, let Kathie know. Then if I can, I will come to you. I could not bear to think that you might ever call for me and I not know it. Will you, Dallas?"

"Yes, darling!"

She turned towards him then, and walking up to him lifted her face to his, trustingly and because she could not help it. He bent and kissed her very tenderly on the lips as one might kiss a child. Both knew that any other kiss might draw them into a whirlpool they had so far avoided and which neither really desired with their minds, even while their bodies ached for one another.

He took her arm and led her to the door of his flat.

"Will you be all right going home?" he asked, as he held it open for her. "I'd take you but—"

"But I'd rather go alone," she said desperately. "Goodbye, Dallas!"

His arms went out impulsively towards her, but with a little heart-breaking cry she had turned and started to run down the stairs. He stood still, listening to the sound of her footsteps; heard them fade away into the distance and then turned and with the steps of a sleep-walker went back into his flat and closed the door.

# Twelve

The next month was torture for Scilla. She supposed that it must be the same for Dallas but she did not know because they never spoke to one another. She felt that it would have been a hundred times easier for each of them had they not had to see one another. But while they did everything they could to avoid any social gathering where they knew the other was also invited, there were always the casual accidental meetings at the Club, on the beach, at private parties. Then their eyes would meet and glance quickly away with a flash of pain and as soon as possible either she or Dallas would leave.

As for her life with Bill, it became more and more difficult for her to continue to play her self-ordained part of carefree, happy young wife. She wondered now how she could ever have supposed that this task could be an easy one; wondered how she could have been so fantastically short-sighted as to enter into a marriage in which love was one-sided. Had Bill loved her less, then again it might have been easier for her; but he was devoted, there was no better word, to his bride and sought her affectionate responses unceasingly, as was only natural since he knew nothing of her innermost feelings.

Kathie alone knew of the struggle that Scilla was putting up. She began to wonder deep inside her how long this tension could continue without a break. Surely something inside her young sister must give way? No one could continue to live on their nerves, day and night, without hope of things improving for many months to come. She knew Dallas would be in Australia by now if a replacement could have been found for him. As it was, he must continue here at least until the new year. Could Scilla stand the strain of those unavoidable meetings until then? It was not as if she could relax in her own home. There the need to put on a convincing show of loving affection for her husband was even more telling.

Then Kathie began to notice a difference in Bill. At first she could not be sure that it was there, but as the days passed, she knew that he had changed . . . indefinably. The once ready charming smile had given way to a quick, nervous laugh. The once natural gesture of reaching out a hand to put on his wife's arm, or to touch her hand, was now curtailed half way. There were lines beneath the unsmiling brown eyes and only when he was conscious of someone's glance on him was he his old, cheerful, irresponsible self.

Had Scilla noticed it? Kathie was not sure of this either. She believed that in fact Scilla was too deep in her own struggle with herself to be aware of any struggle in Bill. How did they manage in their more intimate moments alone together? Another of Kathie's worries was that both were drinking too much. The excessive heat might be partially responsible but Kathie felt she knew the real cause. And Bill was spending money like water. Every time she saw Scilla, her young sister would show her listlessly some new present Bill had given her, or some new luxury for the house, a gold wrist watch, and suddenly a new sports coupé to replace his old car. Even Pete began to notice this lavish expenditure and speculate on how Bill, a junior captain, managed to find the means. Maybe he had private capital, Kathie did not know. And Scilla, except to say that she did wish Bill wouldn't give her so much because it made her feel so guilty, made no comment on their financial status. Kathie was deeply worried but could do nothing. No one could help them except themselves.

Then, as Kathie had half expected, the storm broke . . . or rather, Scilla broke. She telephoned Kathie one afternoon when Bill was out golfing, and weeping incoherently, begged her sister to come round.

Kathie found her in the sitting-room, deathly pale but dry-eyed. She looked ghastly. And she could not keep still.

She wandered round the room, aimlessly touching some of the beautiful ornaments that somehow seemed out of place in an army quarter amongst army furniture, and smoking one cigarette after another.

"I can't go on with it, I can't!" she said as soon as Kathie was seated. Her eyes were enormous and feverishly bright. "I know what you must think of me, Kathie, after my promises, after giving you my word that this wouldn't happen. But I'm not thinking of myself now. It's Bill."

"So I was right!"

"You see it, too?" Scilla asked, and without waiting for Kathie's reply, went on: "He's miserable, Kathie. He knows something is wrong with his marriage but he doesn't know what. At least, I don't think he knows. I nearly told him the other night . . . so nearly. Kathie, I have tried. I've tried desperately to go on as if nothing had happened. I think I could have succeeded if only . . . if only Nancy hadn't told me the truth about that night in Dallas' flat. So long as I despised Dallas for what he had done, I really wanted to forget him and to make a fresh start. But since then although I've tried to want my marriage to be a success, in my heart there has been no belief, no faith, no conviction that it can ever succeed. What am I to do, Kathie? I can stand my own unhappiness. I can even bear the sight of Dallas' face whenever we meet . . . but it's Bill."

"Why don't you explain to him?" Kathie suggested. "Tell him the truth, Scilla. Tell him that if only he will be patient and give you time, you'll get over it. I think that would be fairer to him than letting him think he has failed."

"I am the only one who has failed!" Scilla cried bitterly. "He has been wonderful to me, Kathie, far too good. I can't bear it. If I admire someone's dress, he sends to London for a new one for me. If I mention that green is my favourite colour, next day I find a beautiful jade ring by my breakfast plate. He gives me the earth. I don't know how he can afford it. I suppose he has private means because he obviously can't do it on his pay. He

154

never talks about money to me. When we started off in the flat, he asked me what I wanted for a housekeeping allowance and a personal allowance and I said I'd be able to manage easily for the two of us on half what Pete gives you. But that's the only time he has ever talked about money to me. Yet he must have far more than Pete."

"You met his family, Scilla. Maybe his father gives him an allowance?"

"I don't really see how he can!" Scilla commented wearily. "Bill's father is a retired brigadier and as far as I know lives on his pension. But it isn't that which worries me . . . it's that I feel Bill is giving me all these things in an effort to please me, to make me happy. He knows I'm not. At night it is dreadful. I lie pretending to sleep and now he lies awake, too, pretending that he is asleep and that he thinks I am."

"I can't understand why, if he knows something is wrong, he hasn't spoken about it. Can he suspect anything, Scilla?"

"What is there to suspect?" Scilla replied. "I've asked myself the same question. But he knew I was in love with Dallas once and believes it's all over. He cannot have discovered anything because there is nothing to discover. He can't have heard about Cyrene – only you and Dallas and I knew about that. There was no one else in the hotel who knew we'd spent a day together. And no one saw me go to his flat that afternoon, or leave it. Dallas has never written or telephoned me, and when we meet we act like comparative strangers. What can Bill suspect? I don't talk in my sleep . . . at least, I don't think so. No, Kathie, I don't think he guesses the truth but he knows something has gone wrong with our marriage. He knows I'm not happy and it's making him miserable."

"Then why not tell him the truth?"

"Because I know he'll offer me my freedom and I don't think I could refuse it if he did. It would seem so crazy to go on with our marriage if he knew I was in love with someone else, and that Dallas was in love with me and only he stood between us. Who gains anything? Bill would certainly tell me

155

to go to Dallas . . . and if he did, I don't think I'd have the strength to stay."

"Maybe that would be the best thing, Scilla!" Kathie said after a moment's silence. "If by staying you can't even ensure Bill's happiness, then there is no point in staying, is there?"

"But I might be able to make him happy . . . if only I could get away from here. I think I'll go mad if I have to see Dallas again. We look at each other, knowing what is in each other's heart, knowing by the pain in our own hearts what agony this is for us all. And we say, 'Fancy meeting you', or something equally stupid, and try to get as far away from each other as possible."

"If you told Bill the truth, he'd get a posting!" Kathie reverted to her former idea.

"Yes, I'd thought of that. But, Kathie, Bill loves me. If he knew I was unhappy, he'd give me the earth or my freedom without thought for himself. I know that. If I tell him, our marriage is over."

"Isn't it as good as that already?"

Scilla drew in her breath sharply.

"Not quite, not quite! Kathie, I was married in church and I meant my vows as I made them. I won't go back on them . . . I won't. I could never lift my head again if I failed. The responsibility is all mine because I knew when I married Bill that he loved me and that I didn't love him. I knew it and so everything that follows lies at my door. Do you think I . . . or Dallas . . . could have a moment's peace of mind with the thought of Bill's happiness thrown away so easily?"

"But you say he isn't happy now!" Kathie argued. "Do you think he would be more unhappy without you?"

"I still think I could make him happy if only we could get away. I've told him I have these fictitious headaches. In fact I have had headaches, but I expect it's just nerves. He said I'd be better as soon as the weather got cooler and suggested we went to Cyrene for his next short leave. Cyrene! I couldn't bear to go there again, never, never!"

"Calm yourself, darling," Kathie said gently as Scilla's voice rose hysterically. "Try to be calm. There must be a solution to all this. Let's try and think it out sensibly."

Scilla gave a short laugh and with an effort stopped her pacing of the room and slipped into the armchair.

"Yes, let's be sensible. Let's pretend that all this is happening to someone else and they have asked our advice. What would we say? We'd tell the girl to leave her husband and marry the man she loved. But I can't do it, Kathie. I can't!"

"Yet you say you can't go on like this, and I think that's true. You're in an awful state, Scilla. Do you realise how thin you are? In two months you've lost about a stone."

"That's this climate," Scilla said, not believing it herself. Her voice was suddenly calmer. "I know I did say I couldn't go on, but that's not true. It's never true, is it? I mean, one can do anything at all if one is sufficiently determined. What did Nanny used to say to us? 'There's no such word as "can't"!'"

Kathie smiled briefly and then her face clouded again as she said wistfully:

"That's not really true, Scilla. For one thing, one can't put the clock back. That is the only right solution to what has become of your life."

Scilla lay back in the chair and closed her eyes.

"To go back nine years . . . or even three months Kathie, if I'd only listened to you that night before my wedding. If . . ." Her voice trailed away for a few minutes. Then she said in a different tone, a more normal voice: "Kathie, suppose I did leave Bill, do you think he'd find someone else in time? Do you think if I went now before our marriage was a habit, that he might eventually be happier without me? If I could believe that, I'd go. I want only what is best in the end for Bill."

"I can't answer that!" Kathie said gently. "Only Bill could do that and I don't suppose he could foresee the future. I don't know how he's feeling now. I don't really know him very well.

You are the only one who can judge at all and then it must be a gamble."

"Yes, I know that. But I find I don't know Bill either. I thought I did when I married him. I thought he was just a young, carefree, rather irresponsible young man whose feelings didn't go very far below the surface. I thought that all there was to Bill was the charming, attractive man one could see and understand; whose passions were sincere but never very serious or demanding. I never heard him express a violent opinion about anything or anyone . . . until lately. Now I'm finding a different Bill. I know that he loves me far more than I guessed. That's why I've failed so badly. I counted on the fact that he would make few demands on my inner self; that he would be content with affection and comfort and care. But because he has fallen as deeply in love with me as I have with Dallas, he has begun to want more, to feel more, to see more. Kathie, how can I give him what he asks of me? It is love he wants. Not just a physical response to his physical needs . . . but love. I have no love to give him . . . not that kind of love. I have an affection for him and I'd do anything at all to protect him from hurt, but it is not affection he is asking of me, and I am the only one likely to hurt him. I do hurt him. He gives me some expensive gift and waits for me to throw myself into his arms and hug him impulsively and tell him how much I care about him. But all I feel is unwilling gratitude for things I don't want. I can close my eyes and submit to his embraces but I can't be the initiator of emotions I dread."

"Then I think you should have it out with him, Scilla, and if he agrees that it is best for him, then you must let him divorce you. I know it's an ugly word and that you can't think about it easily or without a nasty taste in your mouth. But the choice should be Bill's."

"You don't agree that it would be shelving my responsibility? Putting the burden on Bill's shoulder when it's of my making?"

"It would be easier if you had not such a rigid conscience,

Scilla!" Kathie said with a smile. "Put that way, I suppose you're right. What do other people do?"

"They either take the easy way and divorce their husbands, or they do the honourable thing and just go on trying to make a go of their marriages. I think in time they probably succeed . . . if nothing snaps before that happens. There isn't any half-way between the two. I made a contract, Kathie, and I've got to stick to it."

Scilla was quite calm now . . . resigned, Kathie thought. It was as if this talk had clarified her mind, strengthened her innermost beliefs and given her the courage to go on. When she left, Scilla even managed a smile as she said:

"Don't worry about me, Kathie darling. If I thought I was responsible for making you unhappy, too, I think I'd walk under a bus. I'll be all right. Really I will."

Kathie made her promise to calm down somehow or other, and also to give up the drinking which was so unlike Scilla; and made her promise to tell her if things became too hard to bear alone again.

That promise was to bear fruit sooner than either of them expected. That night, before Scilla had had time to cement the foundations of her renewed intentions to be a better wife to Bill, he told her he wanted a child.

In the darkness, Scilla clenched her hands beneath the sheet and felt the sweat breaking out in her palms. All her life since she was a little girl, she had loved babies. Since she had grown up she had dreamed of the day she would hold her own baby in her arms . . . but the father of that child had been Dallas. And now Bill had asked for a child.

She heard his voice break the unbearable silence.

"You don't want a baby, Scilla?"

"No . . . not just yet!" she gave her whispered reply. "Not . . . just yet!" she said again.

"Why?" Bill asked. His voice sounded hard and hurt. She felt she could not bear it. Turning a little towards him, she said desperately:

159

"Let's be alone together a little longer, darling."

"Just us two?"

Was his voice sarcastic? She must have imagined it. She said quickly:

"We're both young, Bill. There's plenty of time."

Now his tone sounded weary, defeated.

"I suppose you're right. I only thought . . . well, I don't know. For one thing Mother and Dad aren't young, and they'd be so thrilled with a grandchild. And you know, we could be separated later. When you did think you'd like a baby maybe we couldn't have one. It isn't always easy. I know one chap who waited eight years for his first child."

Scilla bit her lip until she tasted blood. Bill's request was completely justified. The reasons he gave she knew were not the real reasons and she was touched and a little horrified to realise what lay behind them. Without a word being said, she knew that he was trying to tell her he thought a child might be the answer to their unhappiness and might bring them closer . . . make their marriage more real.

Since he did not know the reason why it had so far failed, his answer to the problem was a sensible one. There was nothing at all against the idea and everything in its favour . . . except her own instinctive revulsion to it.

"Bill, aren't you happy as we are?"

The words came from dry lips and she waited tensed for his reply.

"Of course!" he said quickly, too quickly. "It's just that I think a child would make everything perfect. And I think you'd be happier, too. I mean, it must be a bit dull for you hanging round the flat while I'm at work . . . nothing much to do. I know you used to have a job that kept you busy. I expect you're lonely and I thought a baby might be the answer . . ." His voice trailed off nervously.

A baby conceived without love? As an antidote to unhappiness? As a means to strengthen ties that were weak? No! Scilla cried in her heart. Children should be brought into the world because they were wanted . . . not needed. And yet how could she deny Bill what was, after all, his right? What she alone could give him.

"You're very quiet, Scilla!"

"I was thinking about it!" she replied helplessly. "I . . . I don't quite know what to say, Bill. I'm not lonely . . . and I wouldn't want a baby just to fill in time. I think that would be wrong. Of course we'll have a child . . . several children . . . but we've only been married a few months. Let's get to know each other better first."

"But it's so hard to know you, Scilla. I thought I did, but I don't. I often wonder what you are thinking about and I never know. You don't . . . well, you don't tell me things about yourself."

"I'm sorry!" Scilla whispered. "It's just that I'm probably rather reticent . . . I've lived alone for so long. When Kathie got married I had my own flat in town and I became used to being by myself. I suppose I've lost the habit of . . . of talking about me."

For a moment, Bill was silent. Then he said:

"But it isn't just that you don't talk about yourself, Scilla. It's that I can't seem to come near you. Heaven knows I've tried to guess what you're thinking . . . if you're happy . . . why you're looking sad. If you . . . if you regret . . . anything."

"Bill, have you any reason to believe that I regret marrying you? You've been a marvellous husband to me. You're far too nice to me. You're too generous, too. Don't spend so much money on me, Bill. I don't need all those presents."

"No! I'm beginning to think you don't need anything from me."

"Bill!"

"Well, in a way, it's true, isn't it? I thought once that you needed me to love you, to take care of you. But I'm not even sure about that. I almost believe you'd be happier if we weren't married."

She couldn't bring herself to lie directly, yet she couldn't leave that challenge unanswered. She said in a tight little voice:

"Aren't you happy, Bill? Would you rather not have married me? I know I've disappointed you. I know I've failed to give you much that you've given me. I . . . I can't help it. I . . . I need time to get used to being married."

"Well, I suppose that's understandable!" she heard his reply. "It's just that . . . oh, I don't know what's wrong, Scilla. Perhaps that's why I suggested we had a child. I feel that would make our marriage real. I can't explain it, but I don't feel it is real at the moment. It's not your fault . . . nothing to do with you really. Scilla, please let us have a baby . . . please!"

"May I think about it?" Scilla said desperately. "Let me get used to the idea. You know I'll do anything to make you happy, Bill. I want so much for you to be happy . . . for both of us to be so. You mustn't ever blame yourself for anything . . . if . . . if anything is wrong. If there is, it's my fault. I know I'm difficult to understand . . . know it must be hard for you. But, Bill, surely every married couple needs time to adjust themselves to . . . to sharing? Especially if they have been alone as long as I have. If I've seemed to put up a barrier between us sometimes, maybe it's just because I'm still trying to retain a little of my independence."

"I always thought marriage meant a willingness to give up independence. I mean, if you love someone, you want them to be part of you . . . part of your thoughts. Perhaps that is too idealistic. It wouldn't be natural for two people with different natures and characters and upbringings to suddenly want all the same things because they happen to have been to a church and been married. I never really thought of that before. Scilla, what do you want?"

"I don't know!" she whispered. "Nothing . . . only to make you happy, Bill. Then I'll be happy, too."

"Then give me a child, Scilla. Will you?"

"I can't, Kathie, I can't!" Scilla told her sister next day. "I don't want Bill's child . . . Kathie, how can I refuse?" she contradicted her own statement. "I'm his wife . . . and I can't refuse. And it's the only thing he has ever asked of me," she added flatly.

"I think this must be the turning point, Scilla. You've got to make up your mind once and for all what you want to do. If you intend to go on with your marriage, then, as you say, you have no right to refuse Bill a child if he wants one; no matter how much you may not want *his* child yourself. If the idea is really so repugnant to you, then you might as well pack up your marriage. That's obvious. It's stupid to say that in time you'll feel differently. You're only putting off a decision that in all fairness to Bill you ought to make now. Maybe that's why he asked you . . . to force your hand. Maybe he's right and this is what you need to make you settle down. You'll have to go all the way or turn back. Instinctively or wittingly or by chance, Bill has hit on the one thing that can make you act."

"It's not right . . . to use a child as a weapon!"

"That's begging the question!" Kathie said truthfully. "I think you know that, too. I've had children and I know that you love them for themselves, and not just because of the man who happens to be their father. It's not as if you dislike Bill and might dislike those aspects in your child's nature that he passed on to it. You would love your child, Scilla, and loving it, you would not leave it . . . or Bill. I think your reason for refusing, if you do, would be because you'd know then that you'd burnt your boats. If that sounds hard and crude, I'm sorry, darling. But I think you owe it to Bill to make up your mind now."

"Yes, I know!" Scilla agreed. "But I can't do it, Kathie. I could do anything but that. I simply can't give birth to a baby that I have carried inside myself for nine months, wishing all the time that it was Dallas' child . . . his son, to look like him, be like him. You don't know how often I've lain awake at nights dreaming of the day I would hold Dallas' baby in my

163

arms. I wouldn't want another baby . . . and I couldn't bring it into the world not wanting it. I couldn't!"

"Then you'll have to leave Bill. Tell him the truth and leave him, Scilla. This has gone far enough. You can't hope to make a success of such a marriage. Didn't you think before you married Bill that this was bound to happen?"

"Of course I did!" Scilla cried. "But I didn't love Dallas then . . . or at least, if I still loved him, I despised him, too. I thought him a liar and morally weak and a coward, too. I had lost all respect for him and only somewhere deep inside me the love went on, disbelieving the things I thought were true. Because of that, because I believed I hated him, because I wanted to hate and forget him, I could also believe there was a future in my marriage with Bill. In time, I was sure, I would forget . . . would cease to love Dallas. Then I would be free to love Bill and bear his children. That's what I thought, Kathie. If I'd known Dallas was true to himself and to me, I'd never have married Bill . . . *never.*"

"Then you can't go on with your marriage. You don't even have any hope yourself for the future now. Unless you believe there is a time when you'll forget Dallas, you cannot go on living a lie with Bill."

Scilla remained silent. She knew that she would never forget Dallas, never as long as she lived. Not now. A strange calmness now seemed to come upon her as at last she ceased to fight the hopeless battle against that love. One could, after all, only try one's best to meet the terms of a contract. And she had failed. Bill was as unhappy . . . perhaps just as unhappy as she was herself. Their conversation last night had removed any doubt she might have had on that score. Now he had put her to the ultimate test . . . had asked her to prove that she loved him by bearing him a child. And she couldn't do it. She knew that quite definitely. It was one thing to pretend a love for someone and quite another to bring a human being into the world purely to justify a marriage. That she believed with all her heart would be more wrong than to leave Bill, let him divorce her. He would be hurt and she, herself, bitterly ashamed of her failure, but neither would ever have to reproach themselves for failing to give a child the love to which it was entitled.

Kathie had said she would love her baby, no matter who was the father. But in her heart she could not believe that. She knew that if she had a child who looked like Bill and not like Dallas, she would be disappointed in it; if it resembled her, she would feel only pity and fear for its future, that it might grow up with her weaknesses and hurt everything it touched as she had done.

She knew, too, that Dallas would never as long as he lived ask her to leave her husband; but that if she told him it was inevitable, he would open his arms to her, trusting her, without questioning the rightness of such a decision.

Or might he do so? Might he cease to want a woman who had turned back at the first difficult hurdle of marriage? Might he despise her for her weakness? She felt a sudden irresistible desire to talk to him . . . to ask him what she should do. If Dallas directed her, she would do as he said no matter how impossible it might seem.

"Kathie, may I telephone Dallas? Ask him to come here, to your flat? I must talk to him!" she told her sister urgently.

Kathie nodded her agreement. It was clear to her that Scilla had reached breaking point. Maybe Dallas, who was himself involved in this so deeply, might settle the matter once and for all. Kathie had begun to believe that if Scilla was not to become seriously ill, this nervous strain which she had imposed on herself must come to an end. If Dallas could achieve some solution even if it meant divorce, then Kathie would be glad, however much she might pity Bill. Her young sister had been losing weight frighteningly fast and her nerves were in a desperate state. Something would break if she continued as she was doing. Let Dallas share the burden if he could . . . and would.

Half an hour later, Dallas arrived. His face was drawn and anxious as Kathie opened the door to him. Scilla was alone in the sitting-room, but before Kathie told him this, she gave him a brief outline of what had happened and added her own concern for Scilla's physical and mental health. Dallas, himself looking none too well, said nothing but went past Kathie and into the sitting-room. Kathie left them alone.

Scilla was crying. Once she had been too proud for tears. Now she seemed no longer able to control them. She felt hysteria in her weeping and knew that she must keep control of herself. But the relief at seeing Dallas and knowing that he was there . . . that they were alone . . . that she could talk to him, was so enormous that she felt light-headed and faint.

Quietly, Dallas went across the room and took her in his arms. She clung to him with the strength of desperation and for a while they stood without speaking as he gently wiped the tears that ran down her cheeks, and then tenderly pushed the damp curls off her forehead. She grew calmer, as he had known she would, and presently she sniffed rather like a little girl, choked back a sob, and said huskily:

"I'm sorry, Dallas . . . I'm sorry. I couldn't help it . . ."

They sat down on the sofa, the man keeping one arm around her and his other holding tight to hers. He said:

"Kathie's told me, darling. You know that if you are quite sure that you want to come to me, it will make me the happiest man in the world."

"Yes!" Scilla whispered brokenly. "That is probably why I'm so weak, Dallas. That's why it is so terribly hard to make up my mind. I keep reminding myself that Bill will have no one to turn to. I can't bear it, Dallas. I'm afraid . . . afraid to act one way or another. I can't bear to hurt him and yet I can't go on. Dallas, what shall I do?"

"I think the only thing you can do is to tell Bill the truth . . . everything there is to tell. *Then let him decide.* If I were in his shoes, Scilla, I would prefer to lose you than to keep you under the circumstances. If he loves you, he'll want as I would want your happiness above everything. I mean that honestly. If you were now married to me and told me you loved Bill, whatever it might mean to me to lose you, I'd tell you to go. I'm not saying this just because I . . . I love you and want you so badly. You know that I don't believe any man has a right to come between another man and his wife. Unwittingly I have done that, but since it is so, and darling, it is no more your fault than it was mine the way things happened, you must not torment yourself so terribly. You were married under false pretences and it was not your fault that you discovered the truth later. Bill will understand that. I don't think it is fair to keep him in ignorance of the facts. Maybe all this time he has been tormenting himself with the thought that he is somehow failing you. That isn't fair to him."

"All right!" Scilla said helplessly. "I'll tell him. Dallas, I feel awful . . . I just don't seem to have any will-power left. I can't even think coherently. Only one thing makes any sense and that is my love for you. Here, now, in your arms, I am myself. I feel sane. Sometimes lately I've wondered if I was losing my mind. My thoughts controlled me . . . I couldn't control them. I'd find myself out shopping and not knowing what I had come to buy. Dallas, can you love anyone who is so weak? How can you love me, knowing the person I am?"

He smiled down at her.

"I couldn't stop loving you, dearest, even if you told me now that you had murdered Kathie! Because you have been the victim of circumstances that were really beyond your control, I can't and don't think any the worse of you."

"But that isn't true! I knew just what I was doing when I married Bill."

"I know, darling, but isn't it true that in your mind at that time, I was in the past for you, someone you wanted to forget and whom you probably hated? You would not have married Bill if you'd still loved me."

"But I did still love you . . . even while I hated you!" Scilla cried. "You can't make me blameless, Dallas."

"Does it matter who is to blame? Even if it were true that you were in fact responsible, which I don't admit, all that matters now is that the people concerned should be able to sort out their lives in the way that is best for them all. Firstly, of course, there is Bill to consider. I have never believed that he could be happy for long, Scilla . . . not if he loves you. He was bound to sense something vital lacking in you. He cannot be happy himself. If you leave him now, maybe he'll find someone else in time and settle down with her, someone who can love him as he deserves."

"If I could believe that!" Scilla sighed. "Maybe I'm being stupidly vain in imagining that I am indispensable to him. But it isn't that, Dallas. It's just that I imagine myself loving you, married to you, and that you should come to me and tell me you loved another woman. My life would be finished . . . for always."

"Yet it wasn't!" Dallas said with a smile. "You believed I was in love with Nancy yet you still felt there was some future left to you . . . with Bill." He spoke without bitterness. "It's a fact that no one dies of a broken heart . . . at least, not that I have ever heard of."

"I wanted to die of mine!" Scilla told him. "I wished I could die that night I heard Nancy's car and the things she said to you. Then I wanted to salve my pride before I died so I wrote that letter and said the things I said next morning. After you had gone, I wondered how I could kill myself without hurting other people . . . Kathie and Pete and the children. Then I remembered that Bill was coming for the weekend and I stopped thinking about dying. I started to think about the future. At first I think I just wanted to hurt *you* . . . to let you see how little you meant to me. That was when I agreed to marry Bill. Afterwards . . . he was so nice to me, so happy, that I could not bring myself to break off our engagement and hurt him. I let it drift on and suddenly it dawned on me that I might be able to make something of my life after all . . . if I could devote myself to him and keep busy running his home, having his children. It seemed possible then. *I really believed it was possible*. But I didn't know, Dallas. I didn't know how terribly you would haunt me. I ought to have guessed. For nine years I lived with you in my memory. I had no hope of breaking a habit of nine years. And then Bill began to fall in love with me . . . not the way he had loved me before, which wasn't very seriously. He began to feel for me what I feel for you. That made everything impossible. Mere affection wasn't enough for him . . . and I knew I was failing him. I tried, Dallas . . . I tried. But I've failed now. I can't have his child."

"No, darling! Now stop worrying about it. Tell Bill the truth, just as you've told me. I'm sure he'll understand . . . and forgive you. You can go home to England and as soon as my contract is up, I'll come for you. Bill can divorce you and we'll be married as soon as we can."

"You make it sound so easy!" Scilla said brokenly.

"And so it will be, Scilla. We shall make a new life out there in Australia. You will forget all this. And there will be the littlest possible unpleasantness for Bill. You can go home ill and later he can let his friends know that the doctors have advised against your return. When people have gradually got used to the idea that he is finding a bachelor life the better one after all, and I've taken you to Australia, he can divorce you and no one will blame him. They'll all be sympathetic to him and he won't be harmed in any way."

Scilla leaned her head against his broad shoulder and closed her eyes. She felt terribly weary and yet the relief of believing it was all going to be all right in the end was so great that she felt she might weep at any moment. She knew that ahead of her lay the difficult task of telling Bill. But for the moment she would not think about that. She would think of nothing but that the fight was over . . . she was here safe in Dallas' arms . . . believing in him, in the future once again.

But her moment of tranquillity was not to last long. Both heard Pete's key in the lock, his and Kathie's voices in the hall, quiet at first and then Kathie's raised a little. Scilla caught Bill's name and stiffened involuntarily. Dallas stood up and at that moment Kathie and Pete came into the room.

169

Looking at her sister's face, Scilla knew immediately that something had happened . . . something serious.

"Is something the matter with Bill?" she asked tonelessly. Kathie nodded and turned to Pete.

"We'd better all sit down and I'll tell you about it," he said briefly.

"He's not . . . ill?" Scilla asked.

"No, it's rather worse than that!" Pete said.

Scilla heard Dallas say "Steady, darling!" and felt his hand on her arm.

"He's not dead!" Kathie said bluntly. "Tell them, Pete. They've got to know."

They followed Pete's example and sat down. In a quiet, grave voice, he said:

"As you may know, I'm P.M.C. – President of the Mess Committee," he explained, seeing Scilla's puzzled expression. "Bill is Treasurer. I've just been through the books this afternoon and discovered a deficiency . . . a serious deficiency."

"No!" Scilla breathed the word, horrified.

"Naturally, I thought Bill could explain so I got hold of him. But there is no explanation. He has been misappropriating mess funds."

"Not Bill! I can't believe it!" Scilla cried. "There must be some mistake."

"He admitted it as soon as I raised the matter. It was almost as if he'd been expecting me to do so. I'm sorry, Scilla. He asked me to tell you . . . I suppose he felt he couldn't tell you himself."

"But why, why?" Scilla asked.

"Well, it's a court-martial offence," Pete said gently.

"You aren't going to report him?" Kathie burst out. "You can't do that, Pete. He's your brother-in-law!"

"Well, that's all the more reason why I should do it," Pete said quietly. "What am I to do, Kathie? Believe me, I don't want this to come out . . . far from it. I asked Bill if he could possibly make good the deficiencies . . . thinking that if he

170

could, within say the next forty-eight hours, I'd forget seeing the books today and do them again next week. But Bill says there isn't a hope. He's absolutely broke."

"I can believe that!" The hardness of Scilla's voice startled them all. "He has been buying me extravagant presents for weeks. I wondered where he got the money. Kathie did, too, didn't you, Kathie? Once I asked him about it and he told me not to worry about money . . . that it was his prerogative. Pete, he's done this for me. For some childish reason, he believed those expensive gifts would make me happy." Her voice rose hysterically. "Don't you understand? I've failed him. I've let him think he was failing me and this was the only way he could think of to make me love him. You know how young Bill is . . . he's only a boy inside himself. This problem has come up and he's found himself hopelessly unable to understand or deal with it. It's not his fault . . . it's mine. They should court-martial me—"

"Darling!"

The one word from Dallas steadied her and she sank back in her chair, her face white, her eyes enormous. Kathie said:

"I think Scilla is right, Pete. Bill has done wrong, of course, but I don't believe he meant to defraud. I'm sure he meant to pay it all back somehow."

"They all do!" Pete said helplessly. "I had to tell Bill the same thing. He doesn't seem to grasp what might happen. If I can't hush this up, he'll be thrown out of the army. He knows that, of course. He says it will kill his father . . . but it is Scilla he's really concerned about. He knows you'll leave him now."

"The fool! The silly young fool!" Dallas said violently. Only he realised at that moment that now Scilla would never leave Bill. Her sense of guilt and responsibility for what Bill had done would keep her chained to him for the rest of her life. Where Bill's love had been unable to hold her, her own pity for him and guilt would.

"It's all my fault!" Scilla was saying over and over again.

"That's hardly the point!" Pete broke in. "The fact is I can't afford to ignore what I've discovered. I suppose I could overlook it, but only for a few days. And the devil of it is that I can't find the wherewithal to replace what he's taken."

"How much?" Dallas asked bluntly.

"Nearly five hundred pounds. In fact, damn near all the money the mess had! The boy must have been crazy. He can't have hoped to pay it back before it was discovered. He must have known what would happen when he drew the last lot . . . three hundred pounds. That was when he bought the car, he told me. When I told him how crazy that was, he said, 'Scilla always admired drop-head coupés and I did want to surprise her!' I felt it was useless going on discussing the matter any further. He doesn't seem to realise what he's done."

"I'll give you the full amount," Dallas broke in quietly. "Tomorrow."

"No!" Scilla cried. "I'll do it, Dallas. I've nearly a thousand pounds in my account at home. That's what makes this so terrible. I could have given Bill all the money he needed. I didn't know . . . I thought he must have a private income. I never dreamed for one single instant that this could happen. I did once think maybe he was overdrawing from his bank, but he never seemed the slightest bit concerned about money. I always received my allowances regularly . . . and Bill just wouldn't talk about finance to me. Pete, if I can get the money out quickly enough, can you save him from a court martial?"

"Scilla never touched the allowance Father made her, at least not for the last eight years!" Kathie explained to Pete. "The last time she drew on her account was for her training as a model. Father has gone on paying it all the same."

"That's true!" Scilla whispered. "Pete, for goodness' sake tell me you don't have to report this. Bill can resign as Treasurer. I'll see he never takes on responsibility for money for the rest of his career in the army. I'll swear that now."

"I suppose I can . . . blink an eye. I ought not to, as his Colonel . . . and especially not as he's my brother-in-law. But I hate the thought of him being court-martialled. The regiment's name, and the publicity for all of us as well . . . your future, his . . . I don't know. I just can't understand why he did such a crazy thing. He's always been such a good soldier . . . in fact, he would have got his majority next month. Now I don't see how I can let that go through even if I can prevent this other more serious business leaking out."

"You could get him posted, Pete! I don't know why I never thought of that before—" Kathie broke off, suddenly remembering Dallas and the reason for his being here. Scilla had wanted a posting for Bill so that she could get away from Dallas. Now all that might have changed. What had transpired between these two? Judging by their faces, they had resolved to give in to their love, yet Scilla had just promised Pete that she would vouch for Bill for the rest of his army career.

"Scilla!" she said. "What do you intend to do?"

Until that moment, Scilla had had no thought for anyone but Bill. So appalled had she been by Pete's revelation that she had had no room for consideration of how this might affect her and Dallas. She swung round to look into Dallas' face and what she read there only increased the nightmarish horror of this last half hour. Dallas had already accepted the fact that he had lost her once again. She could see nothing but resignation in his hopeless expression. His eyes were infinitely sad and full of understanding.

"Dallas!" she cried.

Kathie took Pete's arm and pulled him out of the room. She had seen enough in those few seconds to guess that these two needed to be alone. As she closed the door, she saw Dallas hold out his arms, and despite her usual placidity, Kathie felt the tears well into her eyes.

"Oh, Pete!" she wept. "What can happen to them now? Scilla will never leave Bill now. I know it, I know it!"

"It's all right, darling, I understand!" Dallas was saying as Scilla clung to him in new desperation. "I don't agree with what you're going to do, but I know that you must and will do it."

"But how could I leave him now? How could I do that to him on top of everything else . . . when I and I alone am responsible?"

"No one is responsible to that extent for another man's actions," Dallas said quietly. "Bill may be young but he is grown up, Scilla, and he knew he was doing wrong."

"But he did it for me!" Scilla cried. "That makes it my fault, too. I can't walk out on him now . . . I can't!"

"You can't hit a man when he's down . . . no matter how he has fallen . . . or perhaps because of the way he has fallen!" Dallas said more to himself than to her. "Well, I shall not try to dissuade you, my darling. I know that you would never find a moment's peace living with me if you came away at this juncture. I can only say that maybe in a little while, you will see all this as I do . . . that it does not really alter the position between the three of us . . . not fundamentally. Then I'll be waiting!"

"I'll never come . . . never!" Scilla cried, as realisation caught her and held her imprisoned in its horrible finality. "I've got to give my life to Bill properly now . . . make up to him for the damage I've done. I'll never be able to tell him the truth about us, Dallas. You must see that. I've got to go back and try to love him. He needs me now."

Dallas said nothing. He, of all people, had no right to try and persuade her. He was too biased in any case to be quite sure of his own judgment although he felt in his heart that Scilla was about to make a sacrifice of herself that could do no real good. If she had been unable to make Bill happy before, how could she achieve it now? What would happen to her in the process of trying? What about the child he wished for? Maybe she could avoid that in view of what had happened, yet what kind of marriage would it be, without love, without children? But he kept silent.

"Dallas, I've got to go to him. He'll be alone at the flat now . . . wondering how I'm taking all this. I've got to go."

Yet she could not bring herself to leave the shelter of his

arms . . . could not bring herself quite yet to do what she had so recently realised was the only course of action left to her. It never occurred to her that she might still divorce Bill . . . that fundamentally her reasons for breaking up her marriage still existed. She had told Dallas she would leave Bill because she had failed to make him happy as his wife. Nothing new had occurred to make her love him more. But her guilt and sense of responsibility were such that she could not walk out and leave him to face the consequences of his actions alone. She knew his need for her would never be greater than it was now. She knew that so long as he did need her, she could not turn her back on him and go to the man she loved. She realised suddenly what this must, in turn, be doing to Dallas. She had raised his hopes only to throw them back in his face.

"Dallas, can you forgive me? Can you?"

"My own dear love, you asked me that before and the answer is always the same, there is nothing to forgive . . . nothing. You could not help this happening. Try to believe that none of this is your fault. You must not get a complex about it, darling. I know that you feel it your duty to stay with Bill, now. I'm not asking you to go against your own beliefs and I know that to do so would make you even more unhappy. Therefore I'm letting you go . . . believing always that some day, somehow, we will be together. I am sure of it, Scilla. We belong together, you and I. You will come to me in the end."

"You are so sure," she whispered. "I wish I could think that . . . I wish I could believe it." She had a sudden mental picture of him waiting through the years for her, growing older, growing slowly disillusioned and still hoping, and the picture brought tears of anguish to her eyes. She cried impulsively:

"You mustn't wait, Dallas . . . promise me not to. You must go back to Australia and find happiness with someone else . . . you must. I can't ever be happy if I know you are somewhere in the world wretched and lonely. Dallas, tell me you'll be happy . . . tell me you will!"

He didn't answer her. He could not do so. So he silenced

her desperate pleading with his lips, and tasted the salt of her tears, which were bitter to his heart.

"Scilla, be sure . . . sure that this time you are not being blinded to the truth."

It was the nearest he could come to pleading with her. But he knew it was useless. She had committed herself in the moment she had said to Pete that she would never allow Bill to handle funds again if Pete would get him out of this scrape. They had been words spoken on impulse, from her heart. She had no doubt then as to what she must do. Perhaps after all she was right. She had promised before God to take Bill as her husband, in good times and in bad. She would not have been the woman he loved so dearly if she could have lightly thrown away those vows.

"All right, darling, it's all right!" he spoke aloud the only words he could think of to comfort her. "If it helps, I will tell you that I think you are acting as any decent person would. I do understand . . . and my dear, my dearest darling, if this is our goodbye, then at least it is a less painful one for me than the last. Now at least I know you do love me; that had the Fates been kinder you really would have been my wife."

They clung together, desperate in their unhappiness and their bitterness for the cruel way Fate had dealt with them . . . and for the foolish way they had dealt for themselves. He kissed her lips, her eyes, her hair, traced the sweet curve of her face with his fingertip and tried feverishly to imprint on his memory this last picture of her. She, too, was seeking to memorise every line of his face. Then her eyes closed as his lips pressed once more on hers and she knew a swift moment of the golden glory of love before his arms dropped away from her and she was standing alone. Then the true knowledge of what she was losing for the third time in her life, and this time for always, hit her as a physical blow. A cold numbed loneliness crept over her body as her mind receded from him. The agony of watching him walk to the door, turn to look into her eyes for the last time, then turn away, became unbearable. She covered her face with her hands so that she should not see him go. As the door closed quietly behind him, they fell away from her eyes and she pressed the back of her hand against her mouth to silence the cry that had risen involuntarily to her lips.

# Thirteen

When Scilla returned to her flat she felt so completely exhausted mentally and physically that she believed herself incapable of any further emotional reaction. When a worried Kathie had suggested accompanying her, Scilla had said:

"I'll be all right, Kathie. I have to see Bill alone, in any case. You needn't worry about me any more. I know now what I have to do and that I have no alternative. I cannot leave Bill. Dallas and I have said goodbye . . . this time for always."

Her flat, her home for the past three months, seemed strangely unfamiliar as she let herself into the hall. Nothing here really claimed her as she had always believed the furnishings of one's first home must do. Glancing at the hall table, the white Indian rugs on the smooth tiled floors, at Bill's army cap on a chair she knew only that she had returned to an empty shell. Were it not for the chains which bound her here she could close the door on all it contained and never know a moment's regret.

"Scilla?"

She drew in her breath and squared her shoulders as she went into the sitting-room in answer to her husband's call. He was sitting outstretched in a chair by the french windows, which had been flung open to trap any cool breeze that might be coming off the sea. His khaki drill shirt was open at the neck, his dark curly hair straggled untidily across his forehead. Beneath the tan, his face was pale and drawn and his eyes, as they looked into hers, utterly miserable.

Pity and remorse filled her. With an impulsive gesture, she

ran the few steps between them, and sliding down to the rug at his feet, clasped both his hands in her own.

"Bill . . . my dear . . . don't worry any more. I think Pete can hush it up . . . it's going to be all right!"

He withdrew his hands from her grasp and gave a short, bitter laugh.

"Is it, Scilla? Do you think it is the end of my career in the army that is bothering me? Do you think that is what I am concerned for? It only proves how little you understand me."

She bit her lip and with an effort once more imprisoned his hands in her own.

"No, Bill! I just wanted to reassure you on that point. I . . . I know what is worrying you . . . and I can reassure you about that, too. I'm your wife, Bill. Nothing can part us."

He stared at her as if he could not believe his ears. Then to her consternation, his eyes filled suddenly with tears and he turned his face away quickly as he fought to control himself. When he spoke, his voice was shaking.

"I suppose I've been out of my mind, Scilla. I can't give you a sensible reason for what I've done. I suppose I realised all along that sooner or later it must be found out. But I wasn't thinking of that. I was thinking all the time that if only I could give you the things you wanted, I could make you happy . . . make you love me."

"I know, Bill, I know!" Scilla broke in. "I do understand your reasons, although they were terribly wrong ones as you must realise now. The blame is mine . . . not yours, because I should have told you long ago that it was not your fault I wasn't happy. I suppose the reason I did not do so was because for a long while I tried to convince myself that you hadn't noticed . . . and then when I was fairly sure you had, I was afraid of hurting you by telling you the truth."

"Then tell me now!" Bill cried desperately. "How have I failed you, Scilla? I suppose I haven't been able to lay that ghost of yours. And of course, he didn't remain a ghost, did he? But you told me it was all over . . . that you hated him.

That's the part I can't understand. I can't believe you would have lied about it. You told me it was finished . . . that you hated him."

Hurriedly, Scilla began to explain everything that had happened. This time she withheld nothing. The only secret she retained was that she had made up her mind to leave him a few hours ago. That she could never tell him.

"Now I begin to understand a lot that was inexplicable before!" Bill commented wearily. "Of course, you realise that you can have your freedom? Even before all this had happened . . . before I ruined our lives the mad way I have . . . I would have let you go?"

"Yes, I knew," Scilla told him gently. "But I wanted to make a success of our marriage, Bill . . . in spite of everything. I still want to and I still think we could do so if we make a new start. It will be so much easier now that you understand."

"You mean . . . you don't want to leave me?" Bill's voice was incredulous. Then his hopeful eyes went dull again and he said: "But don't you see it's too late, Scilla? I have nothing to offer you now. I shall be disgraced . . . chucked out of the army . . . and I'm not trained for any other job. It's best for you that we should call it a day. I couldn't bear to drag your name with mine through the mud."

"There won't be any mud . . . any disgrace!" Scilla told him quickly. "I'm almost sure that Pete intends to say nothing. You see, I can make good the deficiencies. I have plenty of money of my own, Bill. Pete will get you posted . . . he couldn't keep you in his regiment after this . . . it wouldn't be fair to either of you. And it would be best for us both to get right away and make a fresh start. So you see, there is no need for you to turn me away . . . unless you don't want me any longer."

"Not want you!" Bill echoed passionately. "My God, Scilla, don't say things like that. If you only realised *how much* I love you. I'd commit murder for you if you asked it. I suppose that's hard for you to understand . . . and probably unwelcome to listen to under the circumstances, but I've got to say it. You're my life . . . the only thing that matters in my life. If you went, there'd be nothing worth living for. I never believed I could feel this way about a woman. I suppose I never was in love before. But since we were married it's got worse . . . not better. I've loved you more and more and you seem to have loved me less and less."

"That isn't true, Bill. My affection for you has never altered. I couldn't . . . can't give you my love . . . not the kind of love you want . . . the kind you have every right to expect. But if you can give me a little time . . . wait until I'm away from here . . . don't have to see Dallas and be reminded of him all the time . . ."

"You'd be happier if you went to him!" Bill said, suddenly honest. "I can't ask you to stay with me, Scilla, know-ing that."

"But I haven't asked for my freedom!" Scilla countered. "I've known all along that you would have offered to release me if I'd ever asked you to do so. But I still hoped . . . and believe now . . . that we can find happiness together. We'll start again, Bill. Give me another chance to prove that I can be a good wife to you."

With a little cry, his arms drew her to him and Scilla felt her mind slipping away as her body became once more imprisoned. She had won . . . and by winning the battle of duty, had lost her love. Yet while her heart cried pitifully for Dallas her thoughts were strangely calm. She knew that she was doing what was right . . . morally right. She knew with renewed certainty that having made her vows she had never had any real alternative but to stick to them. She had weakened . . . and so nearly given way. By showing his own weakness, his own love for her, Bill had brought her back to her senses. She must never again forget that she was his *wife*.

Later, when he could talk of nothing but his remorse and shame for what he had done, she tried to comfort him, to give him back some self-esteem. Again and again, she reminded him that people could do things utterly foreign to their natures when their nerves were in a bad enough state. He had been desperately worried and for a little time he had gone out of his right mind. She knew, and he knew, that such a thing would never happen again. He had a wonderful past record in the army and he would prove himself a good soldier again in the future. He had years ahead of him to compensate for the wrong he had done.

Gradually, a little of his old confidence and a parody of his old cheerful smile returned. Scilla persuaded him to eat his first meal that day and, while he did not eat much, she could see that her attentions to his comfort, her care of him, was melting all the fear that had lain around his heart . . . his fear of losing her. She knew as she fussed over him maternally that she had after all married a boy . . . not a man. Always in the future she would feel the older of the two . . . the one who must shoulder responsibility. Because he was not as strong as she had believed him, he had been ill-equipped to deal with the sudden emotional upheaval of his unhappy marriage. And for that, she alone was responsible. A stronger man or an older man or a more experienced man might have behaved very differently. But Bill was Bill . . . and if, after all, he was not the broad shoulder on which she had thought to ease her troubles, then the change-over of their roles was perhaps a good thing. She could love the boy far more than she could ever have loved the man. All that was most maternal in her rose to the challenge.

But late that night, as he lay in her arms, she felt her own reaction to the day's terrible strain. Now came the hour of her need for Dallas Now she could have found peace in the strength of his love . . . his care for her. Now, in her loneliness, her heart cried out for him as it had never done so hopelessly, so strongly, in past moments of need. The long years ahead of her, which she had painted so brightly and hopefully for Bill, loomed even more barren and darkly for herself. She had only one tiny spark of comfort – the knowledge that Dallas lay under the same stars, loving her, needing her, longing and regretting and that in this one sense they could never really be parted again.

Dallas was her last conscious thought before she ran to him once more in her dreams.

# Fourteen

Lying in the deck-chair on the lawn, Scilla could smell the roses from the pergola, their scent carrying to her on the faint evening breeze. Mingled with their sweetness was the lovely smell of fresh mown grass drying in the sun. She breathed deeply and lay back in her chair, closing her eyes contentedly. How lovely was England in summer . . . how perfect a garden of roses and how fresh and green the grass. After living in a hot, rainless country like Libya, her appreciation of the English country was more acute than ever.

"Sleeping, Scilla?"

She opened her eyes as Bill's father dropped into the chair beside her. She had grown very fond of her father-in-law in the six months that she had been living with him here in his cottage on the Thames. Her adult relationship with her own father had been so damaged in her adolescence that she had never been able to achieve any real feeling of understanding or sympathy or affection for him. Strangely, it had been Bill's mother and father who really showed her how united a family could be and what a wonderful thing that unity was.

"I feel so lazy!" she admitted to the Brigadier. She called him Brig because Bill always spoke of him as The Brig and the old man was delighted with the name. Far from being a Blimp, he was a charming and simple man in his late sixties, with little about him to remind one that he had once held a position of some importance in the army. To see him now in an old pair of white flannels and V-necked cricket sweater over a crumpled white shirt, it was hard to picture him as he must have been on parade. Only his extreme physical fitness linked him to his army background. He had just mown the lawn, in spite of his age and the fact that the temperature was nearly ninety degrees.

"And so you should be lazy!" he chuckled. "You know I promised Bill I'd be responsible for you and this baby of yours while he's away. A nice walk later when it's cooler I'll permit, but meanwhile you just stay here."

Bill was away on a training course. He had not told her much about it but she was so unusually calm and placid these days . . . since she had got over the first few months of pregnancy sickness, that nothing seemed to bother her very much. This new-found complacency, due probably to the fact that Nature did make a woman placid when she carried a child and perhaps, too, to the happy relationship that existed between her and her in-laws, was still a surprise to Scilla. It was true that she had not yet learned to love Bill, but she did love his family, and her relationship with Bill had become satisfactory to them both. The period of adjustment had not been easy. Nor had those few months during which they had left Libya and gone to the Canal Zone in Egypt. It was the only posting Pete had been able to arrange and it was not by any means a good one for Scilla since she had had to live behind barbed wire in a confined area without even Kathie for company. The fight to put all thought of Dallas from her mind had been a terribly hard one and never completely achieved. But Bill had been wonderfully understanding. He had made no emotional demands on her. He behaved towards her as any good friend might have done . . . trying to arrange little amusements for her, taking her bathing, which was not an easy matter since they had had to go everywhere with an armed guard; curbing always his love for her and giving her only what she asked of him . . . his affection. Gradually, because she knew that she did not *have* to make any responses or gestures that she did not feel she wanted to make, they became easier for her to give. She found she could reach out of her own accord for Bill's hand and that it rested in his without resentment or fear. His pleasure at such moments was touching and her newly discovered maternal tenderness for him prompted her further towards those intimacies that Bill had begun to treasure as proofs of awakening love. Only she had known deep in her heart that to love him as he loved her or as she loved Dallas, would never be possible. Her longing for Dallas burned as brightly and fiercely as ever but was now controlled and hidden so deep in her heart that only in moments of weakness did she permit it to come to the surface of her mind.

Fortunately they remained in Egypt only four months before Bill was posted home. Because they had no house there, and as they were uncertain as to their future, they had accepted the Brig's offer to live with them for the time being. And at about this time, Scilla had learned that she was to have a child.

Bill's delight at the news had been touching. His disgrace . . . although Pete had covered up for him and only the four of them knew about it . . . had humbled him and he had told Scilla that he felt he had no right to bring a child into the world. She had been so busy trying to convince him that that one mistake did not make him a criminal for life, that she had had little chance to consider her own feelings on the subject until later. Then, with Bill away on this training course, she had begun to feel the first thrill of knowing that she was to give birth to a child. She had got over the depressing first months when she had felt sick and a little afraid, and slowly the delight of Bill and his parents had transmitted itself to her, too, and now she was happy about the coming baby.

Sometimes, it was true, she remembered how nearly she might have been carrying Dallas' child . . . how she must try to make herself glad if she gave these three people who loved her a son who resembled Bill. Then her eyes would look sad and there would be a pain in her heart for a little while and she would wander off alone to try to put such thoughts from her.

Brig was so careful of her that she often laughed at him and teased him about it. Bill's mother told her that he had never taken the same care of her when Bill was on the way. He just smiled and said that, after all, a grandchild was a pretty important event and he was quite determined that it should be a boy.

Kathie wrote often from Benghazi and was obviously delighted at the news of her coming niece or nephew. Scilla knew that in Kathie's mind all must be well now since she had been able to achieve the one thing that had so nearly broken up her marriage to Bill before. But then Kathie did not know that the baby was 'a mistake', or to put it more fairly, had not been intended. Nonetheless, Scilla thought nowadays, Fate must have intended it and she knew that Kathie had been right when she told her that she would love her baby for itself alone.

"You're not bored here with us, Scilla?" her father-in-law asked suddenly. "I realise it must be rather dull for you living with two old people. We've got out of the habit of entertaining, you know, since I retired . . . rather fancy a quiet life these days."

"No, I love it!" Scilla told him honestly. "I think I'm terribly lucky to be here. I have none of the worries and responsibilities of housekeeping and yet I can potter about the kitchen and make jam if I feel like it, or turn out a cupboard . . . Mother lets me do just as I please. You both spoil me dreadfully."

"We love to do it!" the old man said sincerely. "You've proved a real daughter to us, Scilla, and we're so proud of you. Bill's a lucky fellow to have got you . . . and I'm glad he knows it."

"I'm lucky to have him, too!" Scilla said. "He's always so kind to me."

Brig looked at her sideways.

"He loves you, Scilla, but then you know that. I never believed that boy would ever feel anything so deeply. But he's grown up since he met you. It isn't just taking on responsibilities, it's a new maturity I see about him. I used to wonder sometimes if he was never going to grow up . . . a kind of lovable Peter Pan, he was. I thought maybe it was because we had him so late in life, and that the gap in years had resulted in keeping him too much of a child. Mother likes him that way, of course, but then women never like their boys to grow up, do they? But it's different for a wife. She needs a man to love and respect."

"Sometimes she can need a little boy to look after, too!" Scilla said softly, not meaning her baby.

"That's a different kind of love, isn't it?" the old man stated, to Scilla's surprise. "I know that's the way you feel for Bill. I've often seen it. Scilla, what happened to the man you really loved?"

She caught her lip and stared at him wide-eyed. She would never have guessed that this charming, simple, elderly man could have been so penetrating . . . so knowledgeable about human nature. Maybe that was why he had been such a good and much loved Brigadier; even now some of his men wrote to him, and at Christmas he had had over a hundred cards from men who had not forgotten him.

"That . . . that's a long story," she said quietly. "It ended a long time ago. How could you have known?"

"Well, I only guessed!" her father-in-law said truthfully. "You see, you're very young in years, Scilla, but quite old in your behaviour. I knew you must have suffered sometime, and I knew that you hadn't suffered any loss in your family. It stood to reason a young pretty woman of your age must have fallen in love before you met Bill. Does it make you unhappy to talk about it?"

"N . . . no . . . not really!" Scilla said doubtfully. "It's just that it seems odd to be sitting here talking on such a subject to Bill's father!"

"Oh, I don't know. I have your happiness at heart almost as much as I have Bill's!" he surprised her again. "I know my son's weaknesses, Scilla, and I know he has been lucky to marry a woman like yourself. I have the greatest respect for you, my dear."

"And I for you!" Scilla said, touching his hand lightly with her own. "But you mustn't feel worried about me. I'm happy and I think Bill is happy, too."

"That's quite certain!" his father said warmly. "He lives and breathes for you, Scilla. Sometimes that kind of love isn't easy to take. It's apt to make demands on you you can't always fulfil. You have to watch every gesture, every word for fear of hurting the other person, and that is difficult. I've never heard you hurt Bill wittingly or otherwise . . . you're far too nice to him."

"You shouldn't say that . . . he gives me everything!" Scilla cried. "I am the one who fails because I can't love him as he loves me."

"But he doesn't know that. I daresay this child you are having has proved your love beyond question."

"But it was not intended!" Scilla whispered. She had never thought she would tell that to a living soul. Her companion did not sound surprised.

"No! But you are happy to have the baby, aren't you? And that is enough."

Silence fell between them for a few moments, then Scilla asked:

"How do you know so much? How is it you understand so much?"

He gave an enigmatic smile.

"Perhaps because I've been through much the same as you. I don't think I'd be harming my wife to tell you, since it is true that I love her now after all these years. She has made me very happy and I owe her everything. But once . . . when I was a subaltern, I fell in love with a married woman. I went on hoping for year after year that she might leave her husband. He was my senior officer and that made it rather difficult for us both. It would have caused an awful scandal if she'd ever left him for me. Then I met my wife and I knew she would marry me if I asked her. For years I couldn't bring myself to make a clean break with this other woman. Then one day I realised that I was ruining three lives by waiting. So I asked my wife to marry me. Those first years weren't easy. Neither of us was very young. Then Bill came and it was suddenly all right. You can see now why we had him so late in life . . . my wife was nearly forty and I was past that age. I've never regretted that I did the right thing. I know if I'd had the chance I'd have taken it all those years ago and clicked my fingers at the disgrace. But it didn't come and now, looking back, I can see it was probably for the best. I've grown to love my wife dearly and I've had a happy life. I want you to have the same."

"I'm glad you told me!" Scilla said. It had given her a new hope for the future. Love could . . . and had grown between two people who had married with love on one side only. Maybe with the years she, too, could grow to love Bill . . . the father of her child.

"I sometimes wonder what became of her . . . the other woman!" Brig said whimsically. "I'd like to have kept in touch but she wisely refused to write."

"I never hear either," Scilla said quietly. "He once promised me that if ever he were ill or needed me, he'd let me know, but I sometimes wonder if he would. I . . . hope he is happy."

The complete silence that Dallas had kept had been a source of pain to her even while she knew that it was better that way. She had written to him, of course, telling him again that she would never leave Bill now; that they were going to Egypt and this was goodbye. She had renewed her own promise to let him know if ever she were free, ill or in need of him and told him for the last time that she would love him always. Next day, she had received from him a small box with the little diamond and pearl engagement ring he had given her so long ago. With it was a note saying:

*Please keep this, my darling, for it should never have been returned all those years ago. I've kept it always believing that the day might come when I could give it to you again, and although its symbol is dead, I want you to have it as proof of the fact that I shall love you all my life.*

*Dallas.*

She had destroyed the note for she knew every word by heart, and the ring she kept in her jewel case and only very very occasionally did she take it out and hold it in her hand for a moment or two in silent communion.

Her father-in-law said suddenly:

"How long to go now, Scilla . . . before the baby arrives?"

"A month!" Scilla told him. "Did I tell you Kathie would be home in time? She and I have always been so close to each other that I'm terribly happy about it. I suppose most girls want their mothers near them but I just want Kathie. I think you'll like my sister . . . and the children are pets. Kathie says if they could find a furnished house near here, they'd take it, as Pete will be at the War Office and is willing to travel up and down every day. They think it would be better for the children than living in London."

"Then we'll start contacting estate agents tomorrow!" Brig said, rising to his feet and helping Scilla out of the deck-chair. "What about that little walk now before the sun goes in?"

As she strolled beside him down the drive where the air was heavy with scent of the wallflowers, Scilla felt that if in the late years of his life Bill were like his father, she could indeed be happy. She loved this man and knew that he loved her. They were the best of friends . . . and their odd relationship made her present contentment almost complete.

Kathie's arrival a few days before Scilla's baby was due coincided with Bill's departure for Kenya. His course had ended a fortnight earlier and he had had two weeks' embarkation leave during which time he had learned he was going to Nairobi. He was delighted with the prospect. The climate there was perfect, Scilla could follow him as soon as the baby was established and she felt well enough to travel; and he had got his majority. His mother's face was less radiant when she reminded him of the Mau-Mau trouble that still existed in Kenya, but both Bill and his father reassured the two women in this respect. Although there was undoubtedly still some trouble in outlying districts, there was no danger in Nairobi itself and very little outside. Maybe by the time Scilla joined him there

191

a satisfactory peace settlement would have been achieved.

In some ways, Scilla was glad that Bill would be gone before Pete arrived. The two men had not met since they had left Benghazi and there must be some awkwardness between the two however much Kathie might write to Scilla saying Pete had all but forgotten about it and was looking forward to seeing Bill again. She knew that Pete could no more forget that incident than could any of them and that it was for her sake and Kathie's that he had acted as he had done in the past, and was willing to behave decently to Bill now.

Bill's goodbye to Scilla was a mixture of optimism and sadness at having to leave her behind.

"I hate leaving you, darling!" he told her on their last night together. "If you could be coming with me, I should be thrilled to death. Still, I quite see that you can't travel at the moment, and while I could probably get compassionate leave, I don't really see much point in it since you don't really need me."

She had suspected a touch of regret in that last sentence and had hastened to reassure him.

"It isn't that I don't need you, Bill. Every woman likes to have her husband near when she's having a baby . . . but I shall have Kathie, and your mother and Brig. And I know you want to go out with your men, almost as much as you want to stay with me! You said yourself that you'd probably only get a week and that means you would only see me for eight hours since the nursing home visiting hours are strict – even for fathers. And you'll worry so if you're here, Bill. It will be much better for you to get the cable saying he or she has arrived."

Bill grinned his old boyish grin which reminded her of the Bill she had met in Benghazi.

"Brig does so want a boy . . . Mother, too. I thought I did until recently and now I think I'd like a girl just like you."

"I'll bear it in mind," Scilla teased him, "and try to suit you, darling, even if it means disappointing Mother and Brig. It's just as well I don't mind one way or another."

For a brief instant, his smile faded and seeing the changed expression, Scilla went on quickly:

"Boy or girl I shall be equally pleased. Whichever it is, we'll have the other in a couple of years' time!"

He was happy again and only at the actual moment of parting did his happiness fade. He held her tightly in his arms and whispered against her ear:

"Oh, Scilla, it's awful saying goodbye. I love you so much. I'll be thinking of you every moment and thanking my lucky stars that you stayed with me after all!"

He had never mentioned that long-past decision before and it touched her that he should have brought it up at this moment when his emotion got the better of him. She said:

"I'm glad, too, darling!" and was rewarded to see him radiant again as he walked away from her to the waiting taxi and waved a last farewell.

Two days later, Kathie moved into the house Brig had found for her not two miles away. Reunited with her sister and the children, Scilla hurried around, helping unpack suitcases and playing games with Dina and Paul. Perhaps because of the excitement and the unusual activity, her baby started to arrive in the early hours of the following morning and it was Kathie who drove her in to the nursing home and held her hand.

"I just arrived in time!" she said, and between the pains Scilla knew that she was glad it was Kathie and not Bill on whom she was leaning at this moment. Bill would have panicked and been worried to death, but Kathie, exhausted though she must be, chatted and advised and comforted and was a tower of strength. She spent the rest of the night in the nursing home and was the first to see Scilla's little daughter, born just before twelve next day.

"What will you call her?" she asked Scilla, who lay with the baby in her arms, her eyes starry, her face both amazed and proud. "You know, darling, she looks exactly like you! I never believed people before when they claimed likenesses for new-born babies. But this poppet isn't pink or crumpled . . . she's like a little miniature edition of you . . . she really is!"

"She can't be . . . she's beautiful!" Scilla said happily. "Oh, Kathie, I'm so lucky. I was often afraid there might be something wrong with my baby . . . I don't know why."

"Most expectant mothers feel that at one time or another!" Kathie said. "There's nothing wrong with your child, Scilla. She's quite the loveliest baby I've ever seen."

"We could call her June," Scilla said drowsily. "Yes, I think, if Bill agrees, we'll call her June."

Kathie went home to telephone both the grandparents. She had not yet met Bill's mother or father but she had heard so much from Scilla in her letters about them that, without thinking, she let them have the news before her own parents. Nor was she really surprised that they should receive the news with such a rush of loving thoughts for Scilla, and her own mother and father with: "Our third grandchild . . . well, Kathie, give Scilla our love and tell her we'll come down and see her in the next few days!"

But Scilla did not need her parents. The Brig and his wife were all she wanted in the way of a family. They welcomed her back to their house with glowing faces and made such a fuss of the baby that Scilla threatened to move to Kathie's house if they continued to spoil her so.

"Of course, you'll be leaving us soon, Scilla dear," Bill's mother said sadly. "We must make the best of the few weeks we still have you both here under our roof. That's the worst of army life . . . you're sent all over the world and families have to be split up. I suppose I should be used to it by now but I shall miss you both when you go. So will Daddy. Promise you'll write often, dear, and send us plenty of photographs!"

"I will!" Scilla said warmly. "And no matter how long I'm away you know I shall always look on this as my real home . . . that I'll always come back to stay with you here."

The first month after June was born were the happiest weeks Scilla had known for eleven years. She was content to let Mother and Brig fuss over her and do nothing herself but lie in the garden in the deck-chair, sewing or knitting and feeding and caring for her baby. It was true that little June resembled her. Everyone remarked on it and even the colour of her eyes gave every indication that the baby blue would turn to Scilla's flecked hazel in a short while.

Bill wrote ecstatic letters from Nairobi. He had a lovely house and garden ready for them. She would like the town and he had already met several wives he imagined she would wish to be friendly with.

*As for little June,* he wrote, *I can't wait to see her. I am sure she is the most beautiful baby in the world, and that you are not biased any more than I am. It seems wonderful that she should be like you . . . now I shall have two Scillas to love and take care of. I'm not a good letter writer so I can't express in the way I would like how wonderfully happy I am and how grateful I am to you for giving me so much happiness . . . yourself and the baby. The chaps here tell me I'm like a cat with ten tails and that I'm so proud of myself and of you that my hat is getting too small for me and I'll need a larger size.*

*I was pleased to hear from Mother that you are so well and I can believe that you are looking lovely as she says, although not 'lovelier than ever' for that would be impossible. That does not sound a very original compliment but I mean it none the less. Only two more weeks and you will be flying out to me. I am planning such a welcome for you. If I could, I'd detail the band to play you off the plane. My only worry now is that anything should go wrong on the flight. Every time I read in the papers of a crash I wish I'd booked you by sea and yet I quite see that air travel will be easier for you with a baby as well as bringing you here to me more quickly.*

*I'm so happy, darling, I could burst with it!*

*Your adoring*
*Bill.*

It was Brig who brought her the news. She was under the cherry tree in the shade, for the heat wave still covered the country. Beside her, little June slept in her carry-cot, a tiny bundle of humanity who would never now see her father. In Scilla's lap lay the feeder she was embroidering and she was never able to bring herself to finish it in the days that followed.

Brig's face was white and suddenly old as he walked across the lawn to his son's wife. Looking up at him, Scilla said anxiously:

"You don't look well, Brig. Does the heat bother you?"

He sat down heavily beside her and unexpectedly, for he was not a demonstrative man and seldom made such gestures, he took her hand. She felt his cold in her warm one.

"I've just had . . . rather a bad shock," he said quietly. "I . . . I don't quite know how to tell you about it."

Various wild surmises chased through Scilla's mind but it still did not occur to her that it might have anything to do with her. She thought perhaps he had lost an old friend.

"You can tell me . . ." she said softly, trying to make it easier for him. "You know we promised always to confide in each other!"

Even then he did not smile and for the first time a little shiver went over her.

"What is it, Brig?" she asked more sharply.

"It's . . . it's about Bill!" he began.

No! Scilla thought. Not that! Don't let him have discovered anything awful about Bill. He wouldn't have done anything bad again. It can't be that.

"What about Bill?" she pressed him, unable to bear the mounting tension. "What about him, Brig?"

"He . . . he . . . Scilla, it's a terrible thing to put into words, but there is no making it easier . . . he's dead!"

# Fifteen

Scilla was so deeply shocked that for a moment she could not understand Brig's words. She apologised and asked him to please begin all over again at the beginning of his dreadful story.

"A telegram came an hour ago from the War Office!" he said, his voice dull and toneless. "I felt I couldn't tell anyone until I had made sure there was no mistake. It does sometimes happen . . . but I telephoned and spoke to the officer who had sent the wire. He gave me a few details, unofficially."

"Please tell me!" Scilla said as he paused. Perhaps in a little while this would seem to be reality not just a ghastly dream which held no meaning for her. Bill could not be dead . . . not on this lovely sunny day . . . not Bill, the father of her little daughter, who lay asleep in her carry-cot, the daughter he had never seen. It could *not* be true.

"It was yesterday . . . he went out on an ordinary patrol. There was no danger attached to it, merely a routine check-up on one or two people they weren't quite sure of. It seems that in one of the village huts some relations had hidden a nephew who had taken the Mau-Mau oath. When it became apparent that he would be discovered, he went beserk . . . rushed out of the hut and fired a gun wildly at any British he could see. Two of Bill's men were slightly wounded . . . and a stray shot got Bill in the head. They rushed him to hospital but he died an hour later. There wasn't a thing they could do for him. His Brigadier used to be one of my junior officers, and knowing Bill was my son, he got these details back more quickly than usual . . . that's how I happen to know so much."

*"Then it is true?"*

197

He reached for her hand and held it almost desperately in his own cold one.

"I'm afraid so . . . afraid so!" he said, his voice breaking. "My son . . . my only child!"

"Brig, don't!" Scilla cried quickly. "You still have me . . . and June. You are all I have, too."

He remembered her again and strove to control his emotions. Only his age and the shock had made him forget that a good soldier can bear even the worst of news with an upright back. And he had Bill's wife to think of now. Scilla must be suffering as much as he . . . yet it was she who was offering him comfort.

"I haven't told my wife yet," he said at last. "I must go and do so. And I expect you'd like to telephone your sister and ask her to come to you."

"No!" Scilla said instantly. "I want to be here with you, Brig, and Mother. She'll need me."

"Yes!" the old man said thoughtfully. "We shall both need you, my dear child. And the baby will be a great comfort to Bill's mother . . . little June is his child."

Scilla's voice broke now as the first numbness of shock had worn off and realisation had slowly seeped into her mind.

"Oh, Brig, why? Why?" she asked helplessly. "Of them all, why did it have to be Bill? It isn't fair!"

"God has His reasons, no doubt!" Brig said quietly. "I'll admit that now I can't understand His reasons but I am a God-fearing man and I believe that such things are ordained. If one did not believe that, a soldier's life would be insupportable. I know it always appears to those of us who are left behind that He picks the very best of our boys. But we must not question Him, my dear."

"Shall I tell Mother for you?" Scilla asked, but Brig shook his head.

"That's my job, Scilla, but I expect she will need you a little later. I think this will break her and you'll have to help me or I

198

fear that she will go out of her mind with grief. He meant so much to her . . . so very much."

"In a way, he was my child, too!" Scilla spoke her thoughts aloud. "And we shan't see him again . . . ever . . . oh, Brig!"

The tears came then . . . thick, choking sobs that he did not try to arrest, for he knew that they would ease her pain. Then the baby woke and cried and Scilla struggled to recover her composure.

"I shall have to go and feed her!" she said, wiping her eyes. "Don't worry about me. Go to Mother, I'll be all right now."

But all was not well. Although feeding her baby had until now been the easiest and most wonderful task she had ever experienced, when she lifted the child to her breast, she could no longer do so. As the baby's cries increased in volume, she felt a fresh bout of weeping overcome her and, hugging the baby to her, rocked the crying child against her heart in a moment of weakness and despair. Then, with an effort that only the baby's cries instilled in her, she went to the phone and asked for Kathie's number.

Half an hour later, Kathie had taken the baby from her and was patiently encouraging it to take the milk she had brought with her from a feeding bottle and teat. Scilla, watching her sister, felt too weak and worn out by the last hour to be of any assistance. She felt that if June continued to cry much longer, she would become hysterical herself. Then suddenly the child began to suck greedily and the silence was like a heavenly blessing to her mother. Kathie looked up and smiled.

"She'll be all right now, Scilla. You go and bathe your face and then lie down."

"I can't do that!" Scilla whispered huskily. "The Brig said Mother was sure to need me and I must go to her. Kathie, thank goodness you're here. I have never felt so helpless or so desperate in my life."

"A sudden shock can do that to a nursing mother and you mustn't worry about it, darling. June is already long past her birthweight and bottle feeding won't set her back. It's possible that you may be able to feed her again yourself in a day or two, but if you can't, it won't matter. Change your dress, darling, if you're going in to Bill's mother . . . and make up your face a little. It will give you courage to help her . . . poor soul."

"Kathie, I think I'll wait a bit longer and take June in with me. Bill's baby will be so much more comfort than I can ever be. I thank God for my baby, not just for myself, but for Bill's parents and for Bill. If he could only have seen her once, Kathie. He wanted a daughter so much and he was so happy because we would have been joining him soon. Now he'll never see either of us again!"

Her voice had risen a tone and Kathie looked at her with concern. It was a bad time for her to have received such a shock when she was not long out of the nursing home and in the emotional after-stages of having a baby. She hoped that Scilla was not going to suffer too much or too long. Her own first reaction had been, inevitably, now she is free . . . free to marry Dallas. But that thought had apparently not crossed Scilla's mind.

Could she, after all, have grown to love Bill so much in their year of married life?

Thoughtfully, she patted the baby's warm little back and waited for the wind to come up, her movements gentle and automatic. Irrelevantly, she decided that she and Pete must have another baby soon. Then her thoughts switched back to Scilla and she said:

"It must comfort you to remember how happy Bill was when he died. He'd had your cable about June, of course."

"And my letter, too. Kathie, he wrote to me such wonderful letters in reply. He was happy . . . wonderfully so. I suppose he couldn't have known he was going to die, could he? It would have been terrible for him to have known he was leaving life just when he was finding it so perfect at last."

"People seldom know they are going to die!" Kathie said reassuringly. "It is the people who are left who suffer."

"Poor Brig! Poor Mother!" Scilla whispered.

As if her pity for the two old people had given her renewed strength, she stood up and began to freshen her face with an astringent. Then she made up carefully and by the time she had changed her frock Kathie had the baby sleepy and contented and with no trace of the unhappy half hour of screams showing. Scilla took her little daughter and hugged her for a moment as she thanked Kathie for coming to the rescue.

"I'll be all right now!" she said. "Don't wait for me. Come over and see us all tomorrow."

"I'm going to send Nanny back with Pete after the children are in bed," Kathie said on an impulse as she stood up. "Nanny knows all about bottle feeding and she can do all that is necessary for June. You'll need a good night's sleep and this is the one way to get it. You must keep well, darling . . . for the baby's sake as well as for your own and for Bill's parents'."

"All right!" Scilla agreed readily. "And thank you again, Kathie."

After her sister had gone, she went back upstairs and taking the now sleeping child from its cot, went along the landing and knocked at her mother-in-law's door.

The Brig rose from beside the bed as she came in, looking at Scilla helplessly.

"She doesn't cry . . . hasn't even spoken a word since I told her," he whispered. "I can't get near her at all. Try to help her, Scilla."

When he had left her, Scilla went over to the bed and sat down beside the motionless form lying there, her face turned away.

"I've brought June in for you to say good night!" she said in a level voice. "She was crying earlier and I thought she might be a little unwell . . ." She saw the shoulders move and went on quickly, "Of course, it has been rather hot all day and I suppose she has reacted to it . . ."

The white drawn face turned slowly round until the poor haunted eyes were looking at the sleeping bundle in Scilla's arms.

"She's . . . not . . . ill?"

Only Scilla understood what an effort it had been to speak those words. Her instinct, however, had been right. Bill's baby crying had brought her grandmother back from the first depths of shock. The baby would achieve the same result with this woman as it had done for herself, for it was her child, too . . . her grandchild.

"No, she's all right now. Kathie says I must wean her, but we'll see. Look, Mother . . . at that dimple by her mouth!"

There was a sudden cry of anguish and then the lined face was buried in the pillows and Scilla knew that the relief of tears had come at last. She put the baby down on the bed and turned to take the older woman in her arms. Her own tears were falling again as she tried to comfort her.

"We haven't really lost him . . . we have his baby, Mother. Don't be too unhappy . . . he wouldn't want to see you like this. He was always such a happy person himself. And for Brig's sake, too . . . you must try to be brave."

When she left the room half an hour later, the doctor whom Brig had telephoned to come went in to find her asleep. He left a sleeping draught with Scilla in case she should wake later in the night, and pronounced his relief on hearing that Nanny was coming to stay.

"You need rest, child!" he told Scilla, seeing the violet shadows beneath her eyes and guessing a little of what these last hours had been like for her. In her post-natal condition, she should have been kept free from worry . . . let alone suffer a shock of this sort. He was deeply shocked himself, for he had known Bill for years and been their family doctor ever since they had come to live here. "Go to bed now and try to sleep," he told Scilla as he left.

But Scilla could not sleep and she went downstairs in her dressing-gown after giving up the attempt and was glad that she had done so. The Brig was sitting alone, late though it was, his face showing his great struggle not to give way to grief.

She made cocoa for them both and sat beside him in the room

she had deliberately flooded with light. He began to revive a little and even smiled when he saw the cocoa, saying:

"Reminds me of night duty in the war!"

"Tell me about when you were young!" Scilla prompted, and, slowly but surely, he began to forget his present unhappiness as he went back in his mind to the past.

They talked for hours . . . quietly, companionably, until the reminiscences joined with the present, and then his voice was steady as he said:

"You will stay here with us, Scilla? For a little while at least? You know you can make your home with us for as long as you like . . . and that it would mean everything to us to have you here. I realise, of course, that the time will come when we have to lose you."

Scilla looked up at him, her eyes suddenly wide with the realisation that had come to her only with this talk of the future. She had given it no thought until now.

The old man was watching her face and saw the light that flashed into the eyes that looked into his in a strange mixture of fear . . . happiness . . . perplexity.

"You are very young, my dear. The time must come when you will marry again. It would be wrong not to, for little June's sake as much as for your own."

Dallas! Scilla's heart left her and reached across twelve thousand miles to the man she had never believed she would see again. *Dallas . . . Dallas!* Then sanity returned and with it the terrible sadness of this moment. Somewhere in the future, there was light, and happiness and love, but she would not belittle Bill's memory by thinking of it now.

"I shan't marry . . . for a long time anyway!" she said at last. "I shall stay here with you and Mother."

The Brig knew then that she had never really loved his son. He had guessed it some time ago when he had spoken to her about it and she had told him a little about this other man in her life. Now he was sure; for she could never have spoken of remarrying at such a time had she really loved his son as he, himself, had once loved. The certainty did not give him any pain for he knew how happy she had made Bill . . . and that was all he would have asked of her. He loved Bill's young wife as his own daughter and now that Bill was gone, he wanted only her happiness. If they must lose her to achieve it, then he would suffer this double loss without regret. He knew that Scilla would never break away from them completely; that she loved them in much the same way as they loved her. And the baby would be a strong link between them always.

Later, he would ask her again about the future . . . when it was not so close to Bill's death that such a conversation must seem to them both to be disloyal to his memory. Maybe she would tell him of her own accord. He wanted to be sure that she would not sacrifice her own happiness for theirs. He must warn his wife when she was better able to face up to things not to let Scilla see what losing her would mean to them both. They must not be possessive or become dependent on her. She must feel free to go whenever her heart desired.

Six months had passed before this moment he had anticipated came to pass. Baby June was a fat, dimpled, laughing little girl just beginning to crawl. She was Scilla's image and neither of Bill's parents, who adored the child, would have had her one wit different, even though they had hoped at one time that she might resemble Bill. Already the deep wound that his death had caused had begun to heal. Scilla, who had lost a lot of weight, had begun to put it on again and the Brig thought he had never seen her looking lovelier than the evening she crept downstairs in her dressing-gown 'for a gossip while you have your night-cap, Brig!' as she told him.

There was no restraint between the young girl and her elderly father-in-law. They were perfect friends and their conversation knew no restrictions of age, or shyness, or restraint. They understood each other so well, and each knew that Scilla had come to tell him something that mattered a great deal to them both.

"I had a letter yesterday!" she said, holding his hand with

both her own. "From Australia. I . . . I thought it would be the best for you to read it, Brig dear. It is from the man I used to be engaged to . . . before I married Bill."

He took the envelope from her and drew out the thin sheet of airmail paper.

*Dear Kid,*

*I read in an English paper some months ago of your husband's death. I wrote to Kathie but she confirmed my own feeling that you might prefer not to hear from me for a little while. She assured me that you were all right. Now I cannot bring myself to keep silent any longer. You know what it is I want to say to you . . . that nothing has changed . . . that I still love you as I always have and always will. When will you come to me, darling? Try to make it soon for we have wasted so many precious years already.*

*Kathie tells me you have a baby daughter who is your image. I never believed that I should be so fortunate as to be able to propose to two Scillas. To you, I say, 'Will you marry me, darling?' And to the tiny Scilla, I say, 'Will you accept me as a father, kid?'*

*Answer for both of you soon.*

*Yours always*
*Dallas.*

"Brig, there are tears in your eyes!" Scilla whispered as he handed back the letter. "I won't go . . . dearest Brig. I won't go. Don't please be unhappy!"

He coughed to clear his throat and recover his composure.

"But of course you will go, Scilla. I am sad, of course, that we should be losing you and June, but I've known it must happen and I'm very, very happy that it should be this way. I think your Dallas sounds a fine fellow . . . and my dear, I know you have loved him a long, long time. Mother and I both understand and we only think more highly of you for pretending so well to Bill and making him so happy. It's your turn now, Scilla. You can go with our blessing. Now there are tears in your eyes!"

"It's just that I can't believe it!" Scilla said brokenly. "I couldn't bring myself to write to Dallas although I thought about it often. It was still so soon after . . . and then there was June. I didn't know how he'd feel about her. Now, getting his letter, I know I want more than anything in the world to go to him. But I couldn't believe that you would be so wonderful about my going. I was afraid you'd be hurt . . . for Bill . . . that you'd think I hadn't really cared for him at all. I did, Brig. I really did love him, but in a different way. It couldn't be more because I had pledged my love years and years ago to Dallas. It was very wrong of me to have married Bill under the circumstances."

"Never say that!" Brig said firmly. "You made him a very happy man before he died. He would never have known that happiness if you hadn't married him, Scilla. And you gave him a place in the future . . . through little June. You have given us great happiness, too, and without you I don't think either of us would have cared much whether we lived or died. It isn't easy to live without anyone to care about very deeply. Now we have you and June . . . and you'll write to us often . . . perhaps come and visit us."

"I will, I will!" Scilla cried. "And Brig, although I think I must go . . . soon . . . I shan't take June with me now. I'll leave her with Kathie for a few months so you'll still see plenty of her. It will be you and Mother who must write and send photographs."

"My dear, are you sure you're doing the right thing? I know how much you love that baby and you'll miss her terribly."

"Yes, Brig, I will. But I feel I must go to Dallas alone. He has been so patient . . . and so understanding. And I think he will be a wonderful father to June . . . I know it. But he will want to be a husband first. Don't you think that is so, Brig dear?"

"Yes!" he agreed thoughtfully. "I think that is so. And I think he will love you even more for thinking of that. Maybe he will love June more because of it, too. You'll come back for her and discover her together. Then she will belong to you both."

"Oh, Brig! Then I can bring Dallas here . . . to meet you both? You won't mind?"

"I expect we shall like him enormously, Scilla. For you to love him so much, he must be a very fine fellow. Tell me about him."

Starry-eyed, Scilla talked on into the night, and Brig listened and nodded his head and, because he loved this young girl so dearly, his last trace of bitterness left him and he knew that he really could welcome this man to his house. He stayed for a little longer after she had kissed him good night, staring into the fire and thinking that it would be rather nice to have another man around the place again . . . some young fellow he could take shooting . . . or down to the village pub for a drink. He dozed a little and woke feeling a little guilty but very contented as he made his way slowly up the stairs to bed.

# Sixteen

London, Rome, Cairo, Bahrain, Karachi, Calcutta, Rangoon, Singapore, Darwin, Sydney, a route map lay spread out on Scilla's lap as she sat in the comfortable seat of the Constellation on the first lap of her journey. An hour ago she had had tears in her eyes when she kissed Kathie and her own darling baby, June, goodbye. But now the tears were forgotten as she felt a mounting excitement within her as she anticipated the glorious end of this flight.

She knew already exactly what she would be doing for the next four days. Tonight, Rome, then an early rise and by lunchtime she would be in Cairo. The very name of this great capital brought back its own memory of a leave Dallas had spent there trying to forget her! A quick stop at Bahrain for refuelling and on to Karachi, which they should reach in the early hours of the next morning. Breakfast would be in Calcutta, and then across the Bay of Bengal to Rangoon. A night stop in Singapore was the last port of call before Australia. She would be touching down in Dallas' native land at Darwin and then at last her destination, Sydney.

Dallas would be meeting her there!

Scilla leaned back in her seat and closed her eyes, trying to believe in this miracle which was at long last bringing her to the man she loved. Purposefully she remembered, and with sadness, the tragedy which had inadvertently led up to this present happiness. Dear, kind, lovable Bill, who had had to lose his life just when he had found his pinnacle of happiness. 'God had His reasons!' Brig had said the day he told her the dreadful news. Now she could believe that maybe one of the reasons was that she and Dallas could find each other again.

208

It seemed easy now to believe there was a Power controlling all their lives. She had had to atone for the marriage she had made so hastily; because she had selfishly desired her own happiness, no matter what the cost to others. At the time, she had convinced herself, and Bill, that she was justified in becoming another man's wife, but she had learned only too soon what she had tried to disbelieve at the time . . . that she still loved Dallas as much as ever . . . that her heart lay within his keeping.

She had nearly failed . . . and now she could feel nothing but gladness that she had not given way to weakness. Had she left Bill when she was in Benghazi, she and Dallas would never have been able to feel at ease with themselves or each other. She could see that so clearly now. By giving up all that was dearest to her because she knew it to be her duty to maintain the vows she had made before God, He had taken pity on her and found His own way to release her from them.

Even Brig and Mother were beginning to recover from the dreadful shock of Bill's death. They so adored Bill's baby that their love and thoughts had had an outlet and they had discovered a new and wonderful reason for living in their old age. Dear Brig, Scilla thought warmly. He had done so much to help her achieve her happiness. He had understood so well what lay in her heart. Had he or Bill's mother been antagonistic to the idea of her remarrying so soon, her present happiness would have been halved and the pure crystal of perfection marred. As it was, Brig had given her his blessing and told her that Dallas would always be welcome in their house . . . that they were both sure they would love him too . . . and that they truly believed she was taking the right step for herself and for the baby.

Even Mother, who might not have been so understanding as Brig, had said the night before Scilla left:

"I don't think Bill would be unhappy if he knew, Scilla dear. He loved you so much and all he wanted was your happiness. I can see that it would not be right for you to go on with your life alone. You are young and need a husband. And June will need a father and brothers and sisters. I hope you will find great happiness, my dear. You deserve it. Brig and I both agree that we could not have loved any daughter-in-law as much as we love you . . . you are like our own child. Don't forget us, will you?"

Weeping in spite of her intentions, Scilla had promised that she would never forget them. While she was away she would write every week; when they came home to fetch June, they would come to stay in this house if they really wanted Dallas as they said. And later, when they went back to Australia, she would send photographs of their little grandchild as often as possible and bring her home on visits whenever Dallas could leave his work to come.

"Dallas has a lot of money, Mother . . . and distance is made much shorter if one is rich. Do you realise that June and I will be only four days' air travel away from you and can come home whenever we like? Dallas told me to tell you that in his last letter. It's strange that I have never thought of Dallas being a rich man. When I first knew him he was living on his R.A.A.F. pay and had no private means at all. My own parents were against the marriage because they thought he would not be able to afford to buy the things they had always given Kathie and me. Now he is far wealthier than Father."

As the four propellers of the giant aircraft hummed in her ears, Scilla's mind flew back to another parting . . . with her own parents. She had taken baby June to see them and to announce her intention of going to Australia to marry Dallas.

At first, she had felt diffident and constrained as she always had done in recent years. But she had suddenly caught sight of her mother's face in the mirror of her dressing-table, and to her concern, seen tears in her eyes.

Impulsively, Scilla had put her arms round the plump shoulders and in that moment the antagonism of years had fallen away and there was love in her heart again. It was as if a long-suffered but hardly recognised pain had suddenly eased and to be able to love her mother again was the most wonderful sensation in the world.

"I'm so glad . . . so glad!" her mother had cried, over and over again. "Daddy and I have never forgiven ourselves for parting you from Dallas all those years ago. Oh, I know you think we didn't care and didn't see how you were feeling. We did. We used to talk about it hour upon hour, night after night. We knew how you blamed us . . . and rightly so. That was why we did not dare to try to make amends. You had left home by then and Kathie told us of the hectic life you were living in London. Daddy had made up his mind to write and tell you that we both regretted that we had stopped you marrying Dallas when you announced your engagement to that fellow in London . . . I forget his name now! So we kept quiet, thinking maybe after all we had been right and you had found happiness with someone else. Afterwards, when you broke it off, Daddy and I hoped you would come home; but then he heard from your bank manager that you never drew on your account and he was terribly hurt. So you see, darling, the Fates were against us right from the beginning, weren't they?"

"Oh, Mummy!" Scilla cried in her turn. "I wish I'd known . . . I wish I had come home!"

"We never lost touch with what was happening to you, darling. Kathie wrote when you were abroad and told us you had met Dallas again. We hoped and prayed that this time it would come right for you. Then you came home, married to Bill. We could see you were not happy and it was unbearable, knowing how much of it was our fault."

"You were not really to blame!" Scilla admitted the truth aloud for the first time. "You advised me . . . that was all. Any parent has the right to do that, whatever their motives. I could have married Dallas . . . I'd planned to run away with him the day he sailed to Australia. I could have done it if I had not been a coward . . . if I had not doubted him. So please don't ever blame yourselves, you and Daddy, again."

"It's so wonderful to have you back, close to us again," her

211

parents said later on. "And awful to think that we must lose you so soon afterwards."

"We'll be coming home in three months' time to fetch June!" Scilla reminded them. "I couldn't be parted from my baby any longer."

"But Dallas won't be able to forgive us as easily as you have done, darling. We treated him even worse than we treated you."

"He won't bear any grudge for what is past!" Scilla said, knowing in her heart that Dallas would forget for her sake those critical remarks about him. His very success would make it easier, for he had proved all his promises.

Her home-leaving had been made quite perfect, except for the parting with her baby. Only Kathie, perhaps, fully realised what it cost her to leave the baby she loved so much. The next three months would make a big difference at such an early age and Scilla might miss June's first steps, her first words . . . and June might not know her mother when she came back. Only her over-riding love for Dallas made that parting bearable. Her common sense had told her that to the baby her going would make very little difference. She was surrounded by love – a mother's love from Kathie, and adoration from her grandparents. She would be well looked after, well trained by Kathie and Nanny, and Dina and Paul would do their best to spoil her! And within a few weeks June would begin to know her mother again and never know that she had been parted from her.

But Dallas needed her love . . . all of it . . . now! He had waited six months since the announcement of Bill's death before writing to her and she knew that had she asked him, he would have flown to England to join her there. It was after very careful thinking and much advice from Brig that she had resolved to be the one to go to Dallas without June. It was not that he would not love the baby . . . and June was so much the exact image of herself in miniature that if he loved her, he must love June; but that they needed time to be alone . . .

quite alone, with nothing in the world to distract their attention. It would scarcely be fair to Dallas to spend their honeymoon pacing the floor with a teething baby . . . or have to curtail the day's activities he had planned because her baby was asleep, or due a feed, or fretful. Adorable as June was, she could be a full-time job and Scilla knew that Dallas would want her exclusively for a little while. Afterwards, he would accept his role of ready-made father and she had no doubts at all that he would be wonderful with her little daughter. To suffer a little herself now at a brief separation would make all the difference in the world to Dallas' future relationship with her baby. The Brig had said so and she knew he was right. If Dallas were in England and took her away for a honeymoon, she knew she would be rushing to the telephone every few minutes to ask Kathie how the baby was!

Now she could not do that; and in any event, she had resolved not to worry. Kathie would write regularly and she must be content with news a week old. If she worried, Dallas would know, and she need not worry . . . she knew that. Even at the actual moment of goodbye, June had smiled contentedly in Kathie's arms and not even held out her little arms to her mother! Hurt though she had been in one way, she was also amused and glad.

Her thoughts swung away . . . forward once more to Dallas. She had all the wonderful love letters he had written to her in her handbag. They had been read and re-read a hundred times. She had sent him a brief cable in answer to his first letter . . . the one she had read aloud to Brig. It had said:

*We accept both proposals. All our love. Scilla and June.*

Almost immediately she had had a cabled reply saying he would leave for England in the next plane if she agreed, and she had been forced to send a second one herself, telling him to wait for her letter.

In this, she had explained to him that she preferred to come to Australia . . . to his country . . . to his home. She would need a little time to prepare for her journey, but if he wished it, she would be ready to marry him on her arrival.

Dallas had been entirely satisfied . . . and quite content to wait another few months. Now that she was free to do so, he hoped she had put his engagement ring back on her finger. He wondered whether she would like to have her present wedding ring melted down and merged with the one he had bought for her. Did she like this idea?

Scilla had been deeply touched by such thoughtfulness. Dallas must have imagined how disloyal it would make her feel to take off Bill's ring and had thought of this wonderful solution to the problem. She had not thought it possible to fall more in love with him and yet this, and the other sentiments expressed in those long letters, had achieved the impossible. She had curbed her inner radiance as far as possible from the Brig and Mother, but now, alone in the plane, it shone forth like a light. Her eyes were like stars, her cheeks glowed and she looked beautiful as only a woman in love can do.

The hours passed in this long, contented day-dreaming. Other passengers talked, played cards, read or slept, but Scilla stared dreamily out of the window at the passing clouds, her thoughts thousands of miles away, and all gloriously happy.

She had left London in winter, but it was summer time when she at last touched down in Australia. She had dressed with care on the aeroplane and when she walked down the steps on to the tarmac she looked cool and dainty. Only her heart was burning with anticipation, her hands trembling a little with sudden shyness as she thought of Dallas' eyes somewhere in the crowd that lined the public enclosure.

She walked into the airport building behind the other passengers and waited while her luggage was checked at the Customs. She had new, matching suitcases, a wedding present from her father, and a completely new trousseau which included her wedding dress. This was of the palest blue shantung, simple but beautifully cut and which, as Kathie had said when she helped her to choose it, made her coppery curls and creamy skin quite perfect. The tiny, flower-petal hat and veil were wrapped in mountains of tissue paper and Scilla was glad that she was not made to unwrap it by the customs officer who chalked all her suitcases without a glance beyond the bright hazel eyes.

Then she moved forward to the Immigration and Health formalities and at last through the doors to the Passenger Reception Hall.

Even before she had had time to look for Dallas he was beside her. She felt his hand holding her arm and, turning, found herself looking into the dark grey of his eyes.

"Dallas!" she whispered, her heart too full for words and all trace of nervousness gone now that she had found him . . . he had found her.

"Darling! How beautiful you look!" he told her, and gently turning her shoulders, put both his arms around her and kissed her lips.

They were oblivious to the crowds milling round them. If people were watching them, they did not care and they did not know. They stood for several long minutes, staring into each other's eyes, reading in their depths the words their hearts were too full yet to say.

Suddenly Dallas released her and looked sharply round. His forehead creased and he said anxiously:

"But darling, where's the baby?"

She smiled at him and caught hold of his hand.

"But you knew I wasn't bringing her! I told you in my last letter I was leaving her with Kathie!"

"I know!" Dallas agreed. "But I thought when it came to the point you'd have had to bring her, too. I wish you had. I so want to see her."

"Oh, darling, I love you for saying that. But we'll have her with us for the rest of our lives. I thought just for three months we'd be together . . . alone . . . just the two of us. Then we'll go home together and fetch her. I want only you now, Dallas!"

She knew then that she had been right . . . Brig had been right. Because he loved her so much, Dallas had shown in every way possible that he wanted her baby, too. But her last words had brought a wonderful light to his eyes and she knew that, after all, they were true. She wanted nothing but Dallas . . . no one but Dallas. No one else existed in the world for either of them but each other.

"Come!" he said breathlessly. "The car's outside and we'll drive into town right away. You must be hungry, sweetheart, and I've so much I want to tell you, to show you."

Starry-eyed, she followed him out to the car-park, waited while he found her luggage and piled the suitcases into the boot. Then, as he climbed in beside her, they were really alone and she was once again in his arms.

"When shall we be married?" she asked as he released her much against his will but knowing they would never get to Sydney if they did not start soon.

"Tomorrow . . . three o'clock in the afternoon at the little blue-stone brick church at The Rock. I wrote and told you about it, didn't I?"

"Yes, darling. And I'm glad it is to be from your home town. I wouldn't have wanted to be married in Sydney . . . or London. Dallas, will your family like me? I'm getting nervous now I am beginning to realise you have a family."

"They're going to love you so much, kid!" he said softly. "Not as much as I do because that is impossible, but so very much. My cousin, Dick, will give you away. Only Mother and Dad and a few of our nearest friends will be there. Then we're having a big party at Dad's house when everyone for miles around will be there. And when it's over, we're going home . . . to our home, Scilla."

"No honeymoon?" she teased him, for they had already decided in their letters that they didn't want to go off to some hotel. Dallas' ranch was waiting for her, redecorated from top to toe, and they could begin their married life where every day would bring some new discovery to Scilla . . . and where every day Dallas could show her a little more of the huge fifteen-thousand-acre farm he had built up, hoping that one day he might be able to offer it all to her.

Scilla felt her heart leap at the thought of the days that lay ahead. Tomorrow she would be driven to Dallas' home . . . meet his parents, whom she knew she would love since he was their son; in the afternoon she would go to the church where Dallas had been christened and at last become his wife.

Then, after the party at which she knew he wanted to 'show her off' to all his friends . . . and she did not mind since she loved his pride in her . . . they would go home. This would be the house where she would spend the rest of her life . . . where she would return with baby June; where in time she and Dallas would have their children, too. This was where she knew she belonged . . . had always belonged, and she felt a fierce impatience to begin her new life.

"Oh, Dallas! I love you so terribly much!" she said as the car drove them slowly through the outskirts of Sydney. "I still can't believe that I am here beside you, driving with you to Sydney . . . that tomorrow I shall really be able to tell myself I am your wife. We need never say goodbye again."

"Nor ever will!" Dallas affirmed. "Nothing must ever come between us again. We both made terrible mistakes in the past; but they don't matter any more except for the lesson they have taught us. You know, I truly believe that we have found a greater, more lasting love than we could have found when we were only children. I shall guard and treasure you, my happiness, until I die!"

Two hours later, they were in each other's arms, dancing at Romano's. Scilla wore a beautiful strapless white evening frock that left her shoulders bare and at her waist were pinned two of the scarlet roses that Dallas had put all over her room at Ushers Hotel. Dallas in a dinner jacket looked strange to her at first, but now, with his arms round her, she knew only a wonderful feeling of rightness and of pride, for every woman in the room was looking at him. Tall, fair, sun-tanned, he was undoubtedly the most attractive man there. Scilla had known a moment of wonder that he should love her.

He was looking down into her eyes, his own plainly adoring.

"Happy?" he asked.

She nodded her reply. Then Dallas signalled to the band leader and almost immediately the saxophone took up a tune that in a moment she recognised, *Cuddle Up a Little Closer, Hold Me Tight!* His eyes grinned mischievously and as her smile answered his, he drew her more closely against him until her cheek lay against his.

Time flew back . . . beyond the unhappy dance at Benghazi, back through the years to the first time they had danced to this tune at the end of the war and she had been seventeen.

"Marry me, Scilla, I love you so!"

Had she only remembered the words or had he spoken them again now? It didn't matter – past, present and future had merged into one. The only things in the world of importance to either of them now were the glory, the wonder and the certainty of their love.

# NEVER SAY GOODBYE

*Recent Titles by Claire Lorrimer from Severn House*

BENEATH THE SUN

CONNIE'S DAUGHTER

AN OPEN DOOR

THE RECKONING

THE RELENTLESS STORM

THE REUNION

SECOND CHANCE

SECRET OF QUARRY HOUSE

THE SHADOW FALLS

A VOICE IN THE DARK

THE WOVEN THREAD


*Non-fiction*

HOUSE OF TOMORROW